She didn't realize he'd stopped in front of their room until she slammed into him.

The contact made her stumble back, and her heels failed to find purchase on the snow-covered walk. She wobbled, her arms pinwheeling as she started to fall. He dropped the suitcase and reached for her, then hauled her upright and held her steady. She exhaled a shuddery sigh of relief before tipping her head back to look at him.

Despite the snow that continued to swirl, the air between them suddenly crackled with heated awareness.

"Are you okay?" he asked gruffly.

She nodded. "Th-thanks."

"What kind of boots are those anyway?"

"Oh. Um. They're Cynthia Bane. She's an up-and-coming West Coast designer—and a client."

"It was a rhetorical question," he told her. "And the right answer would have been 'useless.' Those boots are useless in northern Nevada winter."

"But stylish in California, which is where I bought them."

He suddenly realized he was still holding her and let his arms drop away.

Dear Reader,

Event planner Finley Gilmore was ten years old when her parents divorced, proving that not every walk down the aisle leads to happily-ever-after. Weddings might be the heart of her business, but she has no interest in romance. Then a blizzard strands her in Haven, Nevada, with a sexy stranger, and Finley finds herself with time—and temptation!—on her hands.

College professor Lachlan Kellett isn't in the market for a relationship, either. A short-lived marriage followed by a painful divorce taught him some hard lessons about love, and being snowed in at the Dusty Boots Motel—even with a stunningly beautiful woman—isn't likely to change his perspective.

Morning brings clear skies again, and Finley and Lachlan intend to go their separate ways. Until they realize they are both heading for Northern California and agree to share a ride. The road trip only continues to fan the sparks that ignited during the storm.

But will their return to the real world mean an end to the connection they forged in Haven? Or will they find a way to overcome the obstacles keeping them apart?

I hope you have as much fun reading about these wary lovers as I did writing their story—and that you'll look for more Match Made in Haven titles coming soon.

Enjoy!

Brenda

xo

SNOWED IN
WITH A STRANGER

BRENDA HARLEN

ISBN-13: 978-1-335-59459-4

Snowed In with a Stranger

Copyright © 2024 by Brenda Harlen

Harlequin Enterprises ULC
22 Adelaide St. West, 41st Floor
Toronto, Ontario M5H 4E3, Canada
www.Harlequin.com

Printed in Lithuania

MIX
Paper | Supporting
responsible forestry
FSC® C021394

Brenda Harlen is a former attorney who once had the privilege of appearing before the Supreme Court of Canada. The practice of law taught her a lot about the world and reinforced her determination to become a writer—because in fiction, she could promise a happy ending! Now she is an award-winning, RITA® Award–nominated, nationally bestselling author of more than fifty titles for Harlequin. You can keep up-to-date with Brenda on Facebook and Twitter, or through her website, brendaharlen.com.

Books by Brenda Harlen

Harlequin Special Edition

Match Made in Haven

The Marine's Road Home
Meet Me Under the Mistletoe
The Rancher's Promise
The Chef's Surprise Baby
Captivated by the Cowgirl
Countdown to Christmas
Her Not-So-Little Secret
The Rancher's Christmas Reunion
Snowed In with a Stranger

Montana Mavericks: Brothers & Broncos

The Maverick's Christmas Secret

Montana Mavericks: The Real Cowboys of Bronco Heights

Dreaming of a Christmas Cowboy

Montana Mavericks: What Happened to Beatrix?

A Cowboy's Christmas Carol

Montana Mavericks: Lassoing Love

A Maverick's Holiday Homecoming

Visit the Author Profile page
at Harlequin.com for more titles.

In memory of a treasured stepmom and "gramma"—
Marjorie Anne Stickles.

02 March 1939–27 May 2023

Chapter One

I should have listened to my sister.

From the backseat of the Subaru Forrester in which she was riding, Finley Gilmore couldn't see anything but snow. Whether she was peering through the front or back or side windows, there was only white.

And the way Ozzie was gripping the steering wheel and squinting through the windshield, she doubted that his view was much better.

Apparently ignoring the weather warnings had been a bad idea.

But honestly, how could she have known that today would be the one day the forecasters finally got it right?

"They say it could be the biggest storm this area has seen in a decade," Haylee had cautioned when Finley set her carry-on suitcase by the door.

"They say a lot of things," Finley noted. "And they're usually wrong."

"It's snowing already," her sister pointed out.

And it had been.

But that snow was big, fluffy flakes that seemed to float on the air—nothing at all like the whiteout conditions that her driver was dealing with now.

"I've got a four o'clock flight to Oakland," she'd reminded her sister. "And a busy weekend ahead of me."

Haylee had sighed before turning to her husband. "Tell her to stay."

"You should stay," Trevor Blake had dutifully intoned.

"I appreciate your concern," Finley said. "But I really need to get home."

A horn had sounded from the driveway then, so she'd exchanged hugs and kisses with Aidan and Ellie—her three-year-old nephew and niece—and Haylee and Trevor, then picked up her suitcase (with a Tupperware container of leftover birthday cake nestled safely inside) and headed out to meet her rideshare driver.

The snow had been falling noticeably thicker and faster before they reached the end of Main Street.

"You check with the airport to see if your flight is on time?" Ozzie asked.

"I did and it is," she confirmed.

Then her phone buzzed.

She glanced at the screen, exhaled a weary sigh.

"It *was*," she corrected. "Now it's listed as delayed."

"Delayed often leads to canceled," he warned. "You want me to turn around and take you back?"

"No," she said. "I need to get to the airport."

Ozzie shrugged. "Your call."

Ten minutes later, the driver wasn't shrugging but cursing.

Her phone buzzed again.

Now her flight was canceled.

Damn.

I definitely should have listened to my sister.

"Canceled?" Ozzie guessed.

"Yeah." Finley looked out the window again. "How far are we from the airport now?"

"Too far."

"What does that mean?"

"It means there's no way we're going to make it there before they close the highway."

"Can we go back?"

"I wouldn't," he said.

"What would you do?" she asked, trying to ignore the knots of apprehension forming in her stomach.

Ozzie looked out at the swirling storm for a minute as his vehicle crawled along the road. "We're not far from the Dusty Boots Motel," he noted. "You could call to see if they've got a room available."

It was a good idea, she decided. "Do you need a room, too?" she asked.

"Nah. I've got a lady friend who lives nearby," he said. "She'll let me hang with her until the storm passes."

Finley called the number on the card that Ozzie handed to her. Luckily, there was one room available. She booked it for one night, hoping it was all she'd need.

But staring out at what was nothing less than a full-fledged blizzard, she had to wonder just how long she'd be trapped.

I should have changed my plans.

Unfortunately, the realization came to Lachlan Kellett a little too late, after he'd already started his journey.

But after three weeks in northern Nevada, he was eager to get home to Aislynn.

He'd disregarded the blizzard warning, confident that an early start would put him well out of range when the snow started to fall. His confidence had obviously been misplaced.

He might have been okay if he hadn't detoured into Haven to pick up a pizza to fuel him on his drive. But Jo's Pizza was the stuff of legends, and since his first taste of her pie, more than a decade earlier, he'd never managed to pass by the town without stopping to pick one up.

But the box sat on the passenger seat, its contents untouched, because driving in this storm required every bit of his concentration and skill. And still, there were moments when he wondered if he'd ever make it out of Nevada. Or even out of Haven.

After another twenty minutes of white-knuckle driving, he acknowledged that there was no way he was going to get home tonight. The all-weather tires that were more than adequate for his purposes in California weren't faring so well on roads covered in snow and ice. And of course they did absolutely nothing to improve visibility, which was somewhere in the vicinity of zero. Thankfully he remembered that there was a motel on the lonely stretch of highway he was traveling. The Rusty Spurs or Battered Hat or something like that.

He glanced quickly at the map displayed on the screen of his phone. There it was—the Dusty Boots Motel—half a mile ahead.

When he finally reached the driveway, he gently tapped the brake, slowing his vehicle to a crawl to navigate the turn, and still his SUV skidded on the slick surface. He tightened his hands on the wheel and steered into the skid, fervently praying that he wouldn't end up nose first in a snowbank or a drift. Thankfully, he didn't, but that brief (and scary) moment of uncertainty assured him that seeking shelter from the storm was the right course of action.

There were several other vehicles in the lot, most of them parked in front of numbered units and already buried beneath several inches of the snow that showed no signs of abating anytime soon. Since he didn't yet have a room, he parked beside a pickup truck near the main entrance and stepped out of his vehicle. It was a short trek to the door, but long enough that he could understand how people got thrown off course in snowstorms as he battled against buffeting winds and blowing snow the whole way.

By the time his hand closed around the handle, he suspected

that he bore more than a passing resemblance to the abominable snowman, covered head to toe as he was.

Once inside, he stomped his feet to knock some of the white stuff off his boots and pulled off his leather gloves to dig his wallet out of his pocket. He fished out his driver's license and credit card, then took a few steps further into the reception area to drop them on the counter for the middle-aged desk clerk with platinum-blonde hair piled on top of her head and bright pink lipstick smeared over her mouth.

Shirla—according to the name badge pinned on her thick wool sweater—reluctantly tore her gaze away from the on-line casino game she was playing on her phone to glance up.

The way her heavily mascaraed eyes immediately grew wide confirmed his suspicion that he looked like the mythical Yeti.

"It's snowing out there," he said, hoping the humorous understatement would put her at ease.

Her gaze shifted to the window, and her initial surprise gave way to amusement, as evidenced by the curve of her bright pink lips.

"Checking in?" she asked, in a raspy tone that suggested she'd been a pack-a-day smoker for a lot of her fifty-plus years.

"I hope so," he responded to her question.

She reached for the mouse beside the computer on the desk, sliding it over the pad to wake up the screen.

"Your name?" she prompted.

"Lachlan Kellett."

A pleat formed between her brows as she scanned her computer screen. "Do you have a reservation?"

"No," he admitted. "I'd planned to be back in California and sleeping in my own bed tonight, but that's obviously not going to happen."

"I'm sorry, Mr. Kellett, but we don't have any rooms available."

He sighed wearily and glanced out at the storm again. "So what am I supposed to do now?"

"Depending on which way you're headed, you could try your luck in Haven or Battle Mountain," Shirla said.

He immediately shook his head. "There's no way I'm driving any further tonight."

"Well, there are several sofas in the lounge," she allowed, gesturing vaguely to the far side of the room.

That was when he noticed the row of hooks on the wall behind her. The hangers had numbers above them to indicate the room to which the keys belonged. Had all the hooks been empty, he would have assumed that the motel had upgraded to keycards, but the single key attached to a plastic tag hanging under one of the numbers suggested otherwise.

"I know it's not ideal, but you're welcome to crash there," Shirla continued.

"What about Number Six?" Lachlan asked now, pointing to the lone key on the wall.

"It's reserved."

"Reserved for who?"

Big silver hoops swayed in her ears as she shook her head. "I can't give you that information."

"I understand," he assured her. "What I should have asked is—how late do you hold the room? Because if your guest isn't here now, I doubt very much that he's going to make it."

"A confirmed reservation holds a room until six o'clock," Shirla said.

"So if your guest isn't here by six o'clock, maybe I could buy out the room?" he suggested.

"I guess that would be okay," she agreed.

He glanced at his watch to check the current time and felt a gust of cold air blow through the doors as they opened behind him.

Glancing over his shoulder, he saw a woman—young, blond,

gorgeous—brushing snow off the shoulders of her cardinal red coat.

She caught his eye and offered a smile that he suspected could have melted the three-foot drift outside the door, then she shifted her attention to the clerk as she moved toward the counter.

"My name's Finley Gilmore," she said. "I have a reservation."

"Welcome to the Dusty Boots Motel, Ms. Gilmore." The clerk glanced apologetically in the direction of the man lounging against the counter, then asked her newly-arrived guest for her ID and credit card.

Finley went through the motions of checking in to her room, conscious of the man's gaze on her. As an event planner, she'd dealt with all kinds of people in various situations—from shy quinceañeras and bubbly brides to demanding mothers and implacable fathers—and she handled them all. Julia, one of her business partners, had teasingly nicknamed Finley "the wallet-whisperer," claiming that she had a gift for ensuring that whatever expectations potential clients had when they walked into her office for a consult, every one of them left feeling confident that Gilmore Galas would give them the event they wanted, right down to the tiniest detail.

Finley certainly endeavored to do her best, though there were inevitably snags that occurred—a misspelled name on a cake or the wrong shade of roses in a bouquet or a tardy beer delivery—but Finley made sure that she was the one to deal with those snags, so that the birthday celebrant or anxious bride or happy retiree never had to know there'd been a problem. And that was the real reason Gilmore Galas had an overall five-star rating on Yelp and was fully booked for the next eighteen months.

Yet, despite her purported skill at reading people, she

couldn't quite get a handle on the stranger with the mouth-wateringly broad shoulders, longish dark—almost black—hair, scruffy beard and piercing blue eyes. But something about the way he was looking at her made her insides quiver—not with nervousness so much as awareness.

Which was ridiculous, because brooding, bearded men were not at all her type.

But those shoulders.

And those eyes.

Perhaps it wasn't a wonder that all her female body parts were suddenly humming.

"You'll be in Room Six." The desk clerk swiveled on her chair and reached for the lone remaining key hanging on a hook on the wall.

An actual key.

As if she was checking into a roadside motel in an old movie. Or Schitt's Creek.

Still, she was grateful to have a room. And hopeful that the beds had been replaced more recently than the door locks. Though all she really cared about was that it was clean.

"The room has two double beds and a shower-tub combo," Shirla continued, setting the key on the counter. "There's also cable TV and free Wi-Fi, a mini-fridge, coffee maker and microwave."

"Thank you," Finley said, struggling to slide the oversized plastic tag attached to the key into the pocket of her coat.

"Continental breakfast is served in the lounge—" Shirla gestured to an adjacent seating area with a couple of sofas and several mismatched armchairs in groupings around scarred tables "—starting at seven a.m. and ending when the coffee and pastries run out. Assuming we get our usual bakery delivery in the morning."

"What if I'm hungry now?" Finley asked, suddenly realizing that she was.

"There's a diner down the street."

The automatic response made Finley wonder if the woman had looked outside in the past few hours.

"And what are my options if I don't want to venture out in the storm?" she clarified.

Shirla lifted an arm to point again, this time to a vending machine against the wall.

A vending machine containing only a few bags of chips, a single chocolate bar and two full rows of chewing gum.

Apparently her dinner was going to be the leftover birthday cake in the Tupperware container inside her suitcase.

"Or pizza," the bearded stranger spoke up to say.

Finley's stomach rumbled.

"Pizza would be great," she said. "But I don't think anyone's going to be out delivering in this weather."

"I've got a large cheese and pepperoni in my SUV," he said, jingling his keys as he pulled them out of his pocket.

"Are you offering to share?" she asked hopefully.

"I'd be willing to consider a trade," he said, making his way to the door.

Shirla's gaze followed him as he walked out, then she sighed, a little wistfully. "Did you see those shoulders?"

"Hard to miss," Finley admitted.

"Do you think he got them working out in a prison gym?" the clerk wondered aloud.

"I would have guessed football."

"You could be right," Shirla acknowledged. "But a prison story would be much more interesting."

"Perhaps," Finley agreed dubiously.

The clerk chuckled. "I've always had a thing for bad boys," she confided. "Just the rumble of a Harley's engine gets my juices flowing. Add a leather jacket and some tatts, and I'm a puddle on the floor."

Which was a lot more information than Finley needed to know about the woman working the desk.

"I bet you go for the corporate type," Shirla guessed, assessing Finley. "A guy who wears a shirt and tie to the office every day and golfs with his buddies on Friday afternoons."

It was admittedly close to the mark, and perhaps the reason that Finley felt compelled to respond.

"I couldn't actually tell you the last time I was on a date," she confided. "My job keeps me so busy, I don't have time for much else."

Shirla tsked. "You've gotta make time for the things that matter."

"What matters is keeping a roof over my head." And it was true, even if Finley wasn't really worried about being kicked out of the carriage house she'd been renting from her dad and stepmom for the past half a dozen years.

"Youth is, indeed, wasted on the young," Shirla lamented.

The door opened again, and the man with the mouth-watering shoulders and mesmerizing eyes returned with a blast of icy wind and a flat square box.

At first glance, the stranger's appearance was somewhat intimidating, and Finley could understand why the clerk had pegged him as a bad boy. But nothing about him set off Finley's internal radar. Her hormones, perhaps, but not her radar—though perhaps the tingles in her womanly parts should be heeded as a warning.

Over the years, Finley had learned to be a pretty good judge of character, at least when it came to professional interactions. Unfortunately, her romantic history told a very different story about her personal life.

He stomped the snow off his boots before carrying his pizza through to the lounge.

There was a pot of coffee on the table where Shirla had indicated continental breakfast would be found in the morning. Finley left her suitcase by the desk and ventured over to pour a cup.

She took a tentative sip, shuddered, then emptied a couple of packets of sugar and three creamers into the cup and tried again. It was marginally less horrible now, so she poured a second cup and carried both into the lounge.

"You said something about a possible trade," Finley reminded the stranger, who was already halfway through his first slice of pizza. "So how about I trade you a cup of coffee for a slice?"

He finished chewing and swallowed before responding. "You mean a cup of free, really bad coffee?"

She shrugged. "Desperate times."

"Hardly seems like a fair trade to me," he said conversationally. "Because this is really good pizza."

"Jo's?" she guessed, her stomach rumbling again as the tantalizing scent of the pie teased her nostrils.

"How'd you know?"

"My sister and brother-in-law live in Haven," she told him. "Every time I visit, we have Jo's."

"So you know how good it is." He took another bite of the slice he was holding.

She nodded.

"And you know I'd be a fool to swap a slice of superior pizza for a cup of stale coffee."

"So let me buy a slice." Her stomach rumbled again. "Or two."

His lips twitched. "I probably wasn't going to eat the whole thing in one sitting," he acknowledged. "So you can have a slice."

She set the two cups of coffee on the table and reached into the box before he could rescind his offer.

She lifted a slice to her mouth, not quite managing to hold

back the moan of pleasure that sounded low in her throat as she bit into it.

His lips twitched again.

She was too grateful for the pizza to care that he was silently laughing at her.

She chewed slowly, savoring the combination of flavors and textures: tangy sauce, gooey cheese, spicy pepperoni.

"So where were you headed when the storm brought you here?" he asked, reaching into the box again.

"Airport." She licked a spot of sauce off her thumb. "I had a four o'clock flight to Oakland that was canceled."

"Yours wasn't the only one," he told her. "The whole airport shut down."

"Hopefully the storm will pass quickly so it can reopen in the morning, because I have an engagement party tomorrow night that I cannot miss."

His gaze automatically went to her left hand, bare of rings.

"Not mine," she said, shaking her head for emphasis. "I'm an event planner. Gilmore Galas."

"So what'll happen if you miss the party?"

"I'll have a couple of very unhappy clients on my hands— or former clients."

Dark brows winged up. "Would they really fire you for something completely out of your control?"

"Maybe not," she allowed. "Especially as we're already deep into planning their November wedding. But they'd be disappointed and, truthfully, so would I."

She finished off her slice, her gaze shifting to the remaining slices of pizza in the box.

"Did that take the edge off your hunger?" the stranger asked.

"Only the very tip," she told him.

"So let's talk trade," he suggested.

"I don't know what I have that you might want," she said warily.

"The last vacant room in this motel."

"And I'm not giving it up."

"Do you plan on sleeping in both of the beds?" he asked.

"No. And no."

His brows lifted again. "What was the second no?"

"I'm not going to let you sleep in the other one," she said firmly.

"Why not?" he challenged.

"Because I've seen too many crime dramas on TV to willingly put myself in the middle of a real-life one."

"What if I offered to pay for the room?"

She shook her head. "Then I'd be about seventy-five dollars richer but no less dead."

His lips quirked at the corners. "Do you really think I'm a dangerous criminal?"

"I don't know you, do I?" she pointed out reasonably.

"What do you want to know?"

"A lot more than a quick session of twenty questions is going to tell me."

"So go ahead and Google me," he suggested, pulling his driver's license out of his wallet and offering it to her. "My name is Lachlan Kellett, and I'm a professor of anthropology at Merivale College."

She knew of Merivale College, of course. Not only as a private school in San Francisco but also as a gorgeous venue for both indoor and outdoor events.

"So you're from California, too?" She wasn't sure why that little bit of information seemed reassuring, but it was.

"Born and raised," he told her.

Since he'd invited her to do so, she opened a search engine and punched in the name on his license, along with the name of the school.

"Apparently there is a Lachlan Kellett who teaches anthropology at Merivale College," she acknowledged. "But the thumbnail-sized black-and-white photo on the website doesn't look anything like you."

"The photo's at least ten years old and the beard—" he rubbed the dark hair covering the lower half of his face "—is much more recent."

She wondered if the beard was prickly or smooth, and found herself wanting to find out.

"Pizza's getting cold," he said, reaching for another slice.

Finley felt herself wavering.

"I promise I'm not after anything more than a place to sleep that's a little less public than this," he said, gesturing to the sofa on which he was seated. "I've spent the last three weeks in a falling-down cabin in the mountains and I was really looking forward to sleeping in my own bed at home tonight. Since that obviously isn't going to happen, I'd like to catch a few decent hours of shut-eye before my long drive tomorrow." He glanced out the window. "At least, I hope I have a long drive tomorrow."

She wasn't completely unsympathetic to his plight, but she was still wary. "How about two more slices of pizza for a two-hour nap in my room, after which time I'll wake you up and you'll leave?"

"Two more slices for six hours," he countered.

She shook her head. "I need to get some sleep tonight, too."

"And you're afraid to sleep in the same room as me," he acknowledged.

"I don't know you," she reminded him.

"I don't know you, either," he noted. "But I'm willing to trust that you won't accost me or rob me blind while I'm sleeping."

"Because it's unlikely that I'd get the upper hand on a man who's at least six inches taller and probably fifty pounds heavier than me," she pointed out.

"Would you feel better if I said you could handcuff me to the bed?"

That mental image sparked her hormones again.

"Do you have handcuffs?" she asked.

"No." He winked. "But I was hoping you might."

Her gaze narrowed. "Are you *flirting* with me?"

Now he smiled.

A real smile this time.

The kind of smile that tempted a woman to say "yes" to almost anything.

A different woman, Finley reminded herself firmly.

Perhaps not unlike the woman she used to be, but she was smarter now.

Or at least trying to be.

"And what if I said that I was flirting with you?" he asked her.

"I'd tell you that I appreciate the effort, Professor Kellett, but—"

"Lachlan," he interrupted. "If we're going to be sharing a room, you should call me Lachlan."

"We're *not* going to be sharing a room. I'm offering you two hours in my bed—the spare bed," she hastily amended.

He smiled again, and her heart actually skipped a beat.

Damn. He really was cute in a rough-around-the-edges sort of way.

But now that she was looking at him more closely, she could see the fatigue in his eyes. A bone-deep weariness that tugged at her.

"So what compelled you to spend three weeks in the mountains of northern Nevada in the middle of winter?" she asked him now.

All traces of humor disappeared from his eyes. "The last request of a dying friend."

Her heart squeezed. "I'm sorry."

"Me, too."

She cursed herself for being a fool even as she opened her

phone again to compose a text message to her sister. Since his driver's license was still on the table, she snapped a photo of it to attach to the message.

"You can have the spare bed," she decided. "But I just sent your contact information to my sister, so if housekeeping finds my lifeless body in the morning, the police will be coming for you."

"Good thing I know where there's a cabin in the mountains to hide out," he said, and winked at her again.

She reached into the box for another slice of pizza, because she was almost one hundred percent certain that he was joking.

Chapter Two

Lachlan closed the lid of the empty pizza box.

His soon-to-be roommate had not been kidding when she said she was hungry, as she'd quickly polished off another two slices. He'd devoured four himself and then offered the last slice to Shirla. The desk clerk had gratefully accepted, because even though she'd brought her own dinner, there was nothing better than Jo's pizza.

"We should probably head to our room," he said to Finley.

"It's *my* room," she noted, with a glance at the fancy watch on her wrist. "And it's barely six o'clock."

"And there's a major blizzard raging outside," he reminded her. "If we don't go now, we might not get out the door. Or the wind might knock out the power, and then we'll be bumping around in the dark."

A furrow formed between her perfectly arched brows—a sign of worry that he wished he could soothe.

But the facts were irrefutable, and he had no business wanting anything from this woman—or at least nothing more than the bed that she'd already agreed (with obvious reluctance) to let him have.

"Do you really think we might lose power?" she asked, retrieving her discarded coat from the arm of the sofa and donning it over the snug-fitting dark jeans and cropped pale blue sweater she wore.

Following her lead, he shoved his arms into his down-filled parka and settled his fleece-lined trapper hat on his head. "In a storm like this, we have to at least consider the possibility."

She buttoned up her coat, knotted her scarf around her throat and pulled on a pair of matching mittens.

Cashmere, he guessed. Or some other equally expensive and completely impractical material that was more fashionable than warm. Just like the boots on her feet that barely qualified as such, with chunky little heels and shiny zipper pulls with tassels.

Or maybe he was judging her too harshly.

After all, she was a California girl, possibly unaccustomed to northern Nevada winters and obviously unprepared for the storm that was currently raging.

To be fair, he hadn't been prepared for the intensity of the storm, either. If he had, he would have had chains on his tires and might have been able to continue on his way rather than having to take shelter.

A minor inconvenience, he'd decided, when he'd turned off the highway.

A frustration, he'd amended, upon discovering that the motel didn't have any rooms available.

But now that he'd met the lovely Finley Gilmore, he had to wonder if his lack of preparedness hadn't actually been a stroke of good luck rather than bad.

Shirla managed to tear her attention away from the weather report on the television when they approached the desk to retrieve their bags. "I see you're both heading out."

Finley flushed in response to the clerk's sly smile.

"Ms. Gilmore has graciously agreed to let me crash in her spare bed," Lachlan said, coming to her rescue.

"Not any of my business," Shirla assured them, though her exaggerated wink confirmed that she was speculating nonetheless. "Though I've always said a smart girl makes a man buy her dinner first before she invites him to spend the night."

Finley's cheeks turned an even deeper shade of red.

"Good night, Shirla," Lachlan said firmly.

"I'll probably see you in the morning," the clerk told them. "The girl who usually covers the night shift just called to let me know she can't make it in, so I guess the weather forecasters were right about this one."

"How lucky for us," Finley said dryly.

Lachlan wasn't sure if she was responding to Shirla's comment that she'd see them in the morning or her remark about the forecast, because it seemed equally applicable to both.

"Stay close to the building so you don't get disoriented in the storm," Shirla cautioned, as he reached for the handle of the door.

"Will do," Finley promised.

"I'll lead the way," Lachlan said, as she moved past him.

"I'm not going to get lost." Finley's tone was indignant.

"I wasn't questioning your sense of direction," he assured her. "Just suggesting that you walk behind me, so that you're shielded from the wind."

"I don't need—"

Whatever else she'd intended to say was lost as a blast of wind hit her full on, stealing the words along with her breath.

She took a step back, blinking long, dark lashes dusted with snowflakes. "You can go ahead."

With a shake of his head, he stepped around her and began trudging through the knee-deep snow, creating a path for her to follow. He thought he'd gotten used to the cold over the past few weeks, but the temperature had plummeted even more since he'd set out earlier in the day. With every step he took, he was assaulted by icy pellets of snow, and every breath he drew stabbed like icy needles in his lungs.

He heard Finley mutter a couple of times as she struggled

to maneuver her suitcase through the snow. So he slung his duffel bag over his shoulder and reached back to take her case.

"I can manage," she protested, though not very vehemently.

"I'd like to get to the room before we both get frostbite," he said.

She relinquished her grip on the handle and he lifted the case off the ground before forging ahead, conscious of her scrambling to stay close.

So close that she didn't realize he'd stopped in front of their door until she slammed into him.

The contact made her stumble back, and those silly heels failed to find purchase on the snow-covered walk. She wobbled, her arms pinwheeling as she started to fall. He dropped the case and reached for her, hauling her upright again and holding her steady.

She exhaled a shuddery sigh of relief before tipping her head back to look at him.

Despite the snow that continued to swirl, the air between them suddenly crackled with heated awareness.

"Are you okay?" he asked gruffly.

She nodded. "Th-thanks."

"What kind of boots are those anyway?"

"Oh. Um. They're Cynthia Bane. She's an up-and-coming West Coast designer."

"It was a rhetorical question," he told her. "But the right answer would have been 'useless.' Those boots are useless in northern Nevada winter."

"But stylish in California, which is where I bought them."

He suddenly realized he was still holding her and let his arms drop away. "Key?"

She shoved a mittened hand into the pocket of her coat and pulled out the oversized plastic tag stamped with the number 6.

He opened the door and gestured for her to precede him.

Then he picked up her suitcase again and followed.

Finley halted in the middle of the room, her gaze moving from one bed to the other, that already familiar furrow forming between her brows.

To him, it looked like a typical roadside motel room, with cheap floral spreads covering the beds, flimsy curtains on the window and threadbare carpet on the floor. But perhaps Finley was frowning not over the décor but the close confines of the room, suddenly aware that she would be sleeping only feet away from a virtual stranger.

His gaze shifted back to her face just in time to see the tip of her tongue sweep along her bottom lip, moistening it.

His attention was riveted by the action, his interest piqued by the lushness of her mouth.

He wondered if it could possibly feel as soft as it looked. Not that he had any intention of finding out. Because he suspected that making a move would be a good way to get himself kicked out of her room and onto his ass in the snow.

But it was fun to think about.

And that in and of itself was a surprise, because he hadn't felt the urge to kiss a woman in a very long time. Especially not a woman about whom he knew little more than her name.

Of course, they were going to be spending the night in the same room, which would provide him with the opportunity to learn more.

Or maybe he should forget about making conversation with his reluctant roommate and focus on getting some much-needed sleep before he embarked on the long journey home the next day—providing the inclement weather didn't continue to thwart his plans.

"I'm sure the desk clerk said two double beds," Finley remarked now.

"That's what I heard," he confirmed.

"Do they look like doubles to you?"

He shrugged. "We could push them together to make one big bed, if you want."

"I don't think so."

"You don't think we can?" he asked, deliberately misunderstanding her response.

"We're not going to," she said firmly, as she unwound her scarf and draped it over a hook by the door. Then she slipped off her coat and hung it up, too.

"It's not too warm in here, is it?" she noted, rubbing her hands up and down her arms.

"I'll crank up the heat," Lachlan said, turning away from her to adjust the temperature control on the wall.

"Thanks."

He shrugged out of his coat and placed it on a hook beside hers.

She turned in a slow circle, surveying the room.

"It's not very big," she noted. "But at least it looks clean."

"That's always a plus," he agreed, setting her suitcase on the dresser.

She wandered into the bathroom to continue her cursory inspection.

"There are extra towels, but only one tiny bottle each of shampoo and conditioner," she told him, when she wandered back out again.

"I guess the first one in the shower gets to wash their hair."

"Knock yourself out," she said. "I don't travel anywhere without my own products."

He nodded toward the beds. "Which one do you want?"

"Doesn't matter."

He tossed his duffel onto the mattress of the one closest to the door, then picked up the remote on the nightstand.

"I thought you were desperate to get some sleep."

"I am," he said. "But I sleep better with the TV on. Or maybe I should say that I fall asleep better with the TV on."

"TV stimulates the brain, and they say that a stimulated brain prevents you from getting the deep sleep you really need."

"Who says?" he challenged, selecting a favorite movie.

"Experts," she responded vaguely. "And why does it matter what's on if you're going to be sleeping?"

"Because the experts also say that falling asleep to the sounds of something familiar can reduce stress so that you get a more restful sleep."

"You just made that up."

"Did I?" he challenged.

She dug around in her suitcase, looking for her toiletry bag, he guessed.

"I forgot I had this," she said.

He glanced over as she pulled a Tupperware container out of the case.

"What is it?" he asked.

"Cake."

"Do you always pack cake when you travel?"

"Hardly," she said. "It's leftover from my niece and nephew's birthday party."

"Your niece and nephew have the same birthday?"

"They're twins."

"So yes," he noted, then asked, "How old?"

"Three."

"What kind of cake is it?"

"Probably broken cake after you dropped my suitcase in the snow."

"It was your suitcase or you," he reminded her.

She pried open the lid to inspect the contents. "Well, it doesn't look as if any damage was done."

"What kind of cake?" he asked again.

"Funfetti cake with cherry filling and Italian meringue buttercream icing."

"So you were holding out on me," he mused. "Begging to

share my dinner when, all along, you had cake in your suitcase."

"I didn't beg," she said indignantly.

"Your eyes were begging."

"My eyes were *not* begging."

"Believe me, honey, I know when a woman is begging for something—though it isn't usually to share my dinner."

"My name isn't *honey*."

"Are you going to offer to share that cake, *Finley*?" he asked.

"Maybe I'll wait for you to beg for it," she said.

He grinned, appreciating that she could give as good as she got.

"If it's from Sweet Caroline's, I would beg," he told her.

"Since you obviously have an appreciation for the finer things in life, I won't make you," she decided.

"You consider pizza and cake to be some of the finer things?"

"Pizza from Jo's and cake from Sweet Caroline's are definitely at the top of the list."

"A woman of simple pleasures," he mused.

"I also like good champagne and a grilled filet on occasion."

"Who doesn't?"

"Haylee—my sister and the mother of the twins—actually gave me two slices of cake, so we don't have to worry about cutting it," she said. "But the coffee tray only has stir sticks not spoons, so we'll have to eat with our hands."

"Works for me," he said easily.

She set one of the slices on the lid of the Tupperware container and passed it to him.

"Thanks." He broke off a piece and popped it in his mouth.

He wasn't a big fan of sweets—he'd take chips over cookies any day of the week—but the cake was moist and the tartness of the filling a nice contrast to the sweetness of the icing.

"This is really good," he said, savoring the vanilla flavor of the cake.

"Enjoy it while you can," she advised. "There's a rumor going around Haven that the owner of Sweet Caroline's is planning to sell."

"Maybe the buyer will get her recipes along with the shop."

"That's assuming the buyer continues to operate the space as a bakery. He might want to open an appliance repair shop instead."

"That would be a definite shame," Lachlan noted.

"Bliss in Oakland is the only bakery I've discovered that could give Sweet Caroline's a run for its money."

"Never heard of it," he said.

"They offer eight different cake flavors and twelve unique fillings, and I've probably sampled every single combination."

"How is that possible?" he wondered.

"I'm an event planner," she reminded him. "Clients often invite me to accompany them to menu samplings and cake tastings."

"That sounds like a pretty good job perk to me."

"Except that I pay fifty dollars a month for a gym membership to work off all that free cake."

"There are cheaper—and more satisfying—workouts than going to the gym," he said with a wink, as he popped the last bite of cake in his mouth.

"I think I'll stick with my fifty-dollar-a-month plan," Finley said, just a little primly.

He shrugged. "Your call."

"That *was* good," she said, licking icing off her thumb. "But now I'm thirsty."

"There might be drinks in the fridge."

"And the motel probably charges four dollars for a can of Coke."

He returned the Tupperware lid to her and reached toward the mini-fridge beside the desk.

"I'll pay for the drinks," he said, offering her a bottle of water with a label that read 'Complimentary for Guests.'

Except "guests" was spelled "geusts."

"Your generosity is overwhelming," she noted dryly.

"I did offer to pay for the room," he reminded her.

"You did," she acknowledged, as she uncapped the bottle.

Lachlan did the same with his, then guzzled down half the contents, his Adam's apple bobbing as he swallowed.

Her gaze followed the column of his throat to the line of his jaw. Or what she imagined was the line of his jaw if she could see through the dark hair that covered it. She suspected it was strong and square, and his lips temptingly shaped and surprisingly soft.

And what was wrong with her that she was thinking about such things? Looking at him as if he was a man she might be interested in?

Because he wasn't and she wasn't.

Still, it required more effort than she wanted to admit to tear her gaze away from him and focus it on the bottle in her hand.

"In the age of spell check and autocorrect, how do you make a mistake like that?" Finley wondered, tracing the word "geusts" on her label.

"Laziness," Lachlan suggested. "You should see some of the egregious errors on the papers that my students turn in."

"Egregious, huh?" She smiled. "Now you sound like a professor. You still don't look like one, though."

He reached into the end pocket of his duffel bag and pulled out a pair of dark-rimmed glasses.

"How about now?" he asked, when he'd settled them on his face.

The glasses didn't completely change his look, but they

did add a bit of a scholarly air. Which, on Lachlan Kellett, was incredibly sexy.

"A little bit," she allowed. "Though I still would have guessed that you were a football coach before college professor."

"I never coached, but I did play some football in high school," he told her.

"Ever been to prison?"

To her surprise, he smiled. "Isn't that a question you should have asked before you invited me into your room?"

"You invited yourself," she reminded him.

"I guess I did. And no, I've never been to prison."

"Anyway, it was Shirla who speculated that you'd done time."

"Shirla? The desk clerk?"

She nodded. "She told me she has a thing for bad boys."

He chuckled. "And she pegged me as a bad boy?"

"She was certainly hoping."

"When did you and Shirla have this conversation?" he wondered.

"When you went out to get your pizza."

"Well, I'm sorry if you're disappointed."

"I'm not disappointed. Harleys and tattoos don't do anything for me. Not that I was looking at you in that way," she hastened to assure him.

"What way were you looking at me?"

"Hungrily," she said. "Because you had the pizza."

He chuckled again, the low rumble sliding over her skin like a caress, raising goosebumps on her flesh.

"So what is your type—since it's apparently not bad boys?" he asked.

She rubbed her hands over her arms. "How did we get on this topic?"

"You asked if I'd ever been to prison."

"So I did," she acknowledged. "As for my type, I don't know that I have one. Or maybe it's been so long since I've been on a date that I can't remember."

"Any particular reason you haven't been dating?" he asked.

"Not really. I've just been focused on other priorities."

"Meaning Gilmore Galas?" he guessed.

"Yeah."

"You're too busy planning celebrations for the events in other people's lives that you don't have time to live your own?"

"I'm happy with my life as it is," she assured him.

"Which is what people say when they're really *not* happy with their lives," he remarked.

"I don't know what people you've been talking to," she said. "But in my case, it happens to be true."

"I'm a professor of anthropology," he reminded her. "I talk to all kinds of people."

He finished his drink, recapped the bottle and tossed it into the recycle bin under the desk.

"Okay if I take a shower?"

"The deal was for a bed," she reminded him. "If you want bathroom privileges, too, you'll have to buy me breakfast in the morning."

"Not a problem." He winked. "I always buy a woman breakfast after spending the night in her bed."

"You have your own bed," she reminded him, that prim note sneaking into her tone again.

"But the room is in your name," he pointed out. "So technically they're both your beds."

The chime of her cell phone was a timely interruption, giving her an excuse to turn her back on him so he couldn't see that he'd flustered her. *Again.*

But the soft chuckle she heard as he made his way into the bathroom told her that he knew it anyway.

Just got the kids into bed and saw your message—now tell me more about this hunky guy you're sleeping with tonight!

Finley immediately replied to her sister's message:

I'm not sleeping with anyone! He's just a fellow stranded traveler.

A HOT stranded traveler.

How can you tell from a DMV photo?

You can't. I Googled him.

WHAT? Why?!

Lots of pics online from Merivale College events. VERY. HOT.

How's the weather there?

Don't you dare change the subject!

I just wondered if the storm was starting to let up, because I can't see anything at all outside the tiny window in this room.

So ask the hunky college professor for this thoughts on the weather.

He's in the shower right now.

Which means naked!

Which definitely wasn't something Finley wanted to be thinking about.

Good night, Haylee. Love you.

Are you going to join him in the shower?

No. I'm going to get into my pjs and crawl under the covers of my own bed—on the opposite side of the room.

Hard to believe you're the same sister who told me to stop worrying about finding Mr. Right and be open to finding Mr. Right Now.

Not really hard to believe, considering I'm your only sister. And look what happened—you ended up pregnant.

I have absolutely no regrets.

Finley knew it was true.

But she also knew that there had been weeks—even months—of worry and uncertainty for her sister as Haylee figured out what her future was going to look like. Before she realized that Trevor Blake was as much in love with her as she was with him and finally agreed to let Finley plan their wedding.

She replied to her sister:

I'm glad, because nobody is more deserving of a happy ending than you.

You deserve to be happy, too.

I am happy.

How can you be happy when you haven't had sex in almost a year and a half?

Finley flushed reading the message, quickly typing a response.

Why did I ever tell you that?

Because I'm your sister and your best friend.

I think it's more likely because of the wine.

There was wine, Haylee confirmed.

A lot of wine, if Finley remembered correctly.

But maybe she didn't, as her memories of that night were admittedly a little fuzzy.

The sound of water running in the bathroom suddenly stopped, making Finley realize that Lachlan was finished in the shower. That he was probably, right now, reaching for a towel to rub over his wet, naked body.

Which meant that she needed to hurry if she was going to get changed before he came back.

Good night, she said again.

You'll check in with me in the morning?

As long as I'm still alive, she promised.

xoxoxo

She was rifling through the contents of her suitcase, in search of her pajamas, when the lights flickered.

She hastily exchanged her clothes for her sleepwear just as the room was plunged into darkness.

Chapter Three

Finley heard a crash, followed by a string of inventive curses. She ventured a few steps toward the bathroom—or at least in the direction she thought she remembered the bathroom being located before everything had gone black. "Are you alright?"

"Fine," Lachlan muttered in a tone that sounded anything but fine.

"Do you need ice? I can scrape some up from outside—if I can find the door."

"I don't need ice."

She heard the bathroom door open—the only warning she got that Lachlan was coming out before he barreled into her.

She stumbled back from the impact, and he instinctively reached out to catch her.

"This is getting to be a habit," he remarked, sounding more amused than annoyed now.

"You bumped into me this time," she pointed out to him.

"I guess I did," he acknowledged.

But he didn't immediately let go of her, and she didn't attempt to step away from him.

Instead, she stood there, unable to see anything in the pitch darkness but nevertheless achingly aware of the heat emanating from his body, the tantalizing scent of clean male that teased her nostrils and stirred her blood, the heat of his hands scorching her arms through the flannel sleeves of her pajama top.

"Finley." Her name was barely a whisper from his lips.

"Lachlan," she whispered in response.

Another few seconds passed.

He cleared his throat. "I should, um, find some clothes."

He was naked?

She swallowed. "You're not dressed?"

"I'm wearing a towel."

Lucky towel.

"I forgot to take a change of clothes into the bathroom with me," he explained.

"You should definitely find some clothes."

Still, neither of them moved.

"This probably isn't a good idea," he warned.

"What—" She had to swallow because her throat had gone dry again. "What isn't a good idea?"

"Using the darkness as an excuse to give in to whatever is going on between us."

"Maybe you're only imagining that there's something going on," she suggested.

"I'm not imagining your hand on my chest."

"Ohmygod." She immediately yanked it away, mortified by the brazenness of her own—completely subconscious—action. "I'm so sorry."

"No need to apologize," he told her. "But if you want me to behave like a gentleman, you have to try not to tempt me."

"I'm certainly not trying to tempt you," she assured him, ignoring the fact that her actions told a different story even if she wasn't able to ignore the tingling in her palm where it had been in contact with the warm, taut skin of his hard chest.

"Honey, even in flannel, you're the personification of temptation."

"You wouldn't say that if you could see that my pajamas are covered with cartoon pigs with wings."

"I don't need to see, because I have a very good imagination and I'm a lot less interested in what's on your pajamas than what's underneath them."

She had a pretty good imagination, too. But she didn't want to imagine his naked body, she wanted to explore it.

She wanted *him*.

So much so that she ached.

And though she barely knew the man, she knew it would be foolish to act on the attraction she felt.

There had been a time when she would have thrown caution to the wind and seized the moment—and the man—not caring, as her sister had reminded her, if he was "Mr. Right" so long as he was "Mr. Right Now." What she'd never admitted to anyone was that every time she'd jumped into a relationship (or bed!) with "'Mr. Right Now," she'd secretly been hoping that he would turn out to be "Mr. Right."

After too many disappointments, she'd decided that she needed to be more discerning so as not to set herself up for disappointment again. Remembering that, she took a deliberate step back now, away from Lachlan, away from temptation.

He didn't try to stop her.

"I need to, um, brush my teeth."

She stumbled back to the dresser, where she'd left her suitcase open, and pulled out her toiletry bag.

"The plumbing in the bathroom is backwards," he told her. "Turn the tap left for cold, right for hot."

"Thanks."

It was eerily quiet in the room now, the only audible sound that of the wind howling outside and rattling the panes of glass in the window. It was so quiet, in fact, that Finley heard his towel drop to the floor when he released it.

Now he was completely naked, and every female part of her quivered with awareness of that fact.

There was some rustling then, as he searched in his duffel bag for whatever items of clothing he planned to sleep in.

"Aren't hotels supposed to have backup generators?" she asked now.

"The Rusty Spurs isn't a Ritz Carlton."

"Dusty Boots," she corrected.

"Still not a Ritz Carlton."

She heard him pull back the covers on the bed and took it as a sign that he was no longer naked.

"Then I guess it's a good thing my phone has a torch light," she said, turning it on.

"Which will drain your battery pretty quickly," he pointed out. "And, without power, you won't be able to recharge it."

"You're not helping my efforts to hold back panic. Besides, I'm sure the two minutes I need it to brush my teeth won't kill the battery," she said, using the light to illuminate her path to the bathroom.

Of course, she had to use the toilet and then wash her hands, too, so it was probably closer to three minutes before she exited the bathroom again.

When she did, she discovered that the bedroom was no longer in pitch darkness but was, instead, softly illuminated by a greenish light.

"You had a glow stick?" She was surprised—and relieved.

"I've got a couple of them," he said. "But this one should see us through the night."

"I guess you weren't kidding about being out in the wilderness."

"Why would I kid about something like that?" he asked, his tone puzzled.

She shrugged.

"So much for your plan to fall asleep with the TV on," she remarked.

"I'm so tired, it probably won't matter tonight—so long as your snoring doesn't keep me awake."

"I don't snore," she said indignantly.

"How would you know?"

"No one I've ever shared a bed with has ever complained."

She caught a quick flash of white teeth as he grinned. "Which doesn't mean you don't snore."

She deliberately turned her back on him, tucked the covers under her chin and closed her eyes, though she suspected it would be a long time before sleep came with the sexy professor only a few feet away from her.

Lachlan could tell by the even rhythm of her breathing when Finley's fake sleep gave way to the real thing.

Unfortunately, slumber continued to elude him.

He'd thought he was clever, bartering for the spare bed in her room. But he realized now that it had been a mistake. He'd told himself that he only wanted a quiet place to crash— and it was true—but now that they were alone together, he couldn't seem to stop thinking about the fact that they were alone together. And that Finley Gilmore was the most intriguing woman he'd encountered in a long time.

He'd met her less than five hours earlier, but he couldn't close his eyes without seeing her in his mind. The way her eyes, as blue as a summer sky, shone when she was happy; the way her lips, as perfectly shaped as a Cupid's bow, curved when she smiled; the way she tilted her head, just a fraction, when she was thinking; the way her brow furrowed when she was unhappy with those thoughts.

That stunning face was surrounded by a fall of silky hair that tempted a man to slide his hands into it, tip her head back and cover her mouth with his own.

Yeah, he wished he'd never asked her to let him crash in the extra bed.

But mostly he wished that he'd ignored his conscience when she'd been in his arms. That instead of warning her that it wasn't a good idea to give in to the attraction between them, he'd kept his mouth shut and kissed her.

Because he felt confident that if he'd given in to the urge, she would have kissed him back. One kiss would have led to another, and then his towel and her flannel pj's would have both ended up on the floor.

So maybe it was a good thing that his conscience had kicked in, because the one thing he didn't have in his duffel bag was protection, and he was no longer a twenty-year-old college kid who didn't know not to take chances with birth control.

Which was almost too bad, because he had no doubt that he'd already be fast asleep if he'd found his release with her.

Seize every opportunity.

That was some of the advice his dying friend had given him when they were saying goodbye and pretending it wasn't for the last time.

"Don't be more afraid of life than death," Ben said.

"Dying seems to have made you philosophical," Lachlan responded lightly.

"Dying has made me realize what's important in life," his friend countered.

"And now you're going to tell me?"

Ben shook his head. "You need to discover that for yourself."

"And how do I do that?" he asked, more to humor his friend than because he expected an answer.

"Appreciate every moment, seize every opportunity and find joy in every day."

And while Lachlan might have been tempted to invoke his friend's advice, he couldn't take advantage of Finley's hospitality by making a move. Not even if he felt certain that she was as attracted to him as he was to her.

But damn, it was hard to do the right thing.

Achingly hard.

* * *

Finley woke up a few hours later. She slid out from under the covers and quickly made her way to the bathroom. The temperature in the room had dropped significantly while she slept, and the bathroom tiles were like ice beneath her feet.

She quickly did what she needed to do, washed and dried her hands and hurried back to her bed.

But the cotton sheet and thin blanket provided little comfort in the chilly room. She rubbed her feet together beneath the covers, hoping the friction would help warm them.

A weary sigh emanated from the other side of the room before Lachlan said, "What are you doing?"

"N-nothing."

"I can hear you fidgeting," he said.

"S-sorry." She crossed her feet at the ankles and tried to think warm thoughts: a steaming bath…a crackling fire…hot chocolate…a tropical beach…sweaty sex.

She immediately reined in her wayward thoughts.

Or tried to.

But apparently her mind was enjoying this mental exercise a little too much, because her next thought was: sweaty sex with a hot man on a tropical beach.

And then: sweaty sex with a hot man in a roadside motel.

"I have a long drive tomorrow." Lachlan's reminder interrupted her prurient fantasies. "So I'd really like to get some sleep tonight."

"I'm n-not s-stopping you."

"I can hear your teeth chattering."

"Well, I c-can't help it if I'm c-cold."

"It's not that cold in here," he told her. "Just close your eyes and when you wake up in the morning, the storm will have passed and the power will be back on."

She ignored his advice to push back the covers.

"What are you doing now?"

"I n-need s-socks," she said. "My f-feet are f-freezing."

Though the glow stick continued to provide faint light, he turned on the torch on his phone to better illuminate her search through her suitcase.

Not because he wanted to be helpful, she suspected, but because he wanted her to go back to sleep so that he could do the same.

"Got 'em," she said triumphantly.

He turned off the light and she unfolded the thick socks and pulled them onto her feet.

"Are you going to be able to sleep now?" he asked.

"I h-hope so."

He sighed again and, after a moment of internal debate, finally asked, "Do you want me to sleep with you?"

"What? N-no!"

"I only meant for the purpose of sharing body heat," he clarified.

"Oh." She was silent for a moment, considering his offer. "Would we have to be…n-naked?"

"Naked would make things more interesting," he mused.

"I'll p-pass, thanks," she said, a little primly.

He chuckled softly. "I was only teasing. Of course, we don't have to be naked."

She was silent for a minute, considering. "Can you explain to m-me how it works?"

"You want me to give you a lesson on thermodynamics?"

"Is that w-what it is?"

"That's what it is," he confirmed.

"And how d-does a professor of anthropology know a-about thermodynamics?" she wondered.

"I took several elective courses in physics."

"You took physics *for f-fun*?"

"Physics *is* fun."

"I think we're going to have to agree to d-disagree on that," she said. "But right n-now, I just want to know if the sharing body heat thing really does w-work."

"It really does."

"Okay, then," she finally relented.

He yanked the blanket and sheet off his bed and carried them to hers.

She scooched over on the mattress, making room for him.

He laid the extra covers on top of the bed before sliding beneath them.

Though she was pretty much hugging the edge of the mattress, as soon as he settled beside her, Finley felt the warmth radiating from his body.

"Heat conduction between two bodies occurs at the surface interface between them," he told her.

"C-can you translate that into English, p-please?"

"If you want to share my body heat, your body needs to be in contact with mine."

"Oh."

"Or I can go back to the other bed, if you've changed your mind."

"I haven't changed m-my m-mind." She released her grip on the edge of the mattress and slowly inched toward the middle of the bed.

"I'm not going to jump you, Finley." His tone wasn't just quiet but also sincere.

"I d-didn't think you were."

Hoped, maybe.

But only for a very brief minute.

He snaked an arm around her waist and pulled her closer.

"You really are cold," he noted, sounding surprised.

She nodded.

He held her wrapped in his arms for several minutes, until she stopped shivering and her teeth stopped chattering.

"Think you can sleep now?" he asked then.

She nodded again.

But the truth was, she wasn't sure.

Yes, she was feeling a lot warmer now.

And achingly aware of the man whose arms were around her.

She closed her eyes and drew in a slow, deep breath, inhaling his clean masculine scent.

Well, that wasn't helping.

She held her breath, but of course, that was only a very short-term solution.

"Relax, Finley."

"I'm trying," she admitted. "But I haven't shared a bed with a man in…a very long time."

"Why's that?"

She shrugged. "I've been too busy with work to even think about starting a relationship, and I don't do one-night stands. Not anymore."

"Me, neither," he confided.

"Really?" she asked, surprised and a little skeptical.

"When you get to a certain age, sex for the sake of sex, without any kind of connection, isn't fun anymore."

"And what age is that?"

"Are you asking how old I am?"

"Maybe."

"Then maybe I'm thirty-six."

"I might be twenty-eight," she told him.

"Kind of young to have given up on relationships," he mused.

"I haven't given up," she denied. "I'm just focusing on my career right now."

"And sleeping alone."

"Except for Simon, of course."

"Simon is…a cat?" he surmised.

She frowned into the darkness. "How did you guess?"

"All the single people I know often give their pets human names."

"Well, I didn't name Simon," she told him.

"Who did?"

"My sister."

"The one with the twins?"

"She's the only sister I've got."

"She got the cat for you?"

"No, she adopted Simon from a local shelter. And then she moved to Nevada, so I offered to keep him."

"None of which disproves my point," he noted.

"Speaking of names," she said, eager to change the topic. "I don't think I've ever known a Lachlan before. Is it an Irish name?"

"It is," he confirmed.

"Does anyone ever call you Lach?"

"Only my ex-wife."

"You're divorced?"

"Yep."

"Another question I probably should have asked before I let you share my room," she admitted.

"Or at least before you invited me into your bed," he teased.

"Cuddling was your idea," she reminded him.

"We're not cuddling," he said, making the word sound distasteful.

"Snuggling?" she suggested as an alternative.

"We're sharing body heat."

"For which I'm extremely grateful," she told him.

"And I'm grateful your teeth have stopped chattering," he noted.

"Apparently this thermodynamics thing really does work." She shifted a little, pressing her back against him to absorb more of his body heat.

"Even without you wriggling around," he said through gritted teeth.

"I'm trying to find a comfortable position to sleep, but your body is hard."

"And it's going to get even harder, if you don't stop squirming," he warned.

She immediately stilled. "Oh. I didn't realize... Sorry."

"Don't be sorry," he told her. "Just go to sleep."

If only it was that easy.

"How do you expect me to sleep now that I know you're... um..."

"Semi-aroused?" he finished for her.

"Yeah," she admitted, grateful that it was too dark for him to see the flush of heat that filled her cheeks.

"Don't worry," he told her. "It isn't personal—just a physiological response to your body rubbing against mine."

"I'm not sure if I should be relieved or insulted."

"You should be asleep," he told her. "We both should be asleep."

Finley couldn't imagine being able to sleep now.

But being wrapped in his embrace made her feel warm and safe.

And finally, she slept.

Chapter Four

When she awakened again, Finley's first thought was that it was morning, as evidenced by the sun filtering through the sides of the curtains. Her second thought was that she was alone, not only in her bed but in the room.

Lachlan was gone.

She should have been relieved to be spared any awkward morning-after conversation with the man. Not that anything had happened between them. Nothing except that he'd shared his body heat so that she could sleep.

So why, in the light of day, did that act almost seem more intimate than sex?

Maybe because she understood that sex didn't always require intimacy. That sometimes sex was just a physical act no more significant (though hopefully more pleasurable) than a walk in the park.

To Finley, sharing a bed with a man required a greater level of trust than sharing her body. And she realized now that she'd never just *slept* with a man.

Until last night.

The quiet hum of the heating unit confirmed that Lachlan's assertion that the storm would pass and power would be restored by morning had turned out to be true. She pushed back the covers and slid out of bed, eager to hit the shower, when her phone chimed with a text.

Power meant she could charge her phone before heading to the airport, and she plugged it in before opening the message—an update from the airline notifying her that her rescheduled flight to Oakland was canceled.

"No." Finley shook her head as she scanned the words again. *"No, no, no."*

She first checked the weather report, then the airport status, then she called the customer service number provided in the message.

"I don't understand why my flight's been canceled," she said, after waiting nearly fifteen minutes and dialing through an endless series of voice prompts just to get to a human. "Again."

"Unfortunately, the incoming flight from Denver was grounded by the storm, so we don't have a plane to send to Oakland," the perky customer service rep who introduced herself as Peg informed her.

"What happened to the plane that couldn't take off for Oakland at four o'clock yesterday?"

Peg tapped some keys. "It's boarding passengers now and is scheduled to takeoff for Oakland at 9:20."

"Why was I booked on a twelve thirty flight if there was one leaving more than three hours earlier?"

"Likely because there were no available seats on the morning flight."

She closed her eyes and silently counted to ten before asking, "So what am I supposed to do now?"

"There are seats available on the twelve thirty flight tomorrow."

"But I need to get back to Oakland *today.*"

More key tapping sounded over the line.

"If you can make your way to Salt Lake City, there's a direct flight from there at three-oh-five."

"If I was going to drive to Salt Lake City—" which was a

four-hour trip in the wrong direction "—I might as well drive to Oakland."

"Would you like me to book you a seat on that twelve thirty flight tomorrow?"

"Unless it's a DeLorean leaving at twelve thirty tomorrow, it's not going to get me back to Oakland today, is it?"

"I'm sorry?"

She sighed. "Never mind."

"Is there anything else I can help you with today?" Perky Peg asked.

"No, thank you," she said, and disconnected the call.

Her problems weren't his problems, Lachlan assured himself.

So why, when he saw Finley toss her phone aside with obvious frustration, did he hear himself say, "I could give you a ride."

She whirled around, obviously startled to see him. "I thought you'd already gone. Your duffel bag was gone."

"I tossed it in my truck on the way to get the breakfast I promised you," he said, setting the cardboard tray holding two cups and a paper bag on the table between the two beds. "I didn't know how you take your coffee, so I got cream and sugar on the side."

"I'd take it intravenously if I could," she told him, prying the lid off one of the cups. "And usually black, but having sampled the motel's interpretation of coffee yesterday afternoon, I'm pretty sure it's going to need lots of cream and sugar to make it palatable."

She added both to her cup, stirred with a flimsy plastic stick, then lifted it to her lips for a cautious sip.

"There's a couple of Danishes in the bag," Lachlan said. "One lemon, one blueberry."

"Thanks, but I don't eat breakfast."

"Never?"

"Only the morning af—" She abruptly cut off her own response.

"The morning after what?" he prompted, a smile tugging the corners of his mouth.

She sipped her coffee again. "Clearly I need caffeine to kick in my conversational filter."

"After sex?" he guessed.

"After racquetball."

"I enjoy a spirited game of racquetball every now and then myself. It certainly does work up an appetite."

She reached for the bag of pastries.

"I thought you didn't eat breakfast?"

"Clearly I need to shove something in my mouth to stop talking."

He didn't try to hold back his smile this time.

"Do you want the lemon or blueberry?" she asked.

"You choose."

She chose the lemon.

She didn't speak again until all that was left of the pastry was crumbs. "Did you really offer to drive me to Oakland?"

"It's not exactly out of my way," he pointed out.

"But it's a long time in a car with someone you don't really know."

"Maybe we didn't spend a lot of time talking last night, but we did sleep together."

"We didn't sleep together," she said indignantly.

"I'm pretty sure we did."

"Okay, yes, we did," she confirmed. "But all we did was sleep."

"And you're regretting that this morning?"

"Of course not," she denied.

But the color that filled her cheeks suggested that she wasn't being entirely truthful.

"Can we maybe talk about something else?"

"You didn't have any trouble telling me about your dry spell last night," he mused.

"I simply mentioned that I was on a dating hiatus," she clarified.

"To-may-to, to-mah-to."

"And anyway, it was dark."

"I'm not sure how that's relevant," he said. "Unless you're one of those women who only ever makes love with the lights off."

"*That* isn't any of your business," she retorted.

"Which can be kind of annoying, because most guys want to see the woman they're with—to fully appreciate her attributes."

"I didn't ask."

"I'd definitely want to see you."

"That's *so* not going to happen."

"I'd be lying if I said I wasn't disappointed," he told her.

"Life's full of disappointments, isn't it?"

"Too true." He finished his coffee as she took another tentative sip from her cup.

"Anyway…" Finley hesitated a moment before continuing, "if you were serious about letting me hitch a ride to California, then I accept. Thank you."

"No worries. And there's a lot more room in my vehicle than in a DeLorean."

She grimaced. "You heard that, did you?"

"The neighbors on either side probably heard you," he said.

"I guess I was a little frustrated by that point in the conversation," she acknowledged.

"Travel delays can have that effect."

"Yeah."

"Speaking of travel," he prompted.

"Right." She set her unfinished coffee aside. "Do I have time for a shower?"

"If you can make it quick. We don't know what condition the roads are in or how long it will take us to get out of Nevada."

"I can be quick," she promised.

She found the clothes she wanted in her suitcase and carried them into the bathroom.

Lachlan settled back on the bed he hadn't slept in and turned on the TV, hoping the chatter of the morning show news anchors would drown out the sound of the water in the bathroom.

Because listening to the spray of the water, it was almost impossible not to think about Finley standing under that spray. Naked. Impossible not to picture the water sluicing over her body, washing soapy lather from the curve of her breasts, suds gliding over the indent of her waist, the flare of her hips.

Because after spending the night in her bed, he was achingly aware of every delectable curve of her body. He wouldn't have intentionally copped a feel, but he'd nevertheless awakened with Finley's back snug against his front, one of his knees between her thighs, an arm around her middle, his hand cupping her breast and a rock-hard erection pressing against her tailbone.

Thankfully she'd still been fast asleep when he'd carefully lifted his hand away, dislodged his knee, and gritted his teeth against the ache in his shorts.

A sharp ping from his cell snapped him back to the present. He reached for the device to check the message on the screen.

R u ever coming home? Miss you!

He smiled as the message from Aislynn effectively banished the naked Finley fantasy from his mind.

I should be home later today. And I miss you, too.

Do u miss me more?

Always.

* * *

Finley was in and out of the shower in record time. Not only because Lachlan had told her to be quick, but because she knew it was a long drive to Oakland (the reason she usually preferred to fly!) and she wanted to get on the road so that she would be back in time for Kelly and Paul's event that evening.

Officially it was on her calendar as the "Metler-Grzeszczak Engagement Party," but over the past few months, she'd gotten to know the couple quite well—as usually happened when she was planning an event—and had started to think of them by their given names. (Also, it was a lot easier to say "Kelly and Paul" than "Metler-Grzeszczak.")

She finished drying her hair, twisted it into a loose knot on top of her head, swiped mascara over her lashes, dabbed gloss on her lips and decided that was all the primping she needed to do to spend the next several hours in a car.

She opened the maps app on her phone to check the route from the Dusty Boots Motel to her home in Oakland.

Six hours and forty-three minutes?

Definitely time to get a move on.

She started to tuck her phone away again when it chimed with a message.

Did you survive the night?

She smiled as she tapped out a reply to her sister's query.

It seems I did.

The college professor didn't have any nefarious intentions?

None aside from stealing half my cake.

You shared?!? (The question was followed by a string of shocked-face emojis.)

It seemed like the right thing to do last night. This morning, I'm not so sure.

"Something put a smile on your face," Lachlan remarked, as Finley came out of the bathroom with her pajamas and toiletry bag in one hand and her cell phone in the other. "Was it the handheld showerhead?"

She rolled her eyes. "There was no handheld showerhead."

"Hmm…must have only been in my imagination then."

"For your information, it was my sister."

He shook his head. "Not even my imagination can conjure a woman I've never met."

She tucked her belongings into her suitcase. "I would have expected the mind of a college professor to be occupied by deeper thoughts."

"I'm still a man," he reminded her. "And most of the men I know think about naked women."

"Are you trying to make me change my mind about spending the next six-and-a-half hours in a vehicle with you?"

"It's probably going to be closer to eight hours, factoring in the snow and breaks for food and fuel."

"Eight hours?" She looked worried as she glanced at the time displayed on her phone.

"Give or take."

She zipped up her case.

"And anyway, you're not going to change your mind about riding with me to California, as I'm pretty much the only hope you have of making it home today."

"You're right about that," she confirmed.

"So…was your sister checking in to make sure I didn't kill you in your sleep?"

"Or while I was awake."

"She's not very trusting, is she?"

"She doesn't know you," Finley pointed out. "And neither do I."

"I imagine you'll know me a lot better after an almost five-hundred-mile drive."

"Let's get started."

"So tell me about this engagement party that you can't miss tonight," Lachlan said, when they were finally en route.

"You don't have to feign an interest in my work," Finley told him.

"Maybe my interest isn't feigned."

"What do you want to know? The menu options? The music selections?"

"I guess I'm mostly curious to know why you made the trip to Nevada when you had such an important event coming up in California?"

"Because there was an even more important event happening here."

"Your niece and nephew's birthday party?"

"Of course."

"They're three. They're not going to remember anything about the party, least of all whether or not you were there."

"But I'll remember," she said. "And I would have hated to miss it."

"You mean you would have hated to miss the Funfetti cake."

She grinned. "That, too."

"Do you see your sister and her family very often?"

"Not nearly as often as I'd like since she moved to Haven." She sighed. "And it's kind of my fault."

"Why would you say that?"

"When our cousin Caleb was getting married a few years

back, I nudged Haylee into attending. It was at the wedding that she fell for Trevor Blake."

And into his bed, though that wasn't a detail she intended to share with Lachlan.

"Wait a minute," he said. "Is your cousin Caleb Gilmore?"

"Do you know him?"

"I know the name. And I know that he's part of the family that operates the Circle G—one of the biggest cattle ranches in northern Nevada."

She nodded. "My dad grew up on the Circle G, but ranching wasn't in his blood the way it was his brothers', so when he was eighteen, he made his way to the West Coast and got a job on the docks. He learned the ropes, then started his own company."

"Gilmore Logistics," Lachlan realized.

"You've heard of it?"

"It's an international shipping conglomerate."

"I guess it is," she acknowledged.

"You've got an impressive family," he mused.

She couldn't disagree.

Nor could she deny that she'd traded on her family's reputation, to a certain extent, by using her surname in her company's name.

She'd never anticipated that doing so might make her a target of charming men who wanted her for all the wrong reasons. And she'd dated Gabriel Landon for almost six months before she figured out that her boyfriend's lifestyle was being financed not by his numerous business ventures but his wealthy girlfriends—of which she was only one.

"And I spend my days helping brides decide between cream and blush roses or debating the merits of chiffon versus organza," she said lightly, wanting to make it clear to him that her family's business success—and their wealth—had nothing to do with her.

"Which I'm sure is much more important to them than overseas shipping routes or the market price of cattle," he pointed out.

She was surprised—and pleased—that he could appreciate the value of her work, despite the fact that he likely had less than zero interest in bouquets or fabrics.

"Anyway," she said, attempting to steer the conversation back on track. "Six months after Caleb and Brielle's wedding, Haylee and Trevor were married."

"Did you plan the wedding?"

"Of course."

"So you must like this guy she hooked up with?"

"Trevor's great," she confirmed. "And he makes her happy, which makes me happy."

"Not envious?"

She frowned. "Why would I be envious of my sister's happiness?"

"Because you want what she has?" he suggested.

"I love my brother-in-law, but not in that way," she assured him.

"I was referring to a husband and kids generally rather than specifically."

"Oh." She considered. "Sure, I'd like to get married and have a family someday, but right now, my career takes all of my time and attention."

"Your career—and Simon."

"Right."

The funny thing was, everyone in the family had assumed that Finley would be the first to fall in love, get married and have a family—if only because Haylee had always been so notoriously shy, especially around members of the opposite sex. Now, in addition to being a career woman, Haylee was a wife and a mother, while Finley—previously of the active social life—was so busy planning events for other people that she didn't have time to date or even hang out with friends.

So it probably wasn't surprising that her last relationship (if a handful of dates could even be called a relationship) had fizzled out close to a year ago. Or maybe it had been even longer than that.

Fifteen months?

Eighteen?

She frowned.

She could remember specific details from the Lynch-Sandoval wedding the previous summer (number of guests at the event— 192; color of the bridesmaids' dresses—violet fog; flavor of the cake—red velvet with chocolate mousse filling), but she couldn't remember the last time she'd been on a real date.

She missed dating.

And she missed sex.

At least when she thought about it.

Thankfully, she didn't think about it very often.

But sitting in close proximity to Lachlan for hours after having spent the night sleeping in his arms, she was thinking about it now.

Not so much the physical release (which she could take care of herself, thank you very much) as the intimate connection of being with another person.

She missed having someone to hang out with and talk to. Someone to chat with over dinner or snuggle up with on the sofa to watch a game on TV. Someone to tangle up the sheets with and wake up next to in the morning.

Instead, she had Simon and sole control of the TV remote.

And for now that was…perfectly fine.

Chapter Five

On more than one occasion, his ex-wife had accused Lachlan of having a white knight complex. Of course, Deirdre had said it as if it was a bad thing, but he didn't think there was anything wrong with wanting to help a damsel in distress. And his short-term roommate had obviously been in distress.

Or at least stuck.

Either way, it had been apparent that she was in a hurry to get back to California and, as he was headed in that direction, it seemed logical to invite her to go with him.

Now he was going to be riding in a vehicle with her for most of the day, and he had yet to decide if that was a good or bad thing.

He was accustomed to solo journeys. He'd been making the trip from San Francisco to Haven at least once every summer for the past twelve years. He never minded the solitude. In fact, he preferred listening to his favorite tunes over the forced conversation that sometimes took place on long drives.

But throughout the journey to Haven, all he'd been able to think about was his friend dying, alternating between optimism—hoping that the prognosis wasn't as bad as he suspected—and realism—knowing that Mara wouldn't have reached out to him if her husband wasn't in dire straits. Now, after spending the past three weeks with Ben, he could no longer pretend that his longtime friend wasn't very close to the end of his days.

It was a harsh reality that he didn't want to dwell on, so he was grateful to have company for the drive. And he knew Finley Gilmore would be a very pleasant distraction.

Thank goodness he had a maps app on his phone to illustrate his route, because all he could think about this morning was the glory of her curvy body tucked against his all through the night.

Even in sleep, she'd looked like a fairytale princess slumbering under the spell of an evil witch. Not that he'd stayed awake watching her sleep. Or not for very long, anyway.

It had taken several interminable—and uncomfortable—minutes for his body to accept that her nearness was simply a fact and not cause for celebration, but sheer physical exhaustion had eventually won out and he'd dropped off to sleep.

"Why anthropology?"

Finley's question intruded on his thoughts, drawing him back to the present.

"Where did that come from?" he asked her.

She shrugged. "You said we'd have hours to get to know one another. I'm trying to get to know you. So why anthropology?"

"I was in a computer science program and needed a social science course and anthropology fit into my timetable," he confided. "It wasn't ever supposed to be anything more than a required credit, but the professor was passionate about the subject and inspired in me the same desire to learn about other peoples and their cultures."

"Is there a particular branch of anthropology that's your focus?"

"Ethnology."

"I don't know what that is," she admitted.

"The study of cultures from the point of view of the subject of the study."

"And what was your thesis topic?"

"The influence of the Basque peoples on the ranching culture of the American West."

"I'm guessing you researched this by living in the mountains of northern Nevada?"

"Yeah."

"The friend you were visiting…he's a descendant of the Basques?"

"Yeah," he said again. "I met him when I was doing research for my thesis. In fact, I lived with his family for six months fourteen years ago."

"And you've stayed in contact with him since then?"

"I was the best man at his wedding, and he and his wife named their second son after me, though they anglicized the spelling."

"He's really dying?"

He nodded. "Stage four pancreatic cancer."

Finley grimaced. "That sucks."

"It does," he agreed.

"Want to change the subject?"

"To absolutely anything else," he told her.

She managed a smile. "Your choice."

"Why don't you tell me why you became a party planner?"

"Officially, I'm an event planner, because Gilmore Galas does more than just parties. We also organize company events and corporate retreats and we've even done a few memorials."

"I'm going to take a wild guess here and say that weddings are more fun than funerals."

"Obviously," she said. "But celebrating a life well lived can be enjoyable, too.

"Anyway, I was introduced to the business when I worked part-time for a company called Weddings, Etc. in college. To be honest, I was surprised to discover how lucrative the event planning business was—and how much in demand good planners are."

"And how did your former employer feel about you starting your own business in competition with hers?"

"Actually, Lola encouraged me—"

"Lola?" he interrupted, with a quizzical lift of his brows. "Was she a showgirl?"

"No, she was—and is—a wedding planner."

"Not a Barry Manilow fan, I see."

"Who?"

"He was a little before my time, too," Lachlan noted. "But my mom's a big fan. Anyway, Lola encouraged you to start your own business?"

"She had more work than she could handle, and she wanted to be able to focus on bigger events—society weddings and that sort of thing."

"Why does everything always have to be bigger and better?" he wondered aloud.

"Is that a rhetorical question or a social commentary?"

"It just seems as if weddings today are about excess. Formalwear with designer labels. Dresses with bling. Flowers overflowing from urns. Cocktail hour with a jazz quartet playing while guests sip fancy drinks specifically crafted for the bride and groom's happy day. And then a seven-course meal to precede the cutting of the seven-tier cake decorated with edible gold leaf.

"And, of course, you know the whole affair is costing the bride and groom—or their parents—a fortune, so you, as a guest, feel compelled to buy a bigger, more expensive gift or toss a couple extra C-notes in the card."

"I don't know what kind of weddings you've been attending," she remarked. "But I'm impressed by your attention to detail.

"And I can assure you that I work closely with each and

every couple to set a budget they're comfortable with and then stay within the constraints of that budget to give them a day that they'll remember forever."

"I didn't mean to be critical of what you do. I just think that if couples focused more on their marriages and less on their weddings, maybe more of those marriages would last."

"How many times have you been married?" she challenged.

"Once was enough for me," he said.

Lachlan drove in silence for the next several minutes before he said, "Are you hungry? Or do you not eat lunch either?"

"I eat lunch," she told him. "And yes, I'm hungry."

"How's a burger sound?"

"I don't think it makes any sound—though it might sizzle on a grill."

"I'm going to ignore your sarcasm because I'm starving," he said, taking the next exit off the highway.

Finley had seen the billboard advertising an In-N-Out Burger "half a mile ahead" and assumed that was where he was headed, so she was surprised when he pulled into a vacant parking spot in front of a small square building with neon letters that spelled out "Gigi's Diner."

"Best burgers in town," he said, shifting into Park and turning off the engine.

"But what town?" she wondered aloud.

He grinned. "Clipper Gap."

"How do you find these places?"

"Are you asking about the town or the diner?"

"Both."

"I like traveling off the beaten path," he admitted. "And I'd rather support a local eatery than a multi-million-dollar corporation."

"I can respect that," she said. "Although sometimes, especially when the clock is ticking, the convenience of a drive-through cheeseburger and fries can't be beat."

"This stop won't put us too far behind schedule," he said. "And I promise, you won't be sorry."

They'd spent almost five hours together in his SUV already and more than a dozen hours in the same motel room—the majority of those in the same bed. During that time, Finley had mostly managed to ignore the undercurrents of awareness between them. (The obvious exception being those few minutes right after the power had gone out.)

But that was a task more easily accomplished in the dark of night. Or even seated side-by-side in a moving vehicle.

Sitting across from him in the brightly lit diner, she couldn't help but be aware of his gaze upon her. Nor could she seem to pull her gaze away from him.

There was something compelling about Lachlan Kellett.

It didn't seem to matter that she wasn't looking for any romantic entanglements at this point in her life. Or that she'd never been a fan of bearded men. (Probably because her mom's first boyfriend—following the separation from her husband, of course—had been a guy with a beard. And long hair. And a skull earring. As if Sandra had gone out looking for a man as different from her husband as she could find.)

But Finley was a fan of his eyes. She didn't know that she'd ever seen eyes so blue.

And when he smiled, her body actually tingled.

Which only proved that it had been far too long since she'd been with a man.

She'd been lucky in the friend department, starting with her sister who'd been her BFF from the day Finley was born until they chose different paths after high school graduation. Not that anyone could ever replace Haylee as her best friend, but not seeing her sister every day had required Finley to make new friends in college, and she'd done so, many with whom she still maintained regular contact. Then there were

Julia and Rachel—not just her partners in Gilmore Galas but women she knew she could always count on to have her back, as she had theirs.

When it came to romantic relationships, however, her experience had been very different. She'd had a few boyfriends when she was in high school and had fallen in love for the first time when she was sixteen. Dylan had been on the rowing team and the student council—a sweet and earnest boy who'd aspired to study political science and work in local government someday. But like most young love, theirs had fizzled out during the summer between their junior and senior years.

She'd cried when they broke up, because the end of a relationship, even if inevitable, was sad. But she'd never imagined that she would spend the rest of her life with him. She was far too practical to believe they would love one another forever—and honestly, she had no desire to marry the first boy she loved—but she was still sad to say goodbye to him.

She'd dated casually in college, because she had plans for her life and wasn't ready to get serious. For the most part, the boys she'd dated (and they had been boys, compared to the men she would meet later) had been grateful that she wasn't looking for a long-term commitment.

It wasn't until she was twenty-four and she met Mark Nickel that she actually believed he might be "the one." He was gorgeous and fun, smart and charming, and he'd swept her off her feet without Finley even being aware it was happening. Unfortunately, while she'd been all in with respect to their relationship, Mark had only been going through the motions, because he was still in love with his ex.

Gabriel was her rebound relationship, and she often thought that if she hadn't been so distraught over her breakup with Mark, it wouldn't have taken her so long to see him for the lying, cheating schemer that he was.

That experience had been a wake-up call. That was when

she'd vowed to forget about men for a while to focus exclusively on Gilmore Galas. And her decision had paid off in spades. Not only had the business grown exponentially, but she was now too busy planning events for other people to even think about the fact that she didn't have a social life of her own.

And in any event, she hadn't met anyone who tempted her to break her self-imposed dating hiatus. Although the more time that she spent with Lachlan, the more she found herself wondering if he could be the one.

Thankfully, before her mind could wander too far down that path, a server appeared with two menus. "Nancy" wore a stereotypical waitress uniform consisting of a light blue dress with white collar and cuffs, a white apron tied around her waist and a plastic name tag.

"Coffee, please," Lachlan said to her.

"Same for you?" Nancy asked Finley.

"Yes, please."

The server returned shortly with two mugs.

Noting Lachlan's closed menu, she asked, "Are you ready to order?"

"We are," he said, ignoring the fact that Finley was still perusing her options.

"What can I get for you?"

"Two barbecue bacon cheeseburger platters."

Finley lifted a brow. "Are you really hungry or are you ordering for me, too?"

"I was ordering for you, too, because you were studying that menu as if the contents were going to be the subject of a final exam."

"There's a lot of stuff on this menu."

"And the barbecue bacon cheeseburger platter is the best thing on it," he told her.

"It's true," Nancy said, when Finley looked to her for confirmation. "We have customers who come regular from Sacramento for it."

Finley didn't have a clue how close they might be to Sacramento but assumed the comment was intended to be a recommendation.

"And for our Sunday waffles," the server added.

She handed her laminated menu back. "Apparently I'm having a barbecue bacon cheeseburger platter."

"You won't regret it," Nancy promised.

There was a good amount of food on the platter. In addition to the loaded burger, there was a mound of steak cut fries, a handful of onion rings, a scoop of creamy coleslaw and half a cob of seasoned corn.

Apparently Finley had meant it when she said she was hungry, because when she finally pushed her platter away, only a few random fries and a bare cob remained.

"Should I apologize for recommending a meal you obviously didn't enjoy?" Lachlan asked.

"Is that your way of saying 'I told you so'?"

"Well, I did tell you so."

"You did," she confirmed. "And you were right." She wiped her fingers on a paper napkin. "I considered skipping the onion rings, because I have an event tonight, but I figured onion rings are probably why Altoids were invented."

"Actually, Altoids date back to the late 1780s and the first known recipe for onion rings was published in 1802."

Amusement crinkled the corners of her eyes. "Why would you know something like that?" she asked, sounding baffled—and maybe a little bit impressed.

He shrugged. "I have a good memory for useless trivia. And you have barbecue sauce—" he touched a fingertip to the side of his own mouth to illustrate "—here."

"Oh." She tugged another napkin out of the dispenser on the table and scrubbed the side of her mouth.

"Other side."

She scrubbed the other side. "Did I get it?"

"Yeah."

But he couldn't seem to prevent his gaze from lingering on her mouth. Especially when her tongue swept along her lower lip, as if to moisten it.

He lifted his eyes then, and they locked with hers.

There was a definite zing in the air—a sizzle of attraction that ratcheted up the temperature about ten degrees whenever he was with her. As they'd proven when they'd huddled together during the power outage at the motel last night.

He'd been divorced for nearly a dozen years and, during that time, he'd gone out with any number of undeniably attractive women. He'd even taken a few of them to bed. But none of them had lingered in his mind for very long after they'd parted ways.

And even though he hadn't slept with Finley Gilmore except in the most literal sense, he knew that she wouldn't be so easy to forget. Because being with her, even just sitting across the table from her at a greasy spoon, made his heart feel lighter. And he knew that if he wasn't careful, she might make him forget all the reasons he wasn't looking for a romantic relationship.

"More coffee?"

Lachlan shifted his attention to the server.

"Yes, please," he said, and nudged his mug forward.

Finley managed to release the breath that had stalled in her lungs and tried not to resent Nancy's untimely interruption.

After all, it wasn't as if he was going to lean across the table and kiss her.

Even if she'd wanted him to.

And she had.

In that moment, she'd wanted nothing so much as she'd wanted to feel the press of his mouth against hers, the sweep of his tongue over the seam of her lips—

"Miss?"

Finley blinked. "Sorry?"

Nancy gestured with the pot she was holding.

"Oh, yes. Please."

The server topped up her cup.

"Thank you."

Lachlan settled back in his seat and sipped his coffee, amusement sparkling in those blue eyes. "Taking a little side trip, were you?"

"Actually, I was thinking about work," she told him.

His smirk told her more effectively than any words that he knew she was lying, but he played along.

"So what's the life of an event planner like?" he asked.

"Just an endless string of parties," she said lightly.

"I guess that means you work a lot of Fridays and Saturdays."

"Almost every Friday and Saturday," she confided. "Last weekend was the first weekend I've had off since…probably last March, when I made the trip to Haven for Aidan and Ellie's second birthday party."

"You're obviously close to your sister and her family."

"Except geographically."

"Do you have any other siblings?"

"A brother, Logan, in Oakland, who's an architect. And another, Sebastian, in Palm Beach. He's a high school senior."

"Are you close to them?"

"Logan more than Sebastian, because of the geography thing again, but also because we're closer in age. We get together for lunch every few weeks, though less often during the summer months, because my schedule is so packed."

"So when do you go out?" he asked.

"It seems as if I'm always out."

"I meant, like dating," he clarified.

"I already told you that I don't date. I can't remember the last time I was out with anyone, actually. When I started Gilmore Galas, I didn't let myself imagine that it could be so successful. I certainly never imagined that I'd be booking events two years ahead."

"I'm sure you don't have events every night of the week."

"No," she agreed. "And after an exhausting 2022, I had a meeting with my partners in which we all agreed that we needed to set limits, to ensure our own work-life balance. Which was much more important to Julia, who had a new—and very frustrated—boyfriend at the time, and Rachel, who had a husband and two little ones at home.

"Now we don't schedule more than five events a week and not more than four of those on a weekend, to ensure that we have at least a couple of nights off every week."

"So you *could* date, if you wanted to?"

"Sure," she said. "But there aren't a lot of guys who want to go dancing on a Monday night. Or plan dinner and a movie for a Tuesday."

"Those are your usual nights off? Mondays and Tuesdays?"

She nodded. "Usual but not guaranteed. And our Sunday events are most often daytime events—birthday parties, bridal or baby showers, baptisms or christenings, that sort of thing."

"Good to know."

She wasn't entirely sure what that was supposed to mean.

But the way he was looking at her made her want to consider the possibility that he might be thinking about asking her out.

And to say *yes* if he did.

Then he lifted a hand for the server to bring their check, and the moment was gone.

The last couple hours of their journey passed uneventfully and mostly quietly. Lachlan focused on the drive while Finley kept busy on her phone—responding to emails and exchanging text messages with Julia and Rachel about the evening event.

But she tucked her phone away when he exited the 580, only minutes from her home. She was glad to be back, looking forward to seeing Simon and her dad and Colleen, but she was also a little disappointed that her road trip with the sexy Lachlan Kellett was coming to an end.

He looked from the address she'd punched into his map to the number on the house and then at her.

"This is where you live?" His brows rose. "Apparently the party planning business is indeed lucrative."

"I grew up in the big house, but I live there," she said, pointing to the carriage house (really a renovated detached double garage) set a little further back.

"Still not too shabby," he noted.

"When Haylee and I first started making plans to move out, we were discouraged to realize that there was a significant gap between what we wanted and what we could afford. Or if we could afford a nice apartment, it was because it wasn't in a nice neighborhood.

"My dad thought—probably hoped—we'd give up and stay at home. But who wants to live with their parents forever? It was actually our brother Logan—the architect—who suggested building a second story above the garage.

"And he designed it, too. Kitchen, dining room, living room, three bedrooms, two bathrooms and a rooftop patio and garden."

She was rambling now, sharing details he hadn't asked for and likely had no interest in. But it occurred to her that, so long as they were talking about something else, it wasn't time to say goodbye. Because she wasn't ready to say goodbye.

Except *they* weren't talking.

She was the only one talking.

So she clamped her lips together to give him a chance to respond.

"All that for just you and your sister?" he said.

She nodded.

"So why three bedrooms?"

"Because Logan knew I'd use one as a home office."

"And now that your sister moved out, all that space is yours?"

"Mine and Simon's," she confirmed.

"I hope he took good care of the place while you were away."

"He usually does."

The hint of a smile played at the corners of his mouth as he opened the driver's side door and stepped out of the vehicle, going around the back to retrieve her suitcase.

She exited the passenger side and followed.

"Well, thank you again," she said. "For the ride."

"Thank you again—for the bed."

She lifted a shoulder. "As you pointed out, I wasn't going to be using it, anyway."

"And then I didn't, either."

"The power going out changed both our plans."

"In any event, I appreciated not having to sleep in the lounge." He set her suitcase on the ground. "And your snoring didn't keep me awake *all* night."

"I *don't* snore," she said again.

"How would you know? Only one of us was awake while you were sleeping," he pointed out with unerring logic—and a wink.

She extended the handle of her rolling case. "Are you sure I can't give you any money for gas?"

"I'm sure."

"I kind of feel as if I owe you dinner."

"You bought lunch," he reminded her.

"Because you wouldn't let me pay for gas."

"And now we've come full circle."

She nodded. "Well, maybe I'll see you around."

"I think you probably will."

And since there wasn't anything else to say—and he obviously didn't intend to ask for her number—she turned away.

Lachlan watched Finley make her way to the carriage house at the end of the lane, then retract the handle again so that she could pick up the case and carry it up the long flight of stairs to the side door at the top of the landing.

He should have offered to carry her bag.

He'd been raised to be a gentleman—to open doors for a lady, pull back her chair, stand when she did—and his mother would be appalled if she knew he'd stood there watching instead of helping. His grandmother would cuff the back of his head—after she'd made him bend down so that she could reach it.

But he knew that if he walked Finley to the door, he'd be tempted to kiss her, and he didn't trust himself to be able to resist the temptation.

It was easier—and much smarter, he decided—to let her walk away.

She hadn't seemed to be in a hurry, though. Despite repeated reminders throughout the journey about her urgency to get home and get ready for the evening's Gilmore Gala, she'd stalled when it actually came time to say goodbye.

He knew she'd been waiting for him to ask for her number. No doubt, men were always asking for Finley Gilmore's number. So he decided that, rather than following the expected pattern, it might be fun to keep her a little off-balance and not ask.

In any event, he didn't really need her number.

Because he'd be seeing her again very soon.

Chapter Six

Simon must have heard her key in the lock, because he was waiting by the door when Finley crossed the threshold.

"There's my handsome guy." She set down her suitcase and purse and picked up the cat to cuddle him close to her chest. "Did you miss me?" She nuzzled his fur. "Because I missed you. Haylee misses you, too. But she's got Trevor and Aidan and Ellie now. And if Trevor has his way, they might be adding a dog to the family."

Simon looked at her through narrowed eyes.

"Don't give me that look," she told him. "I'm not getting a dog. I've got everything I want right here."

Apparently Simon believed her, or maybe it was the stroking of his fur that soothed him, because he closed his eyes all the way and purred contentedly.

"I have a great apartment, a wonderful family, terrific friends, a job I love, and the world's most amazing cat. I don't want the complications of a relationship, and I definitely don't need a man who flirted with me every chance he got but then couldn't be bothered to ask for my number."

She continued her rhythmic stroking of the cat.

"But why didn't he ask for my number?"

Of course, Lachlan wouldn't have too much trouble getting in touch with her if he wanted to see her again. He knew her name, the name of her business, and now where she lived.

But he'd given no indication that he might want to see her again, and that was disappointing.

"Why doesn't he want to see me again?"

Simon opened one eye.

"I just don't understand what happened between the time we were in the diner, when he seemed to be on the verge of asking me out, and our arrival here."

She nuzzled the cat again, listening to the comforting purr in his response.

"There was a connection between us. I *know* there was.

"And anyway, he's the one who started the flirting, hinting that he'd let me handcuff him to the bed."

Finley sighed then and set Simon down on the sofa before making her way into the kitchen. "But maybe I did snore in the night.

"Or maybe he's involved with someone—although that's something I'd think he would have mentioned before offering to give me an up-close-and-personal lesson on thermodynamics." She opened the refrigerator and reached for a can of diet Coke. "He did mention that he was divorced, but that doesn't mean he isn't involved with someone else."

She pulled the tab to open her drink and lifted the can to her lips. "Because we know from experience, don't we, that guys aren't always forthcoming about those kind of details?

"Of course, another possibility is that he simply isn't interested," she acknowledged. "Maybe I misinterpreted his flirtation because I'm ready to end this dating hiatus and get out there again. But there are plenty of other guys if I need to scratch an itch.

"In fact, just last weekend when I was in Haven, I got a text message from Calvin Hines. You don't know Calvin," she said to Simon. "He was before your time. But we dated for a few months, had some good times together. And every once in a while, he reaches out and we get together again.

"And if I'd been home when he texted, I might have decided to scratch that itch."

"Oh, sweetie, you can do so much better than Calvin Hines."

Finley let out a startled gasp and spun around to face her stepmother.

"I didn't hear you come in," she confessed, as heat swept up her neck.

"You were pretty deep into your monologue," Colleen noted, sounding amused.

Finley set down her diet Coke to hug her mom.

"How much did you hear?"

"I came in when you were talking about an up-close-and-personal lesson on thermodynamics."

"So almost all of it."

Though, thankfully, not the part about the handcuffs.

"I meant what I said about Calvin—you can do a lot better."

"Calvin's not so bad."

"He's not bad at all," Colleen agreed. "But he's not right for you, which is why you ended your relationship with him—booty calls aside—a long time ago."

"But I know him," Finley pointed out. "Which means I know what I'm getting when I'm with him."

"There can be comfort in the familiar—but the familiar can also lead into a rut."

"Well, my schedule of late hasn't exactly made it easy for me to meet new people."

"Sounds as if you met someone last night."

"A stranded fellow traveler."

"Speaking of stranded, you were going to text your flight details, so that we could pick you up at the airport. The last I heard, your flight had been canceled—again. Which is why I came over to feed Simon."

"My flight *was* canceled again. So I hitched a ride."

Her stepmother frowned.

"I didn't actually stand on the side of the road with my thumb sticking out," Finley assured her. "I got a ride with someone I met at the motel."

"Your stranded fellow traveler?" her mom guessed.

"How do you *do* that?"

"Do what?" Colleen asked innocently.

"Know things I don't tell you."

"A mother's intuition."

"That must be it," she agreed. Because even though Colleen hadn't given birth to Finley—or Haylee or Logan—from the day she'd exchanged vows with Robert Gilmore, she'd been a mother to all of his kids in every way that counted.

"So tell me about him," her mom urged.

Finley didn't know where to begin. With the pizza they'd shared in the reception area of the motel? With the bargain they'd struck to share her motel room? With the storm knocking out the power? She didn't need to mention that he'd wrapped his hard body around her to keep her warm when the temperature plummeted, because Colleen had already heard that part of the story.

"I don't know what to tell you, other than that he's a professor at Merivale College who overheard me on the phone, trying—unsuccessfully—to rebook my canceled flight, and offered to let me ride back with him."

"The flush in your cheeks contradicts your words," her mother noted. "But I'm not going to press for details you're not ready to share."

Finley's already warm cheeks grew warmer.

"Instead, I'm going to invite you to come for dinner."

"So you can grill me after you're done with whatever's on the menu tonight?"

"Pasta carbonara," Colleen said. "No grilling required."

And one of Finley's favorites.

"I wish I could say yes, but I have to be at Harcourt House

for the Metler-Grzeszczak engagement party in less than an hour."

"You also need to eat, and I know you won't eat there."

"Because I don't get paid to eat. And anyway, I had a late—and really big—lunch."

"I'll bring over a plate that you can heat up when you get back."

"Thanks, Mom."

Colleen gave her another hug. "Don't forget to feed Simon before you go."

Going home felt strange.

Driving through the familiar streets of his neighborhood, it was almost as if the past three weeks hadn't happened. Or maybe it was just that Finley's *Back to the Future* reference had stuck in his head. Too much about the woman he'd met twenty-four hours earlier seemed to be stuck in his head.

Anyway, as much as Lachlan was glad that he'd taken the time to be with his friend, he was even more glad to be home.

Three weeks was a long time to be gone. To be away from Aislynn.

He decided that he'd give her a call as soon as he got in, to confirm plans for their weekend get-together. Then he'd tackle laundry and whatever other chores needed to be done around the house. He had a housekeeper who came in once a week to dust and vacuum the common areas, but he took care of his bedroom and home office himself.

He should reach out to Laurel Strickland, too, to thank her again for covering his classes while he was out of town and find out if there were any issues he needed to know about. He'd responded to email queries from his students as much as possible—cell phone service was surprisingly good in the mountains—but mostly he'd redirected his students to Dr. Strickland and promised to follow up when he returned.

After all of that, it might be time to think about ordering dinner. Because he had no idea what might be in his fridge after three weeks away, but he was sure none of it would be edible.

He should have stopped at a grocery store en route but he hadn't, and he had no desire to turn around now. And anyway, now that he was thinking about it, it had been a long time since he'd had Szechuan beef and Shanghai noodles.

As soon as he turned onto his street, he spotted Deirdre's car parked in front of his house and found it was oddly comforting to know there was someone at home to greet him after a long and difficult journey.

"This is a surprise," he said, when he walked in and found both his ex-wife and his daughter in the kitchen. "What are you guys doing here?"

"We wanted to see you." Aislynn threw herself into his arms. "We missed you."

"Aislynn missed you," Deirdre clarified.

"You were gone a really long time." Lachlan didn't have any trouble hearing the accusation in his daughter's tone, even with her face buried in his sweater.

"Longer than I expected to be," he acknowledged.

She drew back a little and tipped her head to look at him with eyes the exact same color as those he saw in the mirror every day. "You missed *three* Wednesday night dinners, a *whole* weekend *and* my spring music concert."

"I'll make it up to you," he promised.

"I don't know that you can," she said peevishly. "But a trip to Disneyland would be a good effort."

He managed a weary smile. "I'll keep that in mind."

"Bonus points if I get to bring a friend."

"That's enough, Aislynn," his ex-wife admonished their daughter.

"I'm just saying."

"And I said that's enough," Deirdre told her. "Your dad just got home from one trip—let him at least unpack before you start nagging him to plan another."

"Too late," Lachlan said, softening his words with a wink for his daughter.

"Why don't you go on upstairs and look for that sweater you've been moaning about not being able to find all week?" Deirdre suggested.

"Because I know it's not here," Aislynn said. "Because I specifically remember packing it to take to your house so I could wear it when me and Harmony went to see *Dirty Dancing*."

"Go look anyway," her mom told her.

With an exaggerated sigh, Aislynn turned and clomped toward the stairs.

"I was sorry to hear that Ben's condition took such a bad turn so quickly," Deirdre said to Lachlan, speaking in a gentler tone now.

"Me, too."

"How's Mara doing?"

"She's putting on a brave face—for Ben and the kids."

"Will you go back…for the funeral?"

He shook his head. "His family will have lots of support then. I'll make a trip in the summer."

"You could take Aislynn with you."

"Yeah, because our daughter likes roughing it almost as much as you do," he noted dryly.

"She might not be a fan of outdoor bathing," Deirdre acknowledged. "But she does like hanging out with her dad."

"At Disneyland."

"Well, who wouldn't?" his ex agreed, with a small smile. "Anyway," she said, ready to move on to another topic. "I picked up a few groceries for you. The basics—bread, milk, eggs. And a bottle of Jack."

"Thanks."

She nodded.

After a beat, she said, "Now would be an appropriate time for you to invite me to stay for a drink."

"I'm not in the mood for company tonight."

Deirdre looked worried. "Which is exactly why you shouldn't be alone."

"I'll be fine."

"Okay," she relented. "But call me if you change your mind."

"I'm not going to change my mind," he told her.

She lifted a hand and laid it on his cheek, rubbing her palm gently against his scruffy beard. "You're going to get rid of this before the party next Saturday, aren't you?"

"You don't like it?"

She tilted her head, considering. "Actually, I think it's kind of sexy," she said. "But I guarantee your mother won't like it."

Deirdre was right about that. After eighteen years in his family—and notwithstanding the fact that they'd been divorced for a dozen years, she was still a member of his family—she knew his parents almost as well as he did.

"I'll get rid of it before the party," he confirmed, just as Aislynn returned with her missing sweater in hand. "In fact, probably before I go back to school on Monday."

"Grandma said she'd take me shopping for a new dress for the party," Aislynn chimed in.

"Lucky you," Deirdre said.

"You could come with us," Aislynn said to her mom. "You probably want a new dress for the party, too."

"I don't know if I'm going to the party," she hedged.

"Why not?"

"Because Philip might be out of town that weekend."

"You don't need to bring a date. Dad's not bringing a date," Aislynn said, before looking to him for confirmation. "You're not, are you, Dad?"

He thought fleetingly of Finley but gave a brief shake of his head. "No, I'm not taking a date."

"See?" Aislynn said.

"Well, that's a decision for another day," Deirdre said. "Right now, we need to be on our way."

"Why?"

"Because your dad's practically asleep on his feet."

"I didn't get a lot of sleep last night," he admitted.

Aislynn sighed. "Okay."

"But I'll see you tomorrow," Lachlan reminded her. "Because it's our weekend this weekend, right?"

"Actually, I didn't know if you were going to be back, so I made plans with Harmony for after school tomorrow."

"I can pick you up at Harmony's."

"Sleepover plans," she clarified.

"Oh."

"But I could come on Saturday."

"Then I'll see you Saturday," he confirmed.

"I'm glad you're back."

"Me, too."

She hugged him again and whispered in his ear. "And don't forget to think about Disneyland."

Finley had planned to be at the venue before the happy couple arrived, so that she could double- (and triple-) check that everything was as it should be. But she fussed a little too long with her hair and changed her shoes three times before she finally made her way out of the house—and then, when she got in her SUV, she saw that her fuel gauge was hovering perilously close to E.

Silently cursing her brother, because she had no doubt it was Logan who'd been zipping around town in her SUV while she was out of town, she detoured from her route to the nearest gas station. While she was fueling up—and continuing to curse her brother—she considered that having to make an unplanned stop wasn't necessarily a bad thing.

Though she trusted both of her partners implicitly, she was admittedly a bit of a control freak when it came to Gilmore Galas. (And justifiably so, in her opinion, as it was her name on the door.) But the truth was, she couldn't run the business without Julia and Rachel, and she knew that showing up a little bit late at an event for which she'd given them the reins weeks ago said far more than any words could about her faith in them.

So after she filled her tank with gas, she took a circuitous route to Harcourt House, ensuring that the party was well under way by the time she arrived.

"I was starting to think that you weren't going to make it," Julia said, when their paths crossed near the coat check.

"I told you I'd be here."

"And that's what I told Kelly and Paul, when they asked for you."

Customer service was key to the event planning business, and Finley prided herself on giving her clients whatever they needed, whenever they needed it. So while the general business line automatically went to voicemail after regular hours, clients who signed with Gilmore Galas were given her direct email and cell phone number so they could feel confident that she was always available to them.

The realization that she hadn't been on-site when the soon-lyweds (the moniker she assigned to brides-to-be and their grooms) were looking for her made her cringe inside, but she had no doubt that Julia had taken care of them.

"Was there a problem?"

"No," Julia said. "They just wanted to thank you person-ally—as they thanked me and Rachel—for ensuring that this party was everything they wanted it to be."

"I'll be sure to speak to them," Finley said. "But you and Rachel are the ones who put in all the work on this."

"We worked our butts off," Rachel confirmed, joining the conversation when her colleagues made their way into the ballroom. "But it didn't seem like it, because Kelly and Paul are both so much fun to work with."

Which was a good thing, Finley mused. Because this little party was going to seem like a walk in the park compared to the wedding that was being planned for November.

But she kept that thought to herself, unwilling to tarnish their shiny moment. Instead, she said, "I want to thank you both, too. Not just for planning this fabulous party, but for being the best partners any woman could ever ask for."

"Someone's in a reflective mood tonight," Rachel noted.

"I just want you to know how much I appreciate you. Because there's no way I could have taken a whole week off to spend with my sister and her family in Nevada if I didn't trust the business in your very capable and talented hands."

"You were Gilmore Galas before we came along," Julia pointed out. "But we're honored to help carry the banner."

Rachel nodded her agreement.

Finley surveyed the room, noting that there were a few guests examining the hot and cold hors d'oeuvres on the buffet table and several more hanging around the bar, but most were on the dance floor, shaking and shimmying to the music. Kelly and Paul were at the center of the group, showing off their moves.

The happy couple were planning a traditional wedding, because it was what their families expected, and they wanted to make them happy—especially as the respective parents were sharing the costs of the affair. So they'd requested an engagement party that would give them a chance to let loose with their friends. They'd assured Finley that they didn't care about themes or menus or flowers and were happy to leave all those decisions up to the professionals. They just wanted to have fun.

"What do you think?" Julia asked.

"It looks like fun is definitely being had," Rachel replied to her question.

Finley had to smile. "And that's why this is the best job in the world."

"One of the reasons," Rachel agreed.

"Another is the number of cute guys who cross our paths," Julia added.

"Says the woman who got engaged a few weeks ago."

"I'm scoping out the prospects for you—not me," her friend said.

"I appreciate your efforts, but I'm really not looking for a man right now."

"And isn't that when they usually come along?" Rachel mused.

"Speaking of—" Julia nudged Finley with her elbow "—check out Mr. Tall, Blond and Tanned checking *you* out."

"Even if I was looking," Finley said. "I wouldn't be looking at the guests at our events."

"Why not?"

"Because they're inevitably friends or relatives of our clients, which would make any…personal interactions…inherently more complicated."

"His name is Craig," Rachel said. "He's a cousin of the bride and also a groomsman in the wedding party. He went to college at UC Davis with Paul and introduced him to Kelly when their paths crossed at a music festival in Long Beach."

"And he's coming this way. Which is why we—" Julia took Rachel's arm "—need to go that way."

As her partners abandoned her, Finley continued to work on her tablet.

"Great event tonight," Craig said.

She glanced up then, as if she hadn't been aware of his approach, and was surprised to discover that he *was* cute, in a stereotypical California boy-next-door kind of way. Tall and lean with sun-bleached dark blond hair, warm brown eyes and an easy smile.

Unfortunately, nothing about Craig gave her tingles.

"Everyone seems to be having a good time," she agreed.

"Kelly and Paul definitely are," he said. "But now you have a problem."

"What's that?"

"They're going to expect something even bigger and better for the wedding."

"That's not a problem," she said. "Plans are already in the works and their wedding will be bigger and better."

"Then I guess I'm the one with the problem," he said.

"What's that?"

"I don't have a plus-one for the wedding."

"Sorry, that's not one of the services we provide."

"I'm not asking you to find me a date—I'm asking you to be my date." He smiled again. "So what do you say?"

"No."

"Ouch. Are you sure you don't want to take at least three seconds to think about it?"

"It's nothing personal," she hastened to assure him. "It's just a really bad idea to mix business with pleasure."

"Then how about being my plus-one for dinner tomorrow night?"

"I can't."

"Because I'm a friend of Kelly and Paul?"

"Because I've got an event tomorrow night."

"Would your answer be different if you didn't have an event?"

"I don't know."

"So tell me when you don't have an event."

"Three weeks from Tuesday… I think. I'll have to check my calendar to be sure."

"You're brushing me off."

"I can see why you'd think that, but my schedule is really crazy right now."

"Uh-huh."

She really didn't have time to date.

And she definitely wasn't looking for romance.

But he was good-looking.

Smart. Charming. Funny.

Not to mention that the bride and groom—both people that she liked—clearly adored him.

Which was why she *should* brush him off, because that connection added another level of complication.

But if she was being perfectly honest with herself, the biggest factor in her decision to *not* brush off boy-next-door Craig was that she was still stinging from the brush-off she'd been given by Lachlan Kellett earlier in the day.

"Are you free Tuesday night?" she asked, before she could talk herself out of it.

"If I'm not, I'll clear my schedule."

"There's a new restaurant—The Wine Cellar—in Bayside Village. The manager invited me to come in for a menu tasting in the hope that we'll add it to our list of recommended venues."

"What time should I pick you up?"

"I've got an appointment in the afternoon, so I'll be heading to the restaurant directly from there."

"Okay. What time should I meet you?"

"The reservation is for seven."

"I'll see you then."

She nodded, surprised to realize that she was looking forward to it.

Chapter Seven

Lachlan had one thing on his mind when he walked into his kitchen Monday morning: coffee.

"Jesus, Dee. It's not even seven thirty in the morning—what the hell are you doing here?"

"It's Monday," she reminded him.

"And?"

"And I often stop by for coffee after dropping Aislynn at band practice Monday mornings so we can talk."

"Weren't you here when I got home on Thursday? Didn't we talk then? Or was that a dream?"

"Aww, you still dream about me?" Deirdre batted her eyelashes playfully. "How sweet."

"Maybe it was a nightmare," he decided.

She poured a mug of coffee for him.

He accepted with a muttered, "Thanks."

"And one of the things Aislynn mentioned on Thursday is what I wanted to talk to you about."

He sipped his coffee, waiting for her to explain.

"I haven't RSVP'd to the invitation to your grandparents' anniversary party yet."

"Why not?" he wondered aloud.

"Because I haven't decided if I should go," she admitted.

He opened the loaf of bread on the counter and dropped two slices into the toaster. "Do you have other plans that day?"

"No."

"Then why wouldn't you want to go?"

"I didn't say I didn't *want* to go. I said I didn't know if I *should* go."

He swallowed another mouthful of coffee. "I'm going to need another minute for the caffeine to kick in to follow this conversation."

Deirdre huffed out a breath. "You know I love your grandparents. Your whole family."

"And they love you." He retrieved a knife from the cutlery drawer, then reached into the cupboard for the jar of peanut butter.

"But we're divorced."

"You're still Aislynn's mother," he pointed out reasonably.

She sipped her coffee. "Will it be weird for you if I bring Philip?"

"Why would it be weird for me?"

"Because we used to be together, and now, I'm with him."

"It might be weird for Philip," he acknowledged with a shrug. "It won't be weird for me."

"You should consider taking a date, too."

When the toast popped up, he slathered peanut butter on both slices, then transferred them to a plate. "You think that will make it less weird for Philip?"

"I think it will make it less…ambiguous…for our daughter."

"Well, now I'm confused," he said, carrying his plate and his mug to one of the stools at the island. "Didn't we agree, way back when, that it would be best not to introduce her to people who might only be a temporary presence in her life?"

"She's not six years old, anymore. She's almost sixteen. Which is something else we're going to have to talk about very soon."

He chewed a bite of toast, swallowed. "Her birthday's not until August."

"August might seem far away right now, but it's her Sweet Sixteen and plans need to be made. However, the anniversary party is a lot closer, and I really think you should take a date."

"As much as I value your insights into my personal life—and I really don't—I'm not dating anyone right now." He bit into his toast again. "And if I *was* dating someone, introducing her to my family for the first time at an event like that would likely lead to her status changing from girlfriend to *ex*-girlfriend."

"So invite a friend. Or even a colleague from work."

"Why is this so important to you?"

Deirdre stole the second slice of toast from his plate and took a bite.

"I figured that if you'd wanted breakfast, you would have made your own."

"I only wanted a bite," she said, returning the toast to his plate.

He didn't bother to sigh; instead he asked again, "Why is this so important to you?"

"Because I overheard Aislynn and Kendra talking one day while you were gone." She licked peanut butter off her thumb. "Kendra was upset because she'd just found out that her dad had asked his girlfriend to be wife number three, and she asked Aislynn if you ever dated girls who were barely out of college."

"Jesus." He lifted his mug to his lips and swallowed another mouthful of coffee. "Is Frank's new fiancée really that young?"

"Twenty-two," his ex-wife told him.

"That's just…wrong."

"Says the man who spends his days hanging out at the local college," she said, tongue in cheek.

He gave her a stern look. "Because it's where I work."

"Anyway, getting back to the girls' conversation…"

He nodded and resumed eating his breakfast, waiting for her to continue.

"Aislynn told Kendra that you don't date very much. Kendra then asked, why not? And Aislynn said it was because you're still in love with me."

"She can't honestly believe that," he protested.

"She's a child of divorce," she reminded him unnecessarily. "Most children of divorce harbor fantasies about their parents getting back together."

"As you pointed out, she's almost sixteen. Isn't she a little old to be fantasizing about a family reunion?"

His ex-wife shrugged. "How am I supposed to know?"

"Well, we can be sure of one thing at least."

"What's that?"

"She clearly has no memories from when we were married, because if she did, she'd have no desire to repeat that experience."

"We're much better as friends than we ever were as husband and wife," she agreed.

"Which doesn't mean I want you butting into my personal life."

Deirdre nodded. "Then find yourself a girlfriend so I don't have to."

Finley loved Mondays.

Most people with traditional jobs looked forward to Friday, because it was the end of the work week and the start of the weekend. And when they wanted to celebrate a special occasion with friends, they generally planned those celebrations for the weekend. Which was why, when everyone else was having fun, Finley was working. And also why, when they all returned to their Monday-to-Friday jobs, she got a reprieve.

Of course, a reprieve didn't necessarily mean a day off. And when Finley's phone rang early Monday morning, she immediately connected the call.

"Good morning, Mrs. Edwards."

Catherine and Douglas Edwards were going to be celebrating their milestone sixtieth anniversary the following Saturday with a party in the Sapphire Ballroom of the Courtland Hotel, San Francisco. From the very first meeting, the octogenarians had been an absolute joy to work with.

They'd come in for a preliminary consult already knowing exactly what they wanted and in sync with respect to every detail. But it wasn't just their complete synchronicity that Finley admired—it was that they were obviously still in love after six decades of marriage. And after every meeting with them, she found herself wondering what it would be like to have that history and connection with another person—and if she'd ever be lucky enough to find it for herself.

"How many times have I told you to call me Catherine?" the client asked Finley now.

"I'm not sure I can give you an actual number, but probably every time we've talked," she admitted. And while she was comfortable on a first-name basis with most of her clients, she'd been brought up to show a certain level of deference to her elders—and Catherine Edwards was certainly that.

"And now you can add this one to the tally."

"How can I help you... Catherine?"

The old woman chuckled. "I can tell that was hard for you, but it will get easier with practice," she promised. "And I'm calling to tell you that I found it."

Finley mentally sifted through the details of their previous conversations for a hint of what "it" might be.

"I knew it was in the attic somewhere," Catherine continued, her voice filled with childlike glee. "And I spent three days in that horrible stuffy space going through boxes and cases and chests, but I finally found it."

"Your original wedding cake topper?" Finley guessed, recalling one of their earliest discussions about the event.

"Our original wedding cake topper," Catherine confirmed.

"That's wonderful."

"Actually, it's hideous."

"I'm sorry?"

"I remembered it being beautiful—but obviously my memory was faulty, because it's not beautiful at all. It's old and ugly. The groom looks like he's wearing the same shade of bright red lipstick as the bride and her eyelashes practically touch her eyebrows. And while the figures are made out of some kind of ceramic, the skirt of the bride's dress is fabric, yellowed with age and fraying at the hem."

"We work with a wonderful company that restores and renews vintage items," Finley said, always glad to be able to provide a solution to a problem. "If you want to bring it in, we can have Mr. Ritchey take a look at it."

"Goodness, no," Catherine said, laughing. "I don't want anyone else looking at this thing. To be honest, I kind of wish I'd never found it. But my Douglas always says I'm like a dog with a bone—which is hardly a flattering analogy but true nonetheless—and I knew it was in that attic somewhere and simply couldn't rest until I'd found it."

"It's your decision, of course," Finley told her. "And if you change your mind, we can add it to the cake later."

"I'm not going to change my mind," Catherine assured her. "Some things from the past are better left there, and this is definitely one of them."

It was good advice, Finley mused, and vowed to do exactly that with her memories of Lachlan Kellett.

Finley had barely walked through the door Tuesday night before her sister initiated a FaceTime call. She connected as she kicked off her shoes and made her way into the kitchen to pour a glass of wine.

"How was your date?" Haylee wanted to know.

"It was good."

"Are you sure? Because it's just after ten o'clock and you're already home—and obviously alone."

"I'm sure." She carried her wine into the living room and settled onto the sofa with her feet tucked beneath her. "The food was fabulous. Squash ravioli with sage brown butter sauce, slow-roasted brined chicken with herbed risotto, seared scallops with grits and sweet corn, grilled tomahawk pork chop with cheesy scalloped potatoes, pan-fried sea bass with watercress salad, and prime rib with horseradish cream and roasted Brussels sprouts."

"You hate Brussels sprouts."

"Apparently I don't hate roasted Brussels sprouts."

"Well, it sounds like you tried everything on the menu."

"It was a tasting menu, so not full portions. But yes, it was a pretty good sampling of the restaurant's offerings."

"And a different wine with every entrée?"

"Of which I only had a couple sips," Finley assured her sister. "Oh, and there was dessert. You would've *loved* all the desserts. My favorite was the apple crisp with vanilla bean ice cream, but there was also a flourless chocolate cake, New York–style cheesecake, a lemon meringue tart, traditional tiramisu and homemade raspberry and lime sorbet."

"And Craig?" Haylee prompted.

"He said the sorbet was the best he'd ever had."

"That's not what I was asking," her sister chided.

"Craig was…great," Finley said.

Because it was true.

In fact, he'd been the perfect date—punctual, attentive and charming. He chewed with his mouth closed, hadn't balked at sharing from his plate and didn't drink too much.

"And the goodnight kiss?"

Finley's mind flashed back to leaving the restaurant with Craig.

"It's not too late," he noted, after he'd walked her to her car. "Do you want to come over to my place? For coffee?"

"We just had coffee," she reminded him.

"I know, but it seemed a little bold to ask if you wanted to come over for sex."

She laughed. "A tempting offer, but one I'm going to have to decline. I've got an early morning and a busy day tomorrow."

"Maybe next time?"

"Maybe." She didn't want to mislead him, and she'd genuinely enjoyed the time she'd spent with him. But while he was an undeniably attractive man, she wasn't attracted to him. She wanted to be—and on the surface, he checked all the boxes—but for some inexplicable reason, she couldn't stop thinking about Lachlan. And getting any further involved with Craig under those circumstances wouldn't be fair to him.

But something in her voice must have given her away, because he said, "There's not going to be a next time, is there?"

"I had a great time tonight, and—"

"I think I'd prefer you to stop right there," he interjected. "It's obvious you're not into me, and while I'm admittedly disappointed, I will at least go home with fond memories of an exceptional meal and a sweet goodbye kiss—with your permission, of course."

She assented with a nod, and he lowered his head to brush his lips over hers.

It was a sweet kiss, and over almost before it had begun.

"The kiss was…nice," Finley said, finally responding to her sister's question.

Haylee sighed. "That bad?"

"I didn't say it was bad."

"You said nice. With a pause preceding the word."

"And nice with a pause is bad?" she asked dubiously.

"What do I know?" Haylee said. "I married the first guy I ever slept with. But I know *you*, and there wasn't any of the excitement in your voice when you talked about Craig that I heard when you talked about Lachlan."

Finley took a long sip—okay, gulp—of wine. "I don't want to talk about Lachlan."

"He hasn't called you?"

"He never even asked for my number," she reminded her sister.

"But he knows your name. And where you work."

"You're right. And any man with half a brain and internet access could find my number easily enough if he wanted to get in touch with me, so clearly he doesn't."

"You also know his name and where he works," Haylee pointed out.

It was true. And in a moment of weakness, she'd actually looked up the faculty directory for Merivale College, so she had the general campus number and the extension for Dr. Kellett in the anthropology department. She'd also found his email address, but she had no intention of using either method of communication to reach out to him.

"I'm not calling him," she said.

"Why not?" her sister wanted to know.

"Because I don't have time to chase after a man and even less desire to do so."

"But haven't you wondered about the odds of two strangers who live in the same general part of California crossing paths five hundred miles away from their respective homes?"

"Not really."

"Well, *I* have," Haylee said. "And I don't think it was chance—I think it was fate."

Finley wasn't sure she believed in fate, but to appease her sister she said, "And if it was fate, then I have to believe our paths will cross again. But no way am I chasing after him."

It had been one of those days.

Actually, it had been one of those weeks in which it seemed as if one crisis had followed directly on the heels of the previous one. It started with a shipment of bridesmaids dresses in the wrong shade of pink (the bride wanted pink tutu but the dresses that arrived were ballet slipper); then a recently engaged couple, both avid hikers, ventured into Muir Woods for an engagement shoot and ended up in the hospital being treated for exposure to poison oak; followed by the guest of honor at a retirement party being caught with his pants down and his secretary saying a very personal goodbye.

And on Friday, at the rehearsal for the following day's wedding ceremony, it was discovered that the ring bearer had chicken pox, leaving the bridal party short two members as both the boy and his mother, one of the bride's attendants, were in quarantine. The drama continued Saturday, with Finley having to send an SOS to a local seamstress for an emergency fix because the bride's dress wouldn't zip up.

She might have been able to anticipate the problem if Naomi had mentioned, at any of her previous fittings, that she would be almost four months pregnant at the time of her nuptials. But the bride had been determined to keep her condition a secret from everyone—specifically from her mother but also, and unfortunately, from the wedding planner. Thankfully, Bridget from "With This Thread" had rescued the day—or at least Naomi's gown.

By seven o'clock, Finley had been on her feet for the better part of twelve hours already and wanted nothing more than to collapse on her sofa with a nice big glass of wine.

Unfortunately, the prospect of both of those things remained elusive. But she'd learned to find moments of Zen during times of chaos, and right now, she was basking in the relative peacefulness of Catherine and Douglas Edwards's sixtieth anniversary celebration while Julia and Rachel were on guard at the wedding across the hall.

As she scanned the room, her gaze snagged that of the man she'd noticed earlier. He was the personification of tall, dark and handsome in a very nice suit, and she'd found herself distracted by him far more often than she wanted to admit.

"Finley."

She broke the connection and summoned a professional smile before turning around. Her expression immediately warmed when she found herself face-to-face with Catherine Edwards.

"What can I do for you, Mrs.—Catherine?" she automatically corrected herself before the other woman could.

"You've done so much, Finley, that I was hoping that you'd let me do something for you."

It wasn't unusual for happy clients to offer a bonus at the conclusion of an event—and Finley tried to ensure that all her clients were happy—but the twinkle in the old woman's eyes warned Finley that she had something different in mind.

"You don't need to do anything for me," she said. "It's been my pleasure to ensure you and your husband are enjoying your celebration."

"It's been absolutely perfect. Or almost perfect."

Finley knew she was being played—and by a champ—but if there was any way she could upgrade the guest of honor's experience from "almost" to "perfect," she had to try.

"Tell me how I can make it perfect," she suggested.

"Let me introduce you to my grandson."

Years of practice allowed Finley to keep her smile in place even during the most awkward moments, like this one.

But still, she struggled to reply. "Oh. Um… Is he single?" she finally asked.

Though it seemed like the answer to her question should be obvious, Catherine Edwards was hardly the first client to want to play matchmaker and, on a previous occasion, it turned out that the client wanted to set her up with a son who was, in fact, married, because he was married to a woman she didn't like.

"Divorced, actually," Catherine responded to her question.

"But I hope you won't hold that against him, because he really is a wonderful man and—" she dropped her voice to a whisper "—my favorite grandson. He's handsome, of course, well-educated, and gainfully employed. A lot of men can't hold a job these days—or don't want to—and a successful woman like yourself has to be careful not to be taken in."

"I'm sure he's every bit as wonderful as you say," Finley interrupted gently. "But I have to stop you there, because I'm already in a committed relationship."

The old woman's brow furrowed. "There's no ring on your finger."

"That's because I'm married to my job."

The furrow eased.

"Unless you're in the business of selling feminine massagers—and I know you're not—then you need a man." The furrow returned. "Or a woman, I guess. Anyway, I'm not one to judge. Except, of course, when I was on the bench and that was my job," she clarified.

Finley gestured to the Bluetooth in her ear, as if she was listening to a communication from one of her associates.

"We're going to have to finish this conversation later," she said apologetically. "I'm being summoned to the bar."

"Oh, dear. I do hope Nathan isn't causing a problem."

"Nathan?"

"Another grandson—not the one I want you to meet," Catherine clarified. "He's been known to overindulge on occasion—most notably any occasion when someone else is paying for the drinks—so I asked the bartenders to keep an eye on him and cut him off if necessary." She frowned again. "Perhaps I should go with you."

"Not necessary," Finley assured her. "Tonight, it's my job to do any worrying that needs to be done and yours to enjoy the party—and the company of the very handsome man who's coming this way right now."

Catherine turned her head, a smile curving her lips as her gaze settled on her husband of sixty years.

"I don't mean to interrupt," Douglas said. "But I need to steal this pretty lady away for a dance."

"A tempting invitation," Catherine said. "But I don't know that these creaky bones can keep up with Beyoncé."

"But they're playing our song," he told her.

"'Single Ladies' most definitely isn't our song," she told him. "It's what happens when you let your grandkids tinker with your playlist before submitting it to the DJ."

The words were barely out of her mouth before the last "oh, oh, oh" faded away and another song started.

"Oh." Catherine's eyes grew misty as she recognized the opening notes of Elvis Presley's "Can't Help Falling in Love." "*This* is our song."

Douglas smiled and led his wife to the dance floor.

Finley loved weddings—the celebration of a new beginning was inherently joyful (though not always without conflict). But if she was being perfectly honest, she loved these milestone anniversaries even more, because they proved to her that love, if it was shared with the right person, really could last a lifetime.

What would it be like, Finley wondered, to love one person for so long? To share a life and a family together?

Of course, there were plenty of couples who stayed married for all the wrong reasons. But looking at Catherine and Douglas, it was apparent that they weren't just bound together by the vows they'd exchanged but by their continued devotion to one another.

Finley indulged herself watching them on the dance floor for another half a minute before heading to the bar to deal with the phantom issue that had interrupted her awkward conversation with Catherine.

On her way, she got a real communication from Rachel.

"Bouquet toss in thirty."

"I'll be there," Finley promised.

But she stopped at the bar first, to grab a glass of soda water with lime from the bartender who'd been keeping her hydrated all night.

"You look like you could use something a little stronger than that."

Finley appreciated the remark even less than the interruption, because it confirmed her suspicion that the expensive concealer she'd bought to hide the dark circles under her eyes wasn't doing its job. Not to mention that she was already juggling two events and not at all in the mood to deflect a guest's attempts at flirtation—even if she'd found her attention inexplicably drawn to this particular guest several times throughout the evening.

But he was the type of man any woman would notice: tall with broad shoulders, short dark hair and deep blue eyes. The first time she'd seen him, she'd experienced an odd sense of recognition, but she'd immediately dismissed the feeling, confident that she'd never crossed paths with him before. And yet, her gaze had gone back to him again and again, as if of its own volition, and the odd sense of familiarity remained.

At another time, she might have been flattered that he'd noticed her, but she didn't have time to indulge in the exchange of flirtatious banter or covert glances tonight.

Her eyes barely flickered in his direction. "That isn't at all a compliment."

"Maybe not," he acknowledged, with a half smile and a small shrug. "I was trying to segue into offering to buy you one."

"Thanks, but I'm working," she said, focusing her attention on the tablet that was always in her hand.

Instead of wandering away, he stayed where he was, apparently unable to take a hint.

"Do I know you?" she finally asked.

"I'm trying to give you the opportunity to know me," he said.

This time, she got the full wattage of his smile, and her knees actually quivered.

"So when do you expect to be finished working?"

"Late," she said bluntly, determined not to let him see how his nearness affected her.

"I'm happy to wait."

"Please don't bother." Her tone was admittedly sharp, perhaps even dismissive. But she really didn't have time for a flirtation with a stranger.

But was he a stranger?

There was something about his shoulders.

And his eyes.

And his voice.

The fragments attempted to come together in her mind, making her think that maybe she did know him. Or maybe she only wanted to.

But that was crazy. She didn't have time for a relationship, and no man had tempted her to wish otherwise in a very long time. Well, no one aside from—

Her gaze narrowed on his face as those fragmented pieces finally clicked into place. "Lachlan?"

Chapter Eight

His lips curved into a smile. "So you do remember me."

"Of course, I remember you," Finley said. "I just didn't recognize you."

"Do I really look so different without the beard?" he asked her.

"Yes." Her instinctive response was followed by a shake of her head. "No," she realized. "It's more than just the absence of the beard. You got your hair cut, too. And you're wearing a suit."

"My grandmother insisted."

"Catherine is your grandmother?"

He nodded. "On my mother's side, obviously."

Shirla, the desk clerk at the Dusty Boots Motel, had guessed that Finley dated "office-type guys who are comfortable in suits," and it was generally true—or had been, way back when Finley had time to date. And as much as this Lachlan Kellett was very much her usual type, she really didn't have time to flirt with him right now—no matter how much she might want to.

"You're the grandson," she realized.

"That's generally how it works," he said. "Her being my grandmother means that I'm her grandson."

"No, I meant that you're *the* grandson."

"Actually, I'm one of six," he told her.

"How many are divorced?"

"Just me," he confessed. "Why?"

"Because your grandmother has been trying to finagle an introduction between me and you."

"Really?" He grinned.

"You're not bothered by her blatant matchmaking efforts?"

"Why would I be when she's chosen a beautiful and interesting woman for me to meet?"

"I see that you can be every bit as charming as your grandfather when you want to be."

"Does that mean I'll get a different answer if I offer again to buy you a drink?"

She shook her head. "Unfortunately, no."

"Because you're working?"

Now she nodded.

"The party seems to be winding down," he noted. "And I don't mind waiting."

"*This* party might be winding down, but the one across the hall is still going strong."

"You've got two events happening right now?"

"That's not unusual for a Saturday," she said, though she was suddenly wishing that it wasn't true for *this* Saturday, because she didn't want to walk away from Lachlan—again.

"Apparently you weren't kidding when you said that you worked weekends."

"I definitely wasn't," she confirmed. "And now, I really do need to be across the hall."

Finley's love of weddings and almost every detail associated with the happy event didn't extend to the tossing of the bridal bouquet. In her opinion, it wasn't just an archaic tradition but borderline insulting to those encouraged to vie for the prize. On the other hand, it was obviously preferable to guests attempting to tear off pieces of the bride's dress in the hope that some of her good fortune would transfer to them, as was apparently the origin of the tradition.

In any event, it wasn't her place to judge or to question, only to give her clients what they wanted. And since Naomi wanted it, the ceremonial bouquet toss had been included in the evening's schedule of events.

"I think I'd rather be in a mob of Black Friday shoppers at Best Buy than in a crowd of single women trying to get their hands on a bride's flowers," Lachlan remarked, as the emcee invited all members of that demographic to gather on the dance floor.

"Then it's lucky that you're not a single woman," she said lightly.

"The garter toss is sometimes even worse," he noted. "Because usually by the time it happens, all the single men are drunk, competitive and reckless."

"Stay tuned," she said. "Or, here's a better idea, go back to the Sapphire Ballroom."

"That party's pretty much over. Grandma and Grandpa are starting to say goodbye to their guests, after which the grandkids will load up gifts and flowers and various memorabilia to take over to their place."

"So that's the real reason you're here—you're ducking out on the work?"

"I think you know the real reason I'm here," he told her.

"You're stalking me?"

"I was hoping to spend some more time with you."

"Then maybe you should have asked for my number two weeks ago, because tonight, I'm working."

"I didn't need your number, because as soon as you mentioned Gilmore Galas, I knew I'd be seeing you here tonight."

"Well, I didn't know I'd be seeing you."

"Are you saying that you wanted to see me again?"

She lifted a shoulder. "I wasn't entirely opposed to the idea."

"Not entirely, huh?" He grinned. "And even with the beard?"

"The beard made you a little more mysterious but not at all unattractive," she noted.

He rubbed his chin. "I could grow it again."

"Your choice," she said. "But the clean-shaven look works, too. It's very classically handsome."

"*It's* classically handsome? Or *I'm* classically handsome?"

"Are you fishing for a compliment, Professor Kellett?"

"A man never objects to being told that a woman finds him attractive," he said.

"*A* man? Or *you*?"

"Busted," he said, and gave her another one of those bone-melting smiles.

"I'm sure you know that I wouldn't be ignoring my responsibilities to stand around talking to you if I wasn't attracted to you."

"And I'm sure you know that I wouldn't have crashed this party if I wasn't attracted to you."

The words sent delicious tingles down her spine.

"This is really bad timing," she told him.

"Are you referring to tonight specifically or your life in general?"

"More the former than the latter, but possibly both."

"So what happens now?" he asked.

"Now the bride and groom will have their last dance, and most of their guests will exit the reception behind them."

"That's not what I was asking."

"I know," she acknowledged. "But it was an easier question to answer."

Right on cue, the emcee announced the newlyweds' last dance, and Finley slipped away to check with the hotel staff that the requested strawberries and (now nonalcoholic) champagne had been delivered to the honeymoon suite in advance of their arrival. From there, she confirmed the timing of last call with the bartenders, made arrangements for the leftover food to be packed up and delivered to a local soup kitchen and then spent several minutes with the weepy mother of the bride, listening to her recount all her favorite moments of the day, of which there were many (and apparently—luckily— no memory of the zipper crisis).

When she returned to the main reception area, Lachlan was still there, chatting with the bartender while he sipped a Coke.

"Is there anything I can help you with?" he asked.

"No. I'm mostly in waiting mode until the band finishes up in—" she glanced at the time displayed on the corner of her tablet "—twenty-two minutes. The last few guests usually trickle out after that and then we can start the breakdown and cleanup."

"Twenty-two minutes doesn't leave much time for me to steal a dance with you."

"I'm the event coordinator, not a guest. And you're not a guest, either."

"Do you really think anyone cares?"

She glanced around. The final headcount for the event had been one hundred and twenty, including the bride and groom, but less than a quarter of that number remained in the ballroom. About a dozen guests were on the dance floor, half that number were lingering at the bar, and the rest were scattered at various tables around the room, picking at the remnants of cake or coaxing the last drops out of bottles of wine.

"Probably not," she finally admitted.

"Then let's take advantage of the moment—and the fact that they're playing our song."

She felt her lips twitch. "We don't have a song."

"Well, this will become our song if you agree to dance with me."

"Apparently you *are* every bit as charming as your grandfather."

"If only that were true," he said, taking the tablet out of her hand and sliding it into the pocket of his suit jacket.

She lifted a brow.

"One dance," he said. "For three minutes, just let yourself forget that you're working."

Another quick glance around confirmed that no one was paying them the least bit of attention. The bride and groom had already said goodbye to their guests and headed upstairs to the honeymoon suite, and their respective parents had likewise called it a night.

"One dance," she relented, because "Wonderful Tonight" had always been one of her favorite songs.

He took her hand in his and drew her close, then set his other hand on her hip.

As soon as she was in his arms, Finley realized her mistake. Because being held by this man made all the unwanted feelings that had stirred to life when they were in close quarters at the Dusty Boots Motel stir again.

She'd had more than a few boyfriends in her twenty-eight years, and she'd even imagined herself to be in love with a few of them. But her heart had bounced back after each of those failed relationships, making her wonder if she might have been wrong about the depth of her feelings.

Despite the time she'd spent with Lachlan in Haven, she still didn't know much about him. But the immediacy and intensity of the attraction she felt seemed to be a warning—that he might be the man she could completely fall for. If she let herself.

And while she was flattered that Catherine Edwards thought she might be a suitable match for her favorite grandson, she hadn't got the impression that Lachlan was looking for a life partner. A flirtation or a fling, sure. But his brief and blunt comments about his marriage gone wrong suggested that he wasn't looking for a long-term relationship.

But maybe she could be satisfied with a flirtation or a fling. Because even a casual relationship with a man whose mere proximity made her body ache in all the right places had to be more satisfying than sitting at home every night with only Simon for company.

The last bars of the song faded away and Finley reluctantly pulled out of his arms. "Are you going to ask for my number now?"

"If I do, and then I call and ask you on a date, will you say *yes*?"

"I'll want to," she admitted. "But as you know, I'm rarely free on a Friday or Saturday night."

"My schedule's flexible," he said. "I'm only teaching three classes this term and none of them are at night."

"So maybe we can figure something out."

"I definitely think we can."

He offered his phone. She added her contact information and returned it to him.

He tapped out a quick message.

Her phone vibrated.

She pulled it out of her pocket.

Now you have my number, too.

She smiled and tucked her phone away again.

"And now I really have to get back to work."

"And I really have to kiss you."

The heat in his gaze combined with the intensity in his words made her knees quiver.

But as much as she wanted him to kiss her, there was no way she would risk damage to her professional reputation by letting it happen here and now.

"I'm working," she reminded him.

And herself.

But she did take a step forward, reach into the pocket of his jacket and retrieve her tablet.

He looked disappointed but not really surprised.

"I'll call you," he promised.

"I hope you do."

Two hours later, Finley, Julia and Rachel had completed a final walk-through of the Diamond Ballroom to pick up anything that might have been lost or left behind by the wedding guests.

"I've got a chandelier-style earring and one of the flower girl's shoes," Julia said.

"I've got a monogrammed cufflink, an abandoned boutonniere and a strapless bra—black satin, 32AA," Rachel announced.

"The boutonniere can be tossed," Finley said. "Everything else goes in the box."

The box was exactly that—a medium-sized cardboard container that served as a portable lost and found. Most event venues had their own policies and procedures for lost-and-found items, but Finley and her team were usually able to reunite misplaced items with their event guests more quickly themselves.

"Can we go now?" Rachel asked wearily.

"We're walking out the door," Finley said, heading toward the exit.

Because in addition to being coworkers, they were friends who looked out for one another. And they had a hard-and-fast rule that none of them was allowed to walk out of an event in the dark of night on her own.

A buzz from her jacket pocket had her shifting the box to check her phone.

Are you finished work yet?

She couldn't help but smile when she saw the message from Lachlan. She'd wondered how long he'd make her wait to hear from him again and was pleased to discover that it wasn't very long at all.

"Problem?" Julia asked, as the sliding glass doors whooshed open and they stepped outside.

"No."

"Man?" Rachel guessed.

"Yeah."

She tapped out a quick reply.

Just leaving the hotel now.

And looking every bit as fabulous as you did two hours ago.

Fabulous? At nearly two a.m. and the end of a very long day, she was more than a little skeptical that anyone would think so.

And anyway, how could he know how she looked unless…

She literally stopped in mid-stride, glancing up from the screen of her phone to see Lachlan standing beside one of the potted trees that flanked the stone columns of the porte cochere.

Her heartbeat quickened.

Her friends paused beside her.

"I'm guessing that's the man," Julia murmured, following the direction of Finley's gaze.

"You guys go ahead," she told them. "I'll meet you at the office in the morning to head over to the baby shower together."

"We have a rule," Rachel reminded her, at the same time Julia took her arm and steered her away.

Finley waited until her friends were out of earshot before approaching Lachlan.

"I can't believe you're still here," she said.

"Not still," he told her. "I helped transport the gifts and flowers and leftover cake to my grandparents' place, and then I came back."

"Did you have some of the cake?"

"I did."

"Was it good?"

"It was… Bliss."

She smiled. "So why did you come back?"

"Because ever since you walked away from me on the dance floor, I haven't stopped thinking about kissing you. Or maybe the truth is that I haven't stopped thinking about you since our road trip."

"I don't know whether to be flattered or scared," she confided.

"Considering that we've already slept together—"

"Only so we didn't freeze to death," she interjected to remind him.

"—and then traveled nearly five hundred miles in the same vehicle, I should hope you know that there's no reason to be afraid of me."

But he was wrong.

She had plenty of reasons to be afraid—for her heart.

Because the more time she spent with him—and the more she thought about him—the more she liked him.

And dancing with him earlier in the evening had reignited the attraction that had first sparked between them more than two weeks earlier, and she suspected that if she let him kiss her now, she wouldn't want him to stop.

Lachlan must have sensed her indecision, because instead of moving in, he said, "But tell me you don't want me to kiss you, and I'll say goodnight again and walk away."

He was letting it be her choice, giving her the space to take responsibility for her own desires.

Finley breached the short distance between them and lifted

her arms to link them behind his head. "I don't want you to kiss me."

Then she drew his mouth down so that *she* could kiss *him*.

It turned out that Finley's lips *were* as soft as they looked, and their flavor even more intoxicating than Lachlan had imagined. He'd only wanted a taste, but as soon as her mouth came into contact with his, he knew that one taste wouldn't be enough.

He held his hands clenched at his sides, because he suspected that if he touched her now, he wouldn't want to stop. But when the tip of her tongue glided over the seam of his lips, the fragile thread of control slipped through his fingers.

He uncurled his fists and lifted one hand to cup the back of her head. His fingers sifted through the silky strands of hair, scattering pins as he adjusted the angle of their kiss. His other hand found its way to her back, his splayed palm urging her closer until their bodies were pressed together from shoulder to thigh and all points in-between.

Their tongues danced a sensual rhythm that heated the blood that pulsed in his veins, and when Finley made a sound low in her throat—a hum of pleasure—it stoked the fire burning inside him.

After a minute—or maybe two or ten—she eased away from him, breathless and panting.

He took a moment to draw air into his own lungs before he said, "Definitely worth waiting for."

"Definitely," she agreed. "Still, it's probably a good idea to slow things down a little."

"It might be a good idea, but it's not what I want right now," he told her.

The confession made her knees quiver.

"Right now, it's not what I want, either," she admitted. "But

I think we should at least go out on a first date before I invite you to come home with me."

"Pizza and cake counts as a first date in my books," he said, in an obviously hopeful tone.

"Well, my standards are a little higher," she told him, fighting the urge to throw herself in his arms again.

"What did you have in mind?"

She decided there was no point in making it difficult to get them to where they both wanted to be. "Dinner in an actual restaurant."

"Tell me when," he said, his easy acquiescence proving that they were on the same page.

"I have a baby shower tomorrow, but I should be free after four o'clock."

He leaned down and brushed another quick kiss on her lips. "I'll pick you up at six."

Chapter Nine

"Are you sure you don't want to come with us to Napa?"

Aislynn didn't look up from the YouTube video she was watching on her phone when she responded to her mother's question. "And sit around with the five-year-olds and their coloring pages while you and Philip get drunk? No, thank you."

"Nobody's going to get drunk," Deirdre assured her. "And if you stay here, what are you going to do all day?"

"I've got math homework to finish." If she could get over to Harmony's to retrieve the textbook she'd left at her friend's house—or convince Harmony to bring it to her.

"To finish? Or start?"

"Have a good time, Mom."

Deirdre took the hint. "You can invite Harmony to come over, if you want."

"Yeah, I might do that," she said.

"But *after* you finish your assignment."

"Yes, Mom."

"And there's leftover roast beef in the fridge for dinner. Enough for both of you, if she wants to stay."

"Leftovers? Yay!"

Deirdre sighed at her daughter's sarcasm. "Or you can order something from UberEats, if you prefer."

"I prefer."

"So…what do you think?" her mom asked, brushing her

hands down the front of her floral chiffon Adrianna Papell dress. "Do I look okay?"

Aislynn was surprised by the question, because it wasn't one her mother usually asked. And why would she when she always looked like she walked off the cover of a fashion magazine?

Deirdre Waterford (she'd never used "Kellett," not even when she was married to Aislynn's dad) was a stunningly beautiful woman. On more than one occasion, Aislynn had heard her grandma say that Deirdre—tall and slender with great bone structure, flawless skin, honey-blonde hair and blue-green eyes—could have made a fortune as a model, if she'd been so inclined.

But Deirdre had been born into a wealthy family, so making another fortune was of little interest to her. Instead, she'd gone to school to learn about things that did. She'd studied history, sociology, anthropology, astrology, criminology and various other topics. She hadn't focused enough on any one subject to earn a degree, but it was in one of her anthropology classes that she'd met Lachlan Kellett. Fourteen months later, they were married, and six months after that, their daughter was born.

Unfortunately for Aislynn, most of her genes came from her dad's side. She had his dark hair, blue eyes and big feet. She hated her feet most of all, because her mom had the most amazing collection of shoes that Aislynn could never borrow because she couldn't squeeze into them.

"Aislynn?" her mom prompted.

"Yeah. You look fine."

"Fine?" Deirdre wrinkled her nose.

She looked up again. "Actually...you look nervous."

"I guess I am. A little."

"First date with a new man?"

Her mom rolled her eyes. "Hardly. In fact, today is the

three-year anniversary of my first date with Philip, and I think he might be planning to ask me to marry him."

"What?" Aislynn had not seen *that* coming. "Why?"

"Because we've been dating three years and a formal commitment is the next step in a relationship." Deirdre's brow furrowed. "You can't honestly be surprised—I've talked to you about the possibility of Philip and I marrying on several occasions."

"I didn't think you were serious."

"Of course, I was serious. I *am* serious." Her mom perched on the edge of the coffee table, facing the sofa where Aislynn was sprawled. "You like Philip, don't you?"

"He's okay, I guess."

"He's a good man," Deirdre said. "And he's known, from day one, that you and I are a package deal."

"Does that mean I get to vote *yes* or *no* on the proposal?"

"No. It means you get to vote on the style and color of the dress you'll wear for our wedding."

Despair enveloped her like a weighted blanket. "You're really going to say *yes*?"

"Why wouldn't I say *yes*?"

"Because…"

Because then there's no way you and Dad will ever get back together.

But of course she couldn't say that aloud to her mom.

Because Deirdre had told her, on more than one occasion, that she had to let go of her silly fantasies about her parents reconciling, because it wasn't going to happen.

But Aislynn didn't believe it. She was sure her mom was just saying that because she didn't want to admit that she was still in love with her ex-husband. And she was equally sure that her dad still loved Deirdre, too.

She didn't know why they'd divorced. She'd been too young to have any memories from way back then. But she did remember hearing her mom and grandma arguing after the fact. (Grandma Waterford did *not* approve of divorce!) Grandma had commented that maybe Deirdre and Lachlan didn't try hard enough to keep their family together and insisted that it was never too late to try again.

Maybe Aislynn could nudge them toward giving it another shot.

Lachlan was absolutely not counting the hours.

If, after a quick glance at the clock, he realized that he would be seeing Finley in a little less than five hours, well, that was just basic mental math.

And anyway, what was wrong with looking forward to spending time with a woman he liked? And who seemed to like him?

Especially considering that he hadn't dated much in recent years.

Not since Victoria.

His most recent ex hadn't broken his heart, but the end of their relationship—or maybe the relationship itself—had left him disillusioned.

Making space in his life for another person required both willingness and effort, but something about Finley made him want to do the work.

Okay, maybe he was jumping the gun a little. After all, it was a long road from a first date—or even a third date—to a relationship, but he was looking forward to taking the first step on that road with Finley tonight.

When his phone pinged, he immediately snatched it up, half-dreading that it might be a message from Finley—because the only reason he could think for her to reach out would be to cancel their plans.

So he was both relieved and surprised when he saw that the message was from Aislynn.

Need ride 2 H's. OK?

H meant Harmony Stevens, his daughter's best friend since kindergarten. The rest of the message seemed clear enough, if a little short on details.

Rather than text a response, he tapped the screen to initiate a call.

"Hi, honey."

She huffed out a breath. "You're supposed to text before you call, to make sure it's a good time for me to talk."

"Considering you just texted me, I didn't think you were busy with something else."

"You're still supposed to text first."

"But now that we're on the phone," he said, eager to move the conversation along, "why don't you tell me why you need a ride to Harmony's house?"

"Because I forgot my math textbook when I was there yesterday and Mom's out with Philip."

"Okay," he said. "I'll be there in ten minutes."

"I can't go right now," she protested.

"Why not?"

She huffed out another breath. "Because Harmony isn't home right now."

"Are her parents there?" he asked, thinking Aislynn just needed someone to let her in the door so she could grab her book.

"No. Her dad's out of town on business and her mom's at her boyfriend's house."

He frowned. "I didn't realize Harmony's parents were separated."

"They're not," Aislynn said matter-of-factly. "She just screws around on him when he's away."

"Or perhaps Harmony is misreading the situation," Lachlan said.

"She caught her mom in the pool house with the boyfriend. Naked."

Okay, not much room for misinterpretation there, he acknowledged, if only to himself.

"Even if she did, you shouldn't be repeating gossip about your friend's mother."

"You asked," she reminded him. "Anyway, Harmony went to Long Beach with her brother today, and they won't be back until five, so I can't pick up my textbook until then."

"And what if I have plans for tonight?"

"You mean, like a date?" The question fairly dripped with skepticism.

"Is that really so unlikely?" he challenged.

His daughter responded by laughing. "Have you had a date in this decade?"

"Tonight could be the first one," he told her.

"Well, even if you did have plans, you'd change them for me," she said confidently. "Because *I'm* the most important girl in your life."

It was what he always told her, because it was true.

Still, he couldn't help wishing that today wasn't the day she needed him to prove it to her.

"Okay," he said. "I'll pick you up at five."

After he hung up with his daughter, he sent a quick text message to Finley.

Something came up. OK if we bump our dinner from 6 to 7?

OK.

Thanks. I'll make it up to you. I promise.

Two desserts?

At the very least.

Lachlan was smiling as he tucked his phone back in his pocket, satisfied that he'd be able to take Aislynn where she needed to go and still make his date—and whatever might come after—with Finley.

Unfortunately, fate had other plans.

Finley sincerely loved her job, because she had the pleasure and privilege of working with couples at some of the happiest stages of their lives.

Of course, every Gilmore Gala was her absolute favorite at the time it was happening, but she had a particular fondness for baby showers. Today was a baby shower in honor of Emily Berringer-Thompson and her three-and-a-half-week-old daughter, Mia Margaret Thompson.

The celebration was taking place at the home of the infant's maternal grandparents—a stunning four-story Victorian in San Francisco's prestigious Pacific Heights neighborhood. The house had been lovingly restored and professionally decorated, so there wasn't a lot of dressing required—just some tasteful accents here and there and, per the hostess's request, lots of flowers.

The menu was similarly understated but elegant, an approximation of British low tea, including finger sandwiches, cream scones with lemon curd, assorted petit fours and miniature fruit tarts. All of it washed down by the guest's selection from a variety of teas—hot and cold—or champagne punch.

"Somebody's got plans tonight," Rachel surmised.

"Why would you say that?" Finley asked her friend.

"Because you've glanced at your watch three times in the past twenty minutes."

"Margaret Berringer wants all of the guests gone by two o'clock so that Emily can nurse the baby on schedule at two thirty."

"No way the new mom has that baby on a schedule at three-and-a-half weeks," Rachel said.

"You know more about babies than I do," Finley assured the mother of three. "But you were at home with your youngest when we did Emily and Ryan's wedding, so you wouldn't know that every single event occurred precisely on schedule that day—from the arrival of the crew to do the bridal party's hair and makeup all the way to the bride and groom's exit from the party."

"That doesn't surprise me," Rachel remarked. "You always have a detailed outline for events."

"And I always build in a buffer, to repair the bride's makeup if any pre-ceremony tears are shed or to accommodate candid photos of the flower girl and ring bearer skipping through the park or drunk Uncle Stanley's rambling toast to the happy couple."

"Because there's always something," Rachel noted.

"Always," Finley agreed. "Except at Emily and Ryan's wedding."

"I don't believe it."

"It's true," she insisted.

"No coffee run for a father-of-the-bride who started celebrating his daughter's impending nuptials with champagne a little too early in the day? No ring bearer playing hide-and-seek when it was time to walk down the aisle? No mother-of-the-groom bitch-slapping her ex-husband's trophy wife?"

"None of that."

"Then it must have been the most boring wedding in the history of Gilmore Galas," Rachel declared.

"It wasn't," Finley assured her. "It was absolutely picture perfect from beginning to end."

"Except for the panties," Julia chimed in.

"I almost forgot about the panties," she admitted, chuckling softly.

"What panties?" Rachel asked, intrigued.

"When we did our walk-through of the event venue after all the guests had gone, we found a pair of pink lace panties in the back corner of the cloakroom."

"The lace panties that all the bridesmaids were wearing," Julia added.

"How do you know what panties they were wearing?"

"I was delivering the bouquets when they were getting dressed—and posing for photos in their undergarments."

"I wonder if those photos made it into the bride's display album."

"Anyway, that's why I'm sure they belonged to one of the bridesmaids. And I have my suspicions as to which one snuck off for a private celebration with her groomsman."

"So there *was* some unplanned extracurricular activity."

"But none that impacted the bride and groom's schedule."

"So what are your plans tonight?" Julia asked, when she caught Finley sneaking another glance at her watch.

"Are they with the hunky guy who was waiting around for you at the hotel last night?" Rachel wondered.

Julia wiggled her brows suggestively. "And did you wake up with him this morning?"

"I have a date," she finally confided to her friends. "Yes, with the guy from last night, and no, I did not wake up with him this morning."

"But maybe you'll wake up with him tomorrow?" Rachel suggested.

Finley couldn't hold back the smile that curved her lips. "I'm not ruling anything out for tomorrow, but first, we need to focus on finishing this event today."

He was going to be late.

It was his own fault for assuming that when Aislynn said she needed to pick up her textbook after five o'clock, it meant that he'd be on his way back home by 5:15. Instead, it was— Lachlan twisted his wrist to glance at his watch again—5:25 and there was still no sign of his daughter's friend.

"Why don't you text Harmony again and ask for an updated ETA?" he suggested.

Aislynn swiped away from the game she was playing on her phone and dutifully sent another message to her friend.

"I'm starting to think you do have plans tonight," she said, her tone accusing.

"I do," he confirmed.

She scowled. "Who is she?"

"Who is who?"

"The woman you're dating."

"We're not really dating," he said, steeling himself for a confrontation. "We're just going for dinner."

"That's not a date?"

"I guess it's a first date," he acknowledged.

Aislynn's scowl deepened.

"Do you have a problem with me dating?"

"Why would I?" she countered.

"I don't know," he said. "That's why I'm asking."

"You can do whatever you want." She shrugged, as if to prove she didn't care. "Just like Mom does."

"Do you have a problem with Philip?" he asked now.

"No." She folded her arms over her chest and stared straight ahead out the window. "But I'm not gonna call him Dad."

"No one expects you to call him Dad," Lachlan assured her.

"Not now," she agreed. "But what about when they're married?"

"Are they getting married?"

She shrugged. "Mom seemed to think he was going to propose today."

Lachlan wasn't surprised by this announcement, considering that his ex-wife had been dating her current beau for close to three years now. And if she was happy with Philip Cohen, then he was happy for her.

His only concern was for his daughter, so he asked her now, "How do you feel about that?"

"It has nothing to do with me."

"We both know that's not true."

"What do you want me to say?"

"Whatever you're thinking," he told her.

She huffed out a breath. "Okay. I think it sucks! I don't want Mom to marry Philip. I want—"

Whatever else she'd intended to say was cut off by the chime of her cell phone.

She glanced at the message on the screen disinterestedly, then her eyes grew wide. "Ohmygod."

"What is it?"

"Harmony's at the hospital. Her brother crashed his car. She's okay, she says, but they're taking Jarrod into surgery."

Aislynn looked at him then, her eyes swimming with tears. "Can we go?"

Lachlan was already backing out of the driveway.

By the time they arrived, Jarrod was in surgery and Harmony was having her arm casted. Marcia Stevens rushed into the waiting room a few minutes later, her face streaked with mascara and tears. She threw herself into Lachlan's arms, obviously desperate for comfort and reassurance.

As a parent, he understood the helplessness and frustration of being unable to fix a child's illness or injury, to take away their pain. He offered her a tissue that he'd plucked from the box on the table and patted her back while they waited for the doctor to give them an update.

Aislynn texted her mom to let her know where she was, so that Deirdre wouldn't freak out when she got home and discovered her daughter wasn't there. Lachlan wasn't surprised when she and Philip came directly to the hospital, so that they could be there to offer support and prayers, too.

It was only when the doctor came out to give an update after Jarrod's surgery that Lachlan thought to look at his watch again.

It was almost eleven p.m.

And he'd completely forgotten about his date with Finley.

Chapter Ten

"You look like hell."

Lachlan set a mug beneath the spout of the Keurig on the credenza in his friend's office and hit the button to dispense a much-needed hit of caffeine. "I feel like hell."

"Must have been quite the party your grandparents had on Saturday if you're still hungover today," Ethan Hayes remarked.

Had the party really only been two days ago?

So much had happened since then, Lachlan felt as if a week had passed.

"I'm not hungover. I'm sleep-deprived." He lifted the mug to his lips. "I was at the hospital with Aislynn until three a.m. this morning."

All signs of amusement vanished from Ethan's face. "What happened? Is she okay?"

"She's fine," Lachlan assured his friend, who had known Aislynn for the whole of her life. "But a friend of hers was in a car accident."

"Is her friend okay?"

"Yeah. The friend's brother, who was driving the car, got banged up pretty good, though."

"That's scary stuff for a kid to deal with," Ethan acknowledged.

He nodded.

"So why are you here? You don't have a class until three o'clock this afternoon."

"Because I need your advice."

"Woman trouble?" his friend guessed.

"I'm not sure."

"How can you not be sure?"

"I haven't actually spoken to her since I did the thing that she might be upset about."

"If you want my advice, you're going to have to be a little more specific about the details."

"I had plans to have dinner last night with a fascinating, smart, gorgeous woman and… I didn't show."

"You stood her up?"

"I was at the hospital with Aislynn," he reminded his friend.

"You called and told her that?"

"No. I, uh, lost track of time and then…it was too late."

"What date number was it?" Ethan asked. "Third? Fourth?"

"First," he admitted.

"You stood her up on what was supposed to be your first date?"

He nodded.

"Forget the apology and cut your losses," his friend advised. "Because there's no coming back from that."

Lachlan swore under his breath.

"Not the answer you were hoping for," Ethan guessed.

"There has to be something I can do."

"You could try finding a good set of kneepads on Amazon and requesting expedited delivery. Because you're going to have to do some serious groveling, my friend."

"I can grovel," he decided.

"And flowers might soften her up for the groveling," Ethan said.

He nodded. "I can do flowers, too."

"Try Oasis." His friend tapped some keys on his computer,

then turned the monitor to show Lachlan the florist's web-page. "Steph likes their arrangements."

"What kind of flowers am I supposed to send?"

"What does she like?"

"First date," he reminded his friend. "I have no idea."

Ethan vacated his seat and gestured for Lachlan to take it so that he could more easily peruse the website.

"Browse by occasion," his friend suggested.

Lachlan frowned at the options on the drop-down menu. "What's the occasion? Make Someone Smile? Love and Romance? Just Because?"

"Just Because," Ethan said. "It's florist code for 'Just Because I'm an Idiot.'"

"Ha-ha."

"You think I'm joking, but I'm not."

"What do you think of this one?" he asked, clicking on an image to enlarge it.

His friend shook his head. "No."

"What's wrong with it?"

"Roses."

"What's wrong with roses?"

"They have *meaning*."

"What are you talking about?"

"There's an actual list. Every color of rose means something different, and the last thing you want to do is give her an opportunity to interpret—or misinterpret—the meaning," Ethan explained. "Carnations, mini carnations, gerbera daisies, chrysanthemums—any of those are fine, but you want to avoid roses."

"Lilies?"

"Lilies are okay."

"This one has sunny lilies, purple asters, green cushion spray chrysanthemums, lavender daisy chrysanthemums and something called Limonium," he said, quoting from the online description.

Ethan looked over his shoulder at the picture on the screen. "Nice," he said approvingly. "Now make it bigger."

"Bigger?"

"There's always an option to upsize," his friend told him, gesturing to the "select size" option on the right side of the page.

He scowled at the prices. "That's a lot of money for flowers."

"Do you like this woman a little bit or a lot?"

He clicked on the "deluxe" button.

"Wow," Ethan mused. "Obviously you like her a lot. So why is this the first time I'm hearing about her?"

"Because unlike you, I like to keep my private life private."

"Until you need my advice, apparently."

"Fair point," Lachlan acknowledged.

"So who is she?"

"Her name is Finley Gilmore."

"Tell me more. And—on a scale of one to ten—how hot is she?"

"I met her when I was on my way home from Nevada. We both got caught in that snowstorm and ended up at the same motel. The next day, her flight was canceled again, so I offered her a ride. She has an event planning business and I am *not* going to insult her by rating her on your stupid scale."

"That means she's a three, maybe a four," Ethan said. "Because if she was a nine or a ten, you wouldn't hesitate to say so."

"Not rating her," Lachlan said again.

"Wait a minute—did you say her last name was Gilmore and she's an event planner?"

"Yeah."

"Gilmore Galas did Steph's sister's wedding last summer."

"The *Beauty and the Beast*–themed event you mocked incessantly?"

"Yeah. I thought it would be tacky—and insulting to the groom, because obviously the bride was the 'beauty,' relegating him to 'beast' status—but it was really well done. From the invitations that said 'Be Our Guest' to the three-armed gold-colored candelabras and pendulum clocks around the room and the 'enchanted rose' centerpieces on each of the tables."

"Sounds as if somebody took detailed notes," Lachlan remarked.

"Steph raved about everything, and I've learned to pay attention when she talks. Most of the time, anyway. And, by the way, Finley's a solid ten."

Lachlan frowned. "You don't get to rate my girlfriend."

"You stood her up on your first date—she's not your girlfriend."

"You're right. Maybe I should forget the flowers—and forget about her altogether." The problem, of course, was that he knew he wouldn't.

"Your call." Ethan shrugged. "But I never took you for a quitter."

"I'm not any good at this," Lachlan told him. "I haven't dated...in a long time."

"You've been focused on your daughter. No one can fault you for that."

"Tell that to Finley."

"You tell it to Finley," Ethan said. "I'm sure if you do, she'll forgive you." He tapped the screen. "But you could add on the teddy bear, for a little extra insurance."

Finley wasn't entirely sure what Lachlan was trying to accomplish with the flowers, but she had to give him an A for effort. The bouquet from Oasis Florists—"A Gilmore Galas Approved Vendor"—was absolutely stunning.

"Oh, wow," Julia said, moving closer to inspect the arrangement of flowers on her friend's desk.

"Nobody does flowers like Oasis."

"Are these from the guy you had dinner with last night?"

"Actually, they're from the guy who stood me up last night," Finley told her.

Julia's jaw dropped. "He was a no-show?"

"Not just a no-show, but no phone call, no text message. Nothing."

"Oh, Fin. I'm so sorry." Julia glanced at the stunning display of blooms again. "And obviously he is, too."

She shrugged.

"He really didn't call—or at least text—with an explanation?"

Now she shook her head. "Not last night. I did get a text message this morning."

"What did it say?"

"Only what the card says." She gestured to the florist card nestled in the flowers.

Julia plucked the note out of the blooms.

I'm so sorry.
-L

"Seriously?" Julia frowned. "That's all he had to say after standing you up?"

"That's it," she confirmed.

"Did you call him?"

"No."

"Why not?"

"Because I wanted to, and my instincts, when it comes to personal relationships, are usually all wrong."

"It's not a weakness to want a connection with another person," Julia said gently.

"I know."

But it was a weakness, at least from her perspective, to want a man more than he wanted her. And if Lachlan wasn't interested enough to show up for their first date, she wasn't going to waste another minute of her time wishing for something that obviously wasn't meant to be.

"You could call him now," her friend suggested.

"I could," she agreed. "Except that I'm working on our presentation for this afternoon, updating our package prices to reflect the latest increases at Bliss Bakery and Flora's."

"I was a little surprised by the price hikes at first," Julia told her. "Until I remembered that I'm surprised at the higher costs every week when I check out at the grocery store."

"We're going to have to consider adding some more budget-friendly vendors," Finley acknowledged. "But I want to be sure that a lower price point isn't indicative of lower quality."

"I actually prepared a list of vendors that I think it would be worth reaching out to." Julia passed the folder in her hand to Finley.

She opened the cover and quickly skimmed the page. "That's an extensive list."

"I thought it made sense to gather as much information as possible before narrowing the field and making any final decisions."

"It does," Finley agreed.

"I'll set up the front parlor for our meeting and then start making calls."

"If you're heading to the parlor, can you take the flowers with you? They'll provide a nice pop of color there."

Julia picked up the vase and Finley turned her attention back to her computer.

A few minutes later, Taylor buzzed from the reception desk.

"There's a Mr. Kellett here, asking to see you."

And Finley's foolish heart actually skipped a beat.

She debated her response for three seconds.

She could send him away.

She *should* send him away.

That would make it clear that she wasn't the type of woman willing to be jerked around by a man.

And really, it was what she should do, because she didn't have time for unscheduled visitors.

But if she sent him away, it was unlikely that she'd ever know why he'd made plans with her and then failed to show up.

And she wanted an explanation, dammit.

Something more than the lame "I'm so sorry" that he'd texted to her and then echoed on an electronically printed card.

"Ms. Gilmore?" Taylor prompted.

"You can send him in," she decided.

When Taylor escorted Lachlan to her office, Finley remained seated behind her desk.

"Hello, Finley."

"Lachlan."

"I considered wearing a hat," he said. "So that I could come in with my hat in hand."

She didn't crack a smile. "Or you could simply tell me why you're here."

"Maybe I should have brought a hat *and* gloves—it suddenly feels as cold as a Haven blizzard in here."

"I have less than thirty minutes before my next appointment and I need at least ten of those to review the client's file, so whatever you came here to say, just say it," she advised.

"Okay," he said. But first he took a minute to survey her office.

Was he looking for the flowers he'd sent? Wondering what she'd done with the obviously pricey arrangement?

"This is quite the place," he noted approvingly.

"We like it," she told him.

"Setting up shop in a renovated home rather than a traditional office building demonstrates a more personal touch for your business. And positioning yourself between a bridal dress boutique and a stationery shop was pretty genius."

"The credit for that belongs to my Realtor."

"Still, you've created a warm and welcoming space here."

"Thank you. Now are you here to schedule a consult?" she asked. "Or was there another reason for your visit?"

He shoved his hands into his pockets. "I'm here to apologize."

"I'm not sure why you felt the need to drop by after sending such a detailed text message and expressing the same sentiment on the card attached to the flowers that were delivered."

"Well, you didn't respond to my text message," he noted, looking around her office again. "And I don't see the flowers."

"I'm not so petty as to throw away a gorgeous arrangement," she assured him. "I had them put in another room for our clients and prospective clients to enjoy."

"But you're still mad."

"I'm not mad," she denied. "We made plans to get together, those plans didn't pan out. There's no point in making a big deal out of something that wasn't."

"It was a big deal to me."

"If it had been a big deal to you, you would have shown up."

"Will you let me explain?"

She glanced at her watch. "You've got three more minutes, then I need to get back to work."

He nodded, wanting to believe that she was a reasonable woman who would accept a reasonable explanation. All he had to do was explain to Finley that his daughter's best friend had been in a car accident. Surely, she wouldn't fault him for forgetting about everything else in order to focus on soothing his distraught child.

The problem, of course, was that he hadn't told Finley that he had a child.

When she'd asked about his marriage, he'd braced himself

for the usual follow-up question about kids—and breathed a sigh of relief when it hadn't materialized. He hadn't wanted to lie to her, but he also hadn't wanted to volunteer any additional details. Because his experience as a single dad in the dating world had shown him that there were a lot of women who didn't want to get involved with a man who shared a child with another woman, and still others who resented that his daughter was his number one priority.

Obviously now was the time to tell Finley about Aislynn, to explain that the only reason he'd stood her up was that his daughter needed him. And if she had a problem with the fact that he had a child, well, it would be better to know sooner rather than later.

But when he opened his mouth, what he heard himself say was, "I had to take a neighbor to the hospital."

And though he inwardly winced at the prevarication, it wasn't really a lie. When he and Deirdre decided to go their separate ways, they'd promised to always put their daughter's best interests ahead of their own wants and needs. Which meant that, in order to simplify the sharing of custody, when it was time for Aislynn to start school, Lachlan had looked for a home in the same neighborhood in which Deirdre was already settled with their daughter.

So? Neighbors.

But still, he felt like kicking himself.

"Ohmygod." Finley's expression immediately changed— her cool indifference giving way to real sympathy. "Is your neighbor okay?"

"Oh. Um. Yeah. She's fine. But her friend was in an accident and she doesn't drive, so I took her to the hospital and stayed with her until she knew that her friend was alright.

"I should have called. I meant to call. But once we got to the hospital…it was just chaos and I completely lost track of time. I'm so sorry, Finley."

She finally pushed her chair away from the desk and rose to her feet. "I think you've apologized enough."

"I don't think that's true. I don't think I can express how truly sorry I am that I didn't get to see you last night. And kiss you last night."

"That's a little presumptuous, isn't it?" she asked, the hint of a smile tugging at the corners of her mouth. "Assuming that I'd let you kiss me on a first date."

"Our first date was pizza at the Dusty Boots Motel."

"That wasn't a date," she chided.

"We had dinner—and dessert—and then we slept together."

"We shared a bed because the power was out and the room was freezing cold."

Still, it had been an intimate experience, even if they'd kept their clothes on, and the memory of that night never failed to stir his blood.

"But even if you did count that as a date—and I don't— how do you get from a first date to a third?"

"Our second date was Saturday night."

"That wasn't a date, either."

"We danced to our song and you kissed me goodnight."

"'Wonderful Tonight' is our song now, is it?"

"It is," he confirmed.

"Good thing I like Eric Clapton."

"I like *you*," he said now. "And I'd really like to reschedule...if you'll give me another chance."

"It so happens that I'm a big believer in second chances," she told him.

He smiled, relieved. "I missed you."

"You saw me two days ago," she reminded him.

"But after last night, I wasn't sure if I'd ever see you again."

"I had no intention of forgiving you," she admitted. "But apparently I'm a sucker for the truth."

He cringed inwardly, because while he'd technically told her the truth, it hadn't been the whole truth.

He would tell her about Aislynn, of course. He just wanted to get to know her a little better first—and for her to know him.

"Pick a date," he said. "You let me know when you're available, and we'll make it happen."

She opened the calendar app on her phone, frowned. "I don't have any nights free this week."

"None?"

"I took five days off last week for my niece and nephew's birthday party," she reminded him. "In order to make up the time away, I have meetings or consults every night this week." She scrolled through her calendar. "Oh, wait. One of my October brides rescheduled her Wednesday night appointment, so I'm free after seven."

He shook his head. "I can do any day *except* Wednesday."

"I guess our rescheduled date will have to wait until next week then," she said.

"Well, I'm not waiting that long for another kiss," he said, drawing her toward him again.

The first touch of his lips against hers was all it took to completely fog her brain, clouding any thoughts of protest. As his mouth moved over hers, heat—like molten lava—spread through her veins. Their tongues touched, then retreated. Once. Twice. More. The rhythm, mimicking the sensual act of lovemaking, created a wave of lust that crashed through her already shaky defenses.

His hand slid up her back, and down again, a slow, sensual caress that melted her bones. She lifted her hands to his shoulders, clinging to him for support.

"Finley."

Her name was a whisper from his lips to her own.

"Yes."

He hadn't asked a question, but that didn't matter. Her answer was *yes*.

Yes to anything.

Everything.

He kissed her again. Like a man who knew what he wanted—and who wanted her.

And she wanted him.

She had just started to consider the possibility of canceling her next appointment so that she could give Lachlan a more complete tour of the building—including the bride's dressing room upstairs, where there was a surprisingly comfortable Victorian chesterfield sofa—when her office door opened again.

"Monica Greer and Peter Topham are—oh."

Finley quickly pulled out of Lachlan's arms.

"Ohmygod," Julia said. "I'm *so* sorry."

"It's okay," Finley told her, grateful that her voice was level despite the fact that her face was burning.

Her friend's gaze skittered to Lachlan, who didn't look the least bit bothered to have been caught in an embrace.

"Julia, this is Lachlan Kellett. Lachlan, meet the indispensable and irreplaceable Julia Morgan."

"Finley always goes heavy on the superlatives after a four-event weekend," Julia noted.

"It's nice to meet you," Lachlan said smoothly.

She accepted his proffered hand. "Lachlan… The sender of the flowers?"

He nodded.

"As you can see, there are no secrets in this office," Finley noted dryly.

"And no locks on the doors," Julia added with a grin.

"I was on my way out, anyway," Lachlan assured her. To Finley he said, "I'll call you to confirm our plans for next week."

"Sounds good."

Julia waited until he was gone before she spoke again.

"Can I just say that he's even hotter up close?" She fanned her face with her hand.

"He stood me up last night," Finley reminded her friend.

"For which he's obviously very sorry. And—considering that you were in his arms when I walked in and he made mention of a date next week—I'm guessing that you've already forgiven him."

Finley forced her attention back to the matter at hand. "You were saying something about the Greer-Topham consult?"

"Right." Julia immediately shifted gears, too. "They're here. They know they're early—Monica noted the wrong time in her calendar—so they're prepared to wait, but I said I'd check to see if we could accommodate their early arrival."

"Is the parlor set up?"

"It is," Julia confirmed. "And Rachel has a pot of fresh coffee on and was arranging a plate of cookies when I checked in with her."

Finley grabbed her tablet. "Then let's get started."

"Before we go…"

She paused.

"…you might want to dab on some lip gloss," Julia suggested, smirking a little. "Because your bare lips look very thoroughly kissed."

As Finley's face heated, her friend's smile widened. "The color in your cheeks looks completely natural though."

Chapter Eleven

As a result of Aislynn and Harmony having been friends since preschool and sharing countless playdates and sleepovers through the years, the parents of each had gotten to know the other child—and her family—quite well. Which meant that Lachlan had known Harmony's brother, Jarrod, since he'd needed five stitches in his chin after diving headfirst into second base playing Little League.

This time, the now eighteen-year-old's injuries were much more significant, including three cracked ribs, a punctured lung, broken collarbone, ruptured spleen and concussion. If he'd been driving his dad's car—a late model Audi A3 with seven airbags—he might have walked away from the crash. Unfortunately for Jarrod, he preferred to drive the classic Plymouth Barracuda that he'd restored in his spare time.

So on his way back to the college after his visit to Gilmore Galas, Lachlan decided to swing by the hospital to check on the teen.

"Chocolate still your favorite?" he asked, offering Jarrod the milkshake that he'd picked up.

The boy managed to nod. "Thanks, Mr. Kellett."

"How are you feeling?"

"Like I've got cracked ribs and a broken collarbone."

"Don't forget the concussion."

Jarrod took a long pull from the straw. "The doctor mentioned something else, too, but I'm having trouble remembering some stuff, on account of the knock I took to the head."

"Glad to see your sense of humor is still intact."

"I think they've got me on some pretty good drugs."

"Your mom's not here?"

"She is. Somewhere." He drank some more of his shake. "I guess she called my dad, because he flew back from New York. He got here a little while ago and suggested they go somewhere to grab a coffee. I think they didn't want to fight in front of me."

"Or maybe they just wanted coffee."

Jarrod offered a wry smile. "My mother doesn't drink coffee, and I don't think my dad wanted a hot beverage so much as he wanted to know who put the hickeys on his wife's neck."

And how the hell was Lachlan supposed to respond to that?

He'd seen the marks on Marcia's throat the previous evening and realized that what Aislynn had said about her friend's mother having a boyfriend was likely true. Still none of his business, except in that it had led him to reflect on his own determination to keep his romantic relationships separate and apart from his time with his daughter. Of course, he now suspected that he might have sheltered her too much, as she seemed to be under the impression that he had no life outside of being a father and a teacher.

"Sorry," Jarrod said now. "It's the drugs letting my mouth run ahead of my brain."

"You don't have to apologize to me," he said. "I'm sorry that you're going to go home to turmoil."

"Yeah, but probably not for another three or four days."

"We don't live too far away," Lachlan reminded the teen. "If you ever want to talk—or just need a break—you know where to find me."

"'S'all good," Jarrod said. "But thanks."

"Take care of yourself."

The boy nodded as he took another pull on the straw.

"Oh. I almost forgot." Lachlan pivoted at the door. "Aislynn asked me to give you this."

Jarrod looked wary. "What is it?"

"A 'Get Well' card, I think."

He accepted the envelope with obvious trepidation.

"I don't think it's anything you need to worry about," Lachlan told him.

"Then you don't know that your daughter's got a crush on me," the boy said.

"Actually, I do know." He'd had his suspicions prior to Sunday night, but the way Aislynn had sobbed for hours, even after being reassured that her best friend hadn't suffered anything more serious than a broken wrist, had confirmed it. "But I also know you're a good kid who wouldn't ever make a move on his little sister's best friend."

Jarrod swallowed visibly. "No, sir."

Lachlan walked away feeling relieved that he'd had a chance to clear the air with Jarrod—and worried that his little girl was growing up too fast.

Teenage crushes were normal. His own high school years weren't so far in the rearview mirror that he didn't remember the excitement and intensity of young love. And while he believed Jarrod had meant it when he said he wouldn't make a move on Aislynn, he knew the boy would likely have more difficulty deflecting any moves she might make.

Obviously he was going to have to talk to Deirdre, to find out if she'd talked to their daughter about boys and hormones and safe sex.

And man, did it make him feel old to consider that his daughter might be thinking about sex, but it wouldn't do him any good to keep his head in the sand.

Still, given a choice, he'd much rather think about his own intimate prospects. And thanks to Finley's forgiveness, they were definitely looking up.

* * *

After the meeting with Monica and Peter, Finley checked her phone for recent messages. There were five texts—one from the mother of her May 18 bride, one from the bride herself, and three from Lachlan.

She forced herself to read them in order.

Just got a very late RSVP from Gina's aunt. Apparently the whole family is planning to come from Spokane for the wedding, so we need meals—and chairs—for six more guests.

PLEASE seat my Aunt Cheryl, Uncle Rick and their 4 kids FAR AWAY from Aunt Diane and Uncle Ron. Long story short: I don't want my dad having to post bail for his sisters the day after my wedding.

Because there were always snags, Finley reminded herself as she opened an email window to communicate the revised final number to the caterer.

She was all too aware that complicated family dynamics could lead to conflict at inconvenient times. While most guests were on their best behavior at formal events, it wasn't unheard of for simmering tensions—fueled by free-flowing alcohol—to boil over. Thankfully her team had proven skilled at reading body language, zeroing in on the source of potential trouble and tactfully de-escalating before fisticuffs erupted. Still, she appreciated the heads-up from the bride and added a note to the file.

With that taken care of, she finally shifted her attention to Lachlan's messages.

Can you give me a call when you have a minute?

Only if it's before 3. After that, I'll be in class.

But class is done at 5.

It was a little disconcerting to Finley that all it took was seeing his name on the display to have her heart skip a beat. Especially as she hadn't been this excited about a new man in her life since…Mark. And in light of how *that* relationship had ended, the comparison wasn't exactly a comfortable one.

But she liked Lachlan, dammit, and she wasn't going to let the ghosts of her romantic past spook her this time.

And since he'd asked her to call, she did so.

"It's two forty-five," she noted. "Am I cutting it too close?"

"My three o'clock class is just across the hall, so this is fine."

The low timbre of his voice in her ear raised goosebumps on her flesh.

"I assume there was a reason you asked me to call."

"There was," he confirmed. "Because I realized, as I was driving away, that we didn't actually set a date for our re-scheduled date."

"I guess we got distracted, didn't we?" she said, her cheeks growing warm again at the memory of his kiss.

"And while I have to say, it was the very best kind of distraction, I'd really like to know when I can see you again."

"Me, too," she said.

"I know you said you were booked all this week, so how does Sunday look?" he asked.

"Like an all-day corporate event at the Fairmont."

"Monday?"

"Usually a good bet," she acknowledged. "But there's a bridal expo in San Jose next week. I'll be there Monday and Tuesday and half of Wednesday. But I should be back by three o'clock. Definitely no later than four."

He sighed regretfully. "Unfortunately, Wednesday doesn't work for me."

She waited for him to tell her what plans he had, as she'd

done to explain why she wasn't available Monday or Tuesday. Not that he owed her an explanation, but his unwillingness to offer one seemed to be a red flag.

Or maybe she was being paranoid because he'd stood her up once already.

And yes, she knew that he'd had a good reason for forgetting about their dinner plans, but that knowledge didn't automatically erase the sense of rejection she'd felt as she'd sat at home watching the clock move past seven o'clock then eight and nine and ten.

It was possible that he had a standing date to play poker with his buddies on Wednesdays. But if so, why wouldn't he just tell her that? Was he trying to be mysterious? Or was he hiding something? Like a standing date with his girlfriend on Wednesday night?

Of course, it was more likely a girlfriend would demand Fridays or Saturdays—and maybe he was unavailable those days, too, but Finley wouldn't know because she never was.

She sighed. "You can probably see now why I don't date."

"We'll figure this out," he promised.

"Maybe we shouldn't even try," she said. "Maybe this is too hard."

"Nothing worth having comes easy," he told her. "And I believe we're worth the effort."

"Okay," she said, because she wanted to believe it, too. "Skipping ahead—how about Tuesday, April 16?"

"I have a lecture at noon, followed by office hours until five, but nothing after that."

"I should be finished around the same time," she told him.

"Do you want to come over for dinner?"

"Are you going to cook for me?"

"I've been told that my enchiladas are legendary."

"Legendary?" she echoed dubiously.

"You can judge for yourself when you try them. How's seven o'clock?"

"I'm putting it in my calendar right now."

"I'll text my address."

"And I'll look forward to your enchiladas on the sixteenth."

"Damn, that seems far away," he said.

"You could use the number I gave you to call sometime between now and then, if you want."

"I'll do that."

The next morning, Lachlan was working on grading the last few essays for his sociocultural and linguistic anthropology class when Stephanie Corrigan knocked on his door. Steph was the head of the math department and also the wife of one of Lachlan's best friends.

He took off his glasses and set them aside to give her his full attention. "What are you doing on this side of campus?"

"I was on my way to the dean's office for a meeting and decided to drop in to find out if the flowers worked," she told him.

He scowled—an expression that didn't faze her in the least because she knew she was one of his favorite people in the whole world.

"Does he tell you everything?"

"Of course," she said easily. "Rule number four in the *Guide to a Successful Marriage*."

"How come I never heard of any such guide when I was married?"

"I have no idea," she said, helping herself to a can of Mountain Dew from the mini fridge in the corner of his office. He kept it on hand for when Aislynn visited him on campus, but his friend's wife was equally addicted to the sugary soft drink. "But the fact that you didn't might explain why you're no longer married."

"Touché."

She popped open the can. "Now answer my question."

"The flowers got me in the door."

"And your Irish charm did the rest?" she guessed.

"I seem to have been forgiven."

"So when are you seeing her again?" She lifted the can to her lips, took a long swallow.

"We're having dinner on the sixteenth."

"The sixteenth? That's two whole weeks away."

"I know," he said glumly. "But she's an event planner, and her schedule is pretty tight this time of year."

"Gilmore Galas." Steph nodded. "Ethan told me. And also that he told you they did my sister's wedding, so I know they're good—and very much in demand. But it's April. Is she really busy every day of the week this early in the season?"

"She's actually free tomorrow night. And next Wednesday."

"Ahh. But you have other plans on Wednesdays."

Now he nodded.

"What are your plans for the sixteenth?" she asked. "Maybe Ethan and I will crash. Check her out."

"And that's why I'm not telling you," he said.

"Come on—it's been a long time since you've been so obviously infatuated with a woman," she pointed out. "Naturally I'd be curious about her."

He glanced pointedly at his watch. "What time is your appointment with the dean?"

She looked at the fitness band on her wrist and swore. "Gotta run," she said, and brushed a quick kiss on his cheek before she did just that.

His phone rang as he settled his glasses on his face again to return his attention to the essays on his desk.

It was Ben's wife, sharing the news that Lachlan had expected as much as he'd dreaded.

Life really was full of ups and downs.

* * *

Finley was pleased that Lachlan took her advice and used the number she'd given him. In fact, he called almost every day, just to say hello and ask about her day. And when they didn't talk, they at least exchanged text messages. Even better, they managed to get together for coffee twice before their official date—once when he was in the vicinity of her office and once when she had an appointment near the college.

Each of those coffee dates had concluded with a quick kiss that gave no outward indication of the heat simmering beneath the surface, but which made Finley wonder if the sixteenth was ever going to come.

Finally the day arrived, and since Lachlan wasn't expecting her until seven, she had time to stop home after work to swap her usual business suit for something a little more informal. She opted for a flirty skirt that hit just above the knees and topped it with a short-sleeved V-neck sweater. Of course, shoes were always the biggest dilemma, and she spent several minutes considering and discarding various options.

If they'd been going out to eat, she would have gone with the wedge sandals with the laces that wrapped around her ankles. But they weren't exactly easy to get on and off, and obviously she'd be taking her shoes off in his home, so she set those aside in favor of Kenneth Cole T-strap sandals with the zippers at the heel.

She made a quick stop on the way to his address, noting that she passed Merivale College en route. It was a nice neighborhood, with established homes, old trees, neatly manicured lawns and well-kept gardens. The kind of neighborhood more suited to families, in her opinion, than a single (albeit divorced) college professor.

Lachlan must have been watching for her arrival, because he opened the door to greet her even before she had a chance to knock.

"Hi." His smile was warm, his gaze warmer.

"Hi," she answered back.

He took her hand and drew her over the threshold, then closed the door at her back and leaned down to kiss her.

It was a casual kiss—light and just a little bit lingering—but like a well-crafted appetizer before a meal, it whetted her appetite for more.

"I brought beer," she said, holding up the six-pack of Dos Equis for his perusal when he drew away from her again.

"Hmm… I had you pegged as a wine drinker."

"I like wine," she confirmed. "But I thought this would go with Mexican food."

"It would," he agreed. "But so would sangria."

"You made sangria?"

He grinned. "Come on into the kitchen and I'll pour you a glass."

She left her shoes and purse by the front door and followed him through the living room to the kitchen.

"Something smells amazing," she said.

"Legendary enchiladas," he reminded her.

She grinned. "I can't wait."

He poured the wine from a cobalt blue pitcher into a stemless glass of the same color.

Through a double-wide arched doorway, she could see into the dining room, where the table was set with woven placemats in bold stripes of orange, pink, green, purple and blue. Green linen napkins were tucked in beaded purple rings, and there were even chunky pink candle holders with fat orange candles.

"It looks like Cinco de Mayo in here."

"Did I go overboard with the theme?"

"No. I'm just surprised. And impressed."

"My mother's influence," he said. "She sells real estate and, though she usually brings a professional in to do the staging, she's picked up a few tricks over the years. And she's adamant that a table always looks better with placemats and napkins."

"And Fiestaware," she noted.

"This is where I have to confess that I borrowed the dishes—and the décor—from her," he said.

"Did she ask why?"

"My mother's pretty smart. I think she figured out that I was trying to impress a woman."

"When you return them, you can tell her that you succeeded."

"And in case you're wondering—no, I did not name names. Not because I didn't want her to know, but because I didn't want her to tell my grandmother, who would be far too smug."

"Aren't your grandparents on an anniversary tour of Europe right now?"

"Not yet. According to my grandmother, they got married in March because they were madly in love and didn't care about the season. But she had no intention of risking a broken hip by taking a once-in-a-lifetime trip in potentially snowy weather."

"That sounds like something Catherine would say," she agreed with a smile.

"Anyway, dinner's ready—whenever you are."

"I'm ready."

He held her chair for her, then topped off her glass of sangria before taking her plate to serve up the food.

"This is a really nice place," she said, when he rejoined her at the table.

"My mom again," he told her. "She knew I was looking for something not too far from the college, but of course, there's almost nothing to be found near a college in the budget of a professor. This one needed a ton of work, so the price was right for me. Of course, all that work required more money, but it didn't all need to be paid up front, and my mom had contacts through her business to put me in touch with the right people."

"How long have you lived here?"

"Almost ten years."

She cut off a piece of enchilada. "So you bought this house when you were...twenty-six?"

"That sounds about right."

"I don't know a lot of twenty-six-year-olds who want the responsibility of home repairs and lawn maintenance."

"Then you don't know a lot of twenty-six-year-olds with parents who constantly espoused the benefits of investing in real estate."

"You're right about that." She lifted another forkful of tortilla stuffed with shredded chicken. "And you're right about these enchiladas, too."

"Legendary?"

She nodded, because her mouth was full.

"I probably shouldn't admit this, but it's a really simple meal to make. I cook the chicken in the crockpot while I'm at work, then throw the rice in the instant pot when I get home, then shred the chicken, assemble the enchiladas and slide them into the oven."

"Simple or not, I'm impressed," she told him. "Most of the guys I know don't know how to do much more than throw burgers or steaks on a grill."

"I can do that, too," he said.

"Of course, you can."

"There's more rice—and more enchiladas. If you want more." She shook her head. "I couldn't possibly eat another bite."

"Are you saying that you don't have room for dessert?" he asked, removing a bakery box from the refrigerator and setting it on the table.

She immediately recognized the embossed logo on the top. "You went to Bliss."

"After I tasted the cake at my grandparents' anniversary party, I had to check it out."

He opened the lid to reveal—

"Dulce de leche cheesecake," she said, unable to hold back the moan that slipped through her lips.

"You like their cheesecake?"

"I *love* their cheesecake."

"So that's a *yes* on dessert?"

"That's a definite *yes* on dessert," she said. "If we hold off until after we've cleared up these dishes."

"You want to tidy up?"

"I'm certainly not going to leave the mess for you after you did all the cooking."

"Finley, I've been waiting two weeks for this night—I don't give a damn about the dishes."

"I just thought it would give us something to do before dessert."

"I've got another idea," he said, and drew her into his arms.

She linked her hands behind his neck and smiled at him. "You want to tell me about this idea?"

"Why don't I show you instead?" he suggested, just before his mouth covered hers.

She knew what to expect from his kisses now—or thought she did.

But every time he kissed her, it was somehow even better than she remembered and even more potent than she antici-pated.

She wondered if, being such a well-educated man, he'd studied the act. He certainly seemed to have perfected his technique.

He nibbled on her lips, teasing her with playful strokes of his tongue that made her tremble and ache and want. But he didn't deepen the kiss. Not yet.

Instead, he drew back and took her hand.

She was a little disappointed when he led her into the liv-ing room. She'd thought he might take her upstairs, because she guessed his bedroom was somewhere on the upper level. She hadn't accepted the invitation to dinner at his place expecting that it would lead to sex, but she hadn't been opposed to the possibility, either.

And she definitely didn't protest when he eased her back onto the sofa.

He kissed her again. This time parting her lips with his tongue, deepening the kiss. At the same time, his hands slid beneath the hem of her sweater. She shivered as his callused palms stroked the bare skin of her torso, an instinctive reaction that caused her breasts to rub against the wall of his chest, sending arrows of pleasure streaking from her already peaked nipples to her center.

It was only their first date.

Or maybe, if she followed Lachlan's logic, it was their third.

And wasn't there some unwritten rule about sex on the third date?

If not, there should be, because she was more than ready to get naked with him.

She tilted her hips, rocking her pelvis against his. She could feel his erection straining against his jeans and gloried in the friction of the denim against the silky fabric of her skirt.

He shifted—and nearly tumbled onto the floor.

"I need a bigger sofa."

"A bed would be even better," she said.

"I have one of those," he told her. "A king-size mattress with fresh sheets on it and a brand new box of condoms in the nightstand...and I just realized how incredibly presumptuous that sounded."

"As a woman whose business relies on precise scheduling, I can appreciate a man who plans ahead."

He rolled off the sofa and rose to his feet, then offered a hand to help her up.

He kissed her again—more promise than passion this time—

using his tongue to give her a preview of what they both knew was going to happen when they moved upstairs to the bedroom.

Suddenly he drew back, his brow furrowed. "Did you hear that?"

"What?" The pounding of her heart made it next to impossible to hear anything else.

"It sounds like…"

She heard it then, too.

Footsteps in the kitchen.

Not light footfalls, as if someone was tiptoeing around, trying to go unnoticed, but clomping treads, as if whoever was there had every right to be.

And then a female voice called out.

"Dad? Are you here?"

Chapter Twelve

Dad?

The word froze Finley in place for a moment.

Lachlan swore softly.

She looked at him, waiting for an explanation, because her mind was refusing to compute the obvious.

"Finley—"

"Dad!"

He took her hands, as if to prevent her from fleeing, before he responded. "We're in the living room, Aislynn."

"Who's we? And why are you in the dark?"

"We were just, uh, hanging out."

Suddenly the lamps on the end tables that flanked the sofa were illuminated. Finley blinked in the brightness, then took a minute to study the girl standing in the doorway.

A girl who could only be Lachlan's daughter.

She had the same dark brown—almost black—hair, though hers fell in loose waves to her shoulders, and the same deep blue eyes. Eyes that were fixed on Finley and filled with equal parts suspicion and animosity.

"This is Finley," Lachlan told the girl. Then he turned to Finley, "And this is my daughter, Aislynn."

He said it as if the name was the only revelation.

But he'd never mentioned having a child. Not once in any

of the numerous conversations that they'd had over the past few weeks.

And she wasn't really a child.

She was a teenager.

So why had he never mentioned that he had a teenage daughter?

It seemed to Finley that was the kind of information you'd share with someone you were starting a relationship with.

"You're new," Aislynn said bluntly, breaking the uncomfortable silence that had fallen. Then her gaze narrowed. "So why do you look kinda familiar?"

Finley had to clear her throat to be able to speak. "I'm an event planner—Gilmore Galas," she said. "You might have seen me at your great-grandparents' anniversary party a couple weeks back."

The girl shifted her attention back to her father. "You picked up the party planner?"

"Don't be rude, Aislynn," Lachlan admonished his daughter. "And no. I met Finley when I was in Nevada."

"Is she why you stayed away so long?" Beneath the suspicion in the question was a subtle note of hurt.

"I met Finley the day before I came home."

His daughter didn't look appeased.

"As much fun as it is to be talked about as if I'm not in the room, I think I should be going," Finley decided.

"You don't have to," Lachlan protested.

"Actually, I do. I've got early meetings in the morning."

He nodded then. "I'll walk you out."

"I can find my way," she assured him.

"I'll walk you out," he said again.

She shrugged, as if it didn't matter.

And it didn't, because she wasn't going to let it matter.

And she wasn't going to waste another minute with another guy who'd lied to her.

But she turned to his daughter and said, "It was nice to meet you, Aislynn."

Then she made her way to the front door, slipped her feet into her shoes and retrieved the purse she'd left beside them.

Lachlan walked out beside her. "Will you at least give me a chance to explain?"

She unlocked her door with the key fob. "A piece of advice—if you shared information beforehand, you wouldn't have to explain after the fact."

"I was going to tell you about Aislynn."

"Aislynn isn't the issue. Your dishonesty is." She opened the door and slid behind the wheel. "Thank you again for dinner."

Then she closed the door and drove away.

"Well, that was awkward," Aislynn said, when Lachlan returned to the house and tracked her down in the kitchen.

Often when she stopped by to see him, her first stop was the kitchen. Because apparently teenagers needed to eat almost constantly. Right now, she was digging into a generous slice of the cheesecake that he'd left on the counter.

The cheesecake he and Finley had been saving for later.

"A little bit," he agreed, trying not to resent that he was in the position of having to smooth over the situation with his daughter instead of Finley, who he suspected was even more upset than Aislynn—and justifiably so.

He squirted soap into the sink and began filling it with hot water. "Did I know you were planning to stop by tonight?"

"*I* didn't know I was planning to stop by," she said. "I was just out for a walk and decided to see what kind of ice cream you had in the freezer." She held up a forkful of cheesecake. "This is even better."

He slid the dishes into the soapy water. "You're not supposed to be out walking alone at night."

"It's a seven-minute walk from Mom's house to yours."

"Alone. At night," he said again.

"I have my cell phone."

He rinsed a plate under the tap and placed it in the drying rack. "And the GPS might help the police locate your body—if whoever kidnaps you didn't think to toss it out the window of his windowless van."

"How could my kidnapper toss it out the window if the van is windowless?" she asked cheekily.

"There are windows in the front." He rinsed the second plate. "Just none in the back."

She shoveled another bite of cheesecake into her mouth.

"I know you think I'm overprotective, but you're a teenager and not nearly as street savvy as you think you are."

"Are you really mad that I was out walking by myself? Or are you mad that I came here?"

"Of course I'm not mad that you came here," he said, scrubbing the cutlery. "This is your home, too."

"But the new girlfriend didn't know that, did she?"

"No." He sighed. "I've always tried to keep my personal life separate from my time with you," he confided. "But now that you're older, maybe it was inevitable that those parts would overlap."

"Overlap how?" she asked suspiciously.

"Like what happened tonight," he said. "You might decide to drop by and discover that I have company."

"Company meaning Finley?" she guessed.

"Well, she's the only woman I'm seeing right now." And, considering the way she'd left, even that was in question.

"But not Wednesdays, right? Wednesdays are *my* night."

"Wednesdays are your night," he confirmed. "And our weekends will still be our weekends."

Of course, that had always been his rule—and a source of contention with some of the women he'd dated in the past. But he didn't imagine that his lack of availability every other weekend would be a problem for Finley, who was booked up almost every weekend.

"But aside from our Wednesdays and our weekends, you have to be prepared for the possibility that Finley might be here—and you have to be polite to her."

Aislynn finished her cheesecake, then carried her plate and fork to the sink. "You can't make me like her."

"I didn't say you had to like her—" though he was certain she would, once she had a chance to know her "—only that you can't be rude to her." He looked at her. "You were rude tonight."

"I was caught off guard," she said in a defensive tone.

"I know," he acknowledged. "But next time you won't be."

"You're sure there's going to be a next time?"

"I hope there will be."

"She's pretty," she noted begrudgingly.

"Yes, she is." He washed and rinsed her dishes.

"Not as pretty as Mom, but still pretty."

He didn't agree with her assessment, but he respected her loyalty to her mom.

"I'm guessing you really like her, if you made your legendary enchiladas for her."

"We're still in the getting to know each other stage," he said, silently acknowledging that there was much Finley hadn't known because he hadn't been ready to tell her. Hadn't wanted to take the chance that she might choose to walk away rather than get involved with a man with a teenaged daughter.

Which is exactly what she'd done.

But to be fair, he was at least partly to blame for what had happened. He hadn't given Finley a chance to decide whether or not she wanted to date a single dad because he hadn't told her he was a single dad.

Aislynn isn't the issue. Your dishonesty is.

And he wasn't sure that there was any way to make up for his snafu—but he knew that he had to try.

* * *

"I didn't expect to hear from you until tomorrow," Haylee said, when she accepted her sister's FaceTime call.

"I'm sorry," Finley's apology was automatic. "Am I calling too late?"

"Only if you expected to talk to the kids."

"No. I just needed to talk to you. I didn't even look at the clock."

"I take it the night didn't go according to plan?"

"Not my plan," Finley said.

"What happened?"

"I found out that he has a child. A daughter."

"You like children," her sister pointed out.

"You're right. I do. I love kids. Especially yours."

"So what's the problem?" Haylee wondered.

"There are two problems. The first is that he never mentioned that he had a child. The second is that she isn't really a child. She's a teenager."

Her sister's eyes went wide. "Oh. Wow."

Finley nodded. "Yeah."

"But if he never mentioned that he had a child—how did you find out?"

"She walked in on us."

"Walked in on you…in the bedroom?"

"No." Thank God for small favors. "In the living room, just as we were about to move things up to the bedroom."

"Well, that was…lucky," Haylee said.

Finley narrowed her gaze on her sister's face. "Are you *smiling*?"

"I'm actually trying very hard not to."

"I'm glad you find the situation amusing."

"Can you blame me? I can only imagine how flustered you must have been—and you're almost never flustered."

"I was completely blindsided," she admitted. "How could he have failed to mention that he has a teenage daughter?"

"In all fairness, you haven't known the guy that long."

"I was ready to sleep with him." And he was obviously ready, too, with his clean sheets and new box of condoms.

"And not for the first time."

Finley chose to ignore her sister's teasing remark.

"I really liked him, Haylee. For the first time in a long time, I met someone that I really liked. Someone who made me think that a relationship might be worth the effort."

"And now that you know he has a teenage daughter, you suddenly don't like him?"

"It's not the daughter—it's the lying."

"Did he ever tell you that he didn't have a child?"

"A lie of omission is still a lie."

"Maybe."

"At the very least, it's a secret. And you know how I feel about secrets. And why."

"I know," Haylee confirmed. "But you've got to stop assuming every guy you meet is like Mark."

"But I didn't assume that Lachlan was like Mark—and then it turned out that he was."

"And you ran out without giving him a chance to explain," her sister guessed.

"I didn't run," Finley denied. "I thanked him again for dinner and walked out at a dignified pace."

"And blocked his number, I'll bet."

She hadn't. Not yet.

But it was a good idea.

"He lied to me," Finley said again.

"When was he supposed to tell you?"

"Any point in time prior to his daughter walking through the door would have been good."

"Give him a chance to explain, Fin."

"I can't believe you're saying that to me. I thought you'd be on my side."

"I am on your side. One hundred percent. All the time. And it's because I'm on your side that I don't want to see you shut out the first guy you've really liked in a long time."

"It's not what I want, either," Finley said. "But I'm not going to be duped again."

He sent her a cheesecake.

Finley might have thought it was the cheesecake they hadn't had for dessert the night before if she hadn't been there when it arrived and saw the delivery man with the Bliss logo on his shirt.

There was no note. No personal—if brief—apology this time, only her name on the delivery slip.

And it made her wonder what kind of game he was playing.

Did he think he was being clever?

That she'd feel compelled to call him to ask if he'd sent her a cheesecake?

Of course, she knew it was from him.

Who else would send her favorite cheesecake from her favorite bakery?

Or maybe he was counting on her sense of propriety urging her to make a call, to thank him for the thoughtful gesture.

If that was the case, she had a gesture for him.

She stared at the bakery box in the middle of her desk, trying to decide what to do with it.

Her bruised heart urged her to dump it into the wastebasket beside her desk.

Her logical mind was appalled by the idea of such wastefulness.

Her empty stomach voted for grabbing a fork and digging in.

It was just a cheesecake. In the grand scheme of things, the fate of the cheesecake was irrelevant.

Except that she knew whatever decision she made about the cheesecake was really a decision about Lachlan. And if experience had taught her anything, it was that she always seemed to make the wrong decisions when it came to her personal relationships with men.

Did that mean that she'd made the wrong decision in walking away?

Give him a chance to explain.

With her sister's voice echoing in the back of her head, she grabbed her purse and headed for the door—then turned back to pick up the cheesecake and put it in the refrigerator for safekeeping.

Lachlan had office hours between two and four on Wednesdays for students to drop in at their convenience, but the reality was that students who wanted to chat usually contacted him via email first to make sure that he was available.

No one had made an appointment for today, so he wasn't expecting any particular students to stop by. Still, the knock on his door wasn't a surprise.

The surprise was when he looked up and saw Finley standing there.

He removed his glasses and rose to his feet. "Finley."

"I should have called first. But I didn't, because even though I left my office with the intention of coming here to see you, I wasn't entirely sure I would follow through.

"And I very nearly didn't make it," she continued her explanation. "The layout of this campus is ridiculously confusing, and I had to stop three different people to ask for directions."

"I'm glad you're here," he said. "I'm not sure why you're here, but I'm glad you are."

"I decided to give you a chance to explain."

"Why don't you sit down?" He gestured to the pair of leather club chairs facing his desk.

"I'm happy to stand."

Which he interpreted to mean that she had no intention of letting down her guard enough to get comfortable, so he remained standing, too.

"Can I start by saying I'm sorry?"

"What exactly are you apologizing for?" she asked. "The fact that your daughter interrupted what was happening? Or the fact that you never told me that you had a daughter?"

"Both."

"So why didn't you tell me? And don't you dare say that it didn't come up in conversation, because while that might technically be true, having a child is the type of thing that you should make darn sure comes up in conversation."

"You're right," he agreed. "The truth is, I haven't dated a lot in recent years. And before that, when Aislynn was younger, I was careful to keep my personal life separate from her, because I didn't want to confuse her by introducing her to women who might or might not stick around."

"You said when she was younger—how old is she?"

"Almost sixteen."

Wow.

"So you were twenty when you became a dad?"

He nodded. "Deirdre got pregnant when we were in college, when safe sex was more of a guideline than a rule, especially when alcohol was added to the mix. We both wanted the baby, so we got married and managed to stay together for almost four years before we realized that neither of us was happy. Not only that, we were taking our unhappiness out on each other, constantly sniping and finding fault, forgetting that we'd been friends before we became parents.

"So we decided to go our separate ways and share custody of Aislynn, and we've been co-parenting amicably since then."

"I'm sure you both deserve credit for that," she said. "But right now, I'm still wrestling with the fact that you lied to me."

"I might not have told you the whole truth about my failed marriage, but I didn't lie. If you'd asked if I had any kids with my ex, I would have told you."

"So because I didn't ask, you didn't have any obligation to tell me that you had a teenage daughter?"

"That's not what I'm saying," he protested.

"Then what are you saying?" she challenged.

"That it was…a failure to communicate."

"A failure to communicate?" she echoed.

"And that I'm sorry. Really, really sorry."

She sighed. "So where do we go from here?"

"Where do you want to go?" he asked cautiously.

"I want to have a baby."

His brows lifted. "With me?"

"No!" Her response was immediate and perhaps a little too vehement. "I mean, I don't know. I only meant that, someday I'm going to want a family of my own and obviously you've already been there, done that, so maybe you won't want to do it again."

"Are you asking me if I want to do it again?"

"I guess I am," she admitted. "But in a conversational way, not a propositional way."

"Then, in a conversational way, I'd say that I need to give the idea some thought. Or maybe not. Because now that I am thinking about it, I feel confident that, if I was planning a future with a woman, I could imagine children in that future."

She frowned.

"Not the answer you were looking for?"

"I guess I thought that, if you said you didn't want any more kids, it would justify me walking away."

"And you want to walk away?"

"I don't know what I want."

His brows lifted.

"I haven't had a lot of success with relationships," she reminded him.

"You've mentioned that once or twice," he acknowledged.

"My sister thinks that I look for excuses to end relationships before they have a chance to run their course."

"And I just took away the excuse you were planning to use to end this one."

"Maybe you should be looking for an excuse to end this relationship. Obviously, I've got some issues to work through."

"Everyone has issues."

"That's probably true," she acknowledged.

"So what's our next step? Assuming that you'll give me another chance and there will be a next step."

"I'd like to try the date thing again. But we're going to have to work on our communication," she told him. "And you need to understand that secrets and lies are a hot button for me."

"Then, in the interest of full disclosure, I'll tell you that the night I stood you up, it was Aislynn's best friend who was in the car accident."

Her cool façade melted a bit further. "Of course your focus would have been entirely on her."

He nodded.

"And your Wednesday plans?" she prompted.

"I pick Aislynn up from band practice after school on Wednesdays and then we have dinner together."

"Well, that's a lot better than what I was thinking."

"You thought I was seeing someone else?" he guessed.

"It didn't seem out of the realm of possibility."

"I'm really not that kind of guy," he told her.

"Well, I hope I have the chance to get to know what kind of guy you are."

"And I hope I won't have to wait another two weeks to see you again." His phone emitted a sound like an old-fashioned alarm clock. "That's my reminder to leave campus so I'm not late getting to the high school."

"And I don't want you to be late on my account."

"Can I walk you to your car?"

"You could, but then you would be late," she told him. "I'm parked on the opposite side of campus."

"Why would you park on the opposite side of campus?"

"Because I had no idea where the Social Sciences building was."

"I could drive you to your vehicle," he suggested as an alternative.

"Not necessary," she said. "But if you want, you can call me later tonight."

"I will."

"In that case, I should unblock your number." She pulled out her phone then and swiped across the screen a few times.

"You blocked my number?"

"It was my sister's idea."

"Your sister told you to block my number?"

"Well, no. She assumed that I had already blocked your number, which gave me the idea. But she's also the one who told me to give you a chance to explain."

"In that case, I'm glad you listened to her."

"Me, too." She kissed his cheek. "And thank you for the cheesecake."

Chapter Thirteen

In the two weeks that had passed since the night of the legendary enchiladas (and the teenage daughter reveal), Finley and Lachlan had managed to get together once more for coffee, once for lunch and once for drinks before a Friday night wedding rehearsal. Though they continued to talk almost daily, Finley wanted more. She wanted face-to-face time with him.

Naked face-to-face time would be even better.

She scrolled through her calendar on her way back to her office after an emergency meeting with a couple who wanted to move up their wedding date—by five months!—because they'd just learned that the bride-to-be was also a mommy-to-be. And while Finley prided herself on being very good at her job, there was simply no way she could expect the venue to be available on the earlier date and all the third-party vendors that she'd secured to provide services (flowers, cake, music and more) to be able to accommodate an earlier date. Because it was not and they could not.

And now she was likely going to be late for a site visit on the campus of Merivale College, after which she was meeting Lachlan for another coffee date.

Finley hated being late—even if it was only a few minutes. And having to answer a call from her mother while she negotiated the traffic between Oakland and San Francisco did nothing to improve her mood.

She was three minutes behind schedule when she parked at the college. But at least she arrived before the bride and groom, who showed up five minutes later with their respective mothers. The plan was to tour Alumni Hall as a potential venue for the upcoming nuptials, as Pamela and Mason had met at Merivale College, had gotten engaged on campus (Mason proposed at the very spot where they'd shared their first kiss) and wanted to be married there, as well. Their mothers had other ideas, so Finley's job was to help them see the potential of the setting and tactfully remind them that the day was about their children.

An hour later, she walked into the campus coffee shop to find Lachlan waiting.

"I'm sorry I'm late."

He glanced at his watch. "Yeah, a whole three minutes. I was just about to walk out the door."

"I hate being late."

"I know." He touched his lips to hers briefly. "Should I order you a decaf?"

She frowned. "When have I ever ordered decaf?"

"Never," he admitted. "You just seem a little...wound up."

"It's been one of those days," she confided.

"Let me get the coffee and then you can explain."

He returned a few minutes later with two oversized mugs.

"Thanks." She wrapped her hands around the cup. "And sorry. I guess I am a little wound up."

"Difficult bride?" he guessed.

"Difficult brides, I can handle," she said. "My mother is another story."

"You were in a great mood after shoe shopping with her last week."

"Well, shoe shopping always puts me in a good mood," she said. "But also, that was Colleen. My stepmom."

"I was sure you told me you'd been shopping with your mom."

"I usually refer to Colleen as 'Mom,' because she's been a part of my life since not long after my parents split."

"How old were you when they did?"

"Nine." And she'd been certain it was the end of her world—or at least her family. Because when you're a kid, your family pretty much is your world.

"I think the hardest part, for me, was that Sandra didn't think about Haylee or me or Logan, she just decided that she didn't want to be married anymore and walked out. And it didn't seem to occur to her to take us with her."

Maybe her kids would have balked at leaving the only home they'd ever known, but the fact that she just walked away…

"You felt abandoned," Lachlan guessed.

She nodded.

"My dad seemed as confused as we were. I mean, I was a kid, so what did I know about what went on between them when we weren't around? But he seemed sincerely baffled to discover that she wanted out of their marriage.

"I know he asked her to stay, because I overheard bits and pieces of that argument one night. He told her that even if she didn't love him anymore, she owed it to us to try to make the marriage work.

"Obviously she wasn't persuaded by his argument, and for the next few years, Haylee and me and Logan shuttled back and forth between our dad's house and our mom's apartment, as they tried to do the shared custody thing—a lot less successfully than you and your ex-wife."

"So your mom lives in Oakland, too?"

Finley shook her head. "Not anymore. She moved to Florida after she and Dalton were married."

"You did mention a brother in Palm Beach," he recalled now. "So I guess you don't see your mom very often."

"Maybe once or twice a year. And that's only been since Haylee's wedding. Prior to that, it was more like once every two or three years."

"And she's in town now?"

"Yep. She called completely out of the blue today, wanting to go for lunch, never considering the possibility that I might be unavailable. Because for so many years, I was so desperate for any little bit of attention from her, I would drop whatever I was doing to spend even a few minutes with her."

"You could have skipped coffee with me if you wanted to catch up with her," he said.

"I know I could have," she said. "But I wanted to have coffee with you. Because spending time with you—even if it's only thirty minutes in the middle of the day—makes me happy."

"I'm glad to hear that."

"But what would make me really happy," she continued, "is if you said that you didn't have any plans tonight."

"As a matter of fact, I don't," he told her. "But I thought you had something on your calendar."

"A consult," she confirmed. "Canceled. The bride and groom decided that instead of spending their hard-earned money on a fancy wedding, they're going to put it toward a down payment on a house and have a private ceremony at city hall."

"So what do you want to do now that you have a free evening? Dinner and a movie?"

"How about pizza at my place? We can Netflix and chill—and not worry about being interrupted."

"Sounds promising," he said. "I remember there was a pizzeria around the corner from your place when I drove you home from Haven—do you order from there?"

"Carlos's," she said, nodding.

"Why don't you order whatever you want for seven o'clock and I'll pick it up on my way?"

* * *

Lachlan told himself not to read too much into her invitation. He was pleased that she had a free night and wanted to spend it with him, but when she said "Netflix and chill," it was possible she just meant watching TV and relaxing.

And he'd be okay with that, really. Considering the missteps he'd made at the beginning of their relationship, he decided to let her set the pace going forward.

And if that meant more cold showers in his future, well, he was starting to get used to them, anyway.

He carried the pizza (and the bottle of wine he'd picked up to enjoy with the pie) and made his way up the stairs to her carriage house.

He knocked—and winced when the back patio lights of the main house came on.

Maybe they were on a timer. He certainly hadn't knocked loudly enough to attract the attention of anyone inside the house. But maybe Finley's dad had some kind of paternal instinct that warned him when someone was sniffing around his daughter. And Lachlan had definitely been sniffing—and hoping to do a lot more—but now he was having second thoughts about anything more with her parents so close by.

Then Finley opened the door.

She was standing behind it at first, so he couldn't see her until he crossed the threshold and she closed the door at his back. And then, when he could see her, he couldn't seem to do anything but stare.

"You're not saying anything," she noted.

"I'm...speechless."

Her lips curved.

Lips that were painted the same cherry red color as the satin babydoll she was wearing.

"We agreed that we needed to work on our communication," she reminded him. "So I thought a visual aid might help illustrate why I invited you to come over tonight."

He swallowed. "It wasn't only because you wanted your pizza delivered?"

"It was not." She took the box and the bottle out of his hands and set them on the coffee table. "And one of the best things about pizza is that it tastes just as good cold."

"I want to respond with something clever, but all the blood seems to have drained out of my head."

"Is that because you like what you see?"

"More than you can know."

"I don't often wear red," she said. "I'm not sure it's my color, but I saw this in the window of a little lingerie shop not far from my office and thought you might like it."

He swallowed again. "You were thinking of me...when you bought that?"

She nodded. "And when I put fresh sheets on my bed. And when I tucked a box of condoms in the nightstand."

"A whole box?"

"I don't expect we'll use them all tonight," she said.

"I'll give it my best effort," he promised.

She smiled at that, then took his hand and led him to her bedroom.

She'd set the scene in there, too. With candles flickering around the room and music playing softly in the background.

"I must say, I appreciate your clear communication."

"I didn't want there to be any doubt about how much I want to be with you."

"Do I need to tell you how much I want to be with you?"

Her gaze slid down his body, to where his erection was clearly straining the zipper of his jeans. "I don't think so."

He lifted a hand to toy with the bow tied over one of her shoulders, hooked the loop of satin with his finger and tugged. The bow loosened, then released, the ends of the tie falling apart, leaving her shoulder bare and exposing the curve of her breast. He dipped his head to press his lips to her skin.

She shivered.

"Cold?"

She shook her head.

He repeated the process with the other bow, kissed her other shoulder.

He could see the points of her nipples straining against the fabric. He cupped her breasts in his hands, stroking the turgid peaks with his thumbs. She made a sound low in her throat that was almost a whimper, then lifted her hands to frame his face and draw his mouth down to hers.

It had been a long time since Finley was intimate with a man. She usually enjoyed sex—and even more so when it was with someone she felt close to—but it had been a long time since she'd dated a man she liked and trusted enough to take that next step with. And now that Lachlan was finally here, she had no intention of being a passive participant.

She hastily unfastened the buttons of his shirt, desperate to touch him as he was touching her. The rest of his clothes—along with her babydoll and matching thong—followed, then he eased her down onto the mattress and covered her naked body with his own.

His tongue slid between her lips, to tease and tangle with hers as his palms moved over her torso, stroking her body, stoking her desire. Her hands slid up his arms, tracing the muscular contours. His shoulders were broad and strong—more indicative of the football player he used to be than the college professor he was now.

His whole body was lean and tough, and she wanted to explore every inch of it. She started by reaching down and wrapping her fingers around his rigid length.

He groaned in appreciation as she stroked him slowly, from base to tip and back again.

He let her play for another minute before he captured her wrist and pulled her hand away. "I'm not sure I can take much more of that."

"So take me," she said.

"I'm going to," he promised. "But first…"

He lowered his head to nibble on her throat, the scrape of his unshaven jaw against her delicate skin raising goosebumps on her flesh. She moaned softly as his hands roamed over her body in a leisurely but very thorough exploration.

He continued the exploration with his mouth, tracing the ridge of her collarbone, nuzzling the hollow between her breasts, licking and suckling her nipples. Sparks zinged through her veins; liquid heat pooled at her center. His hand slid between their bodies to part the soft folds at the juncture of her thighs and test her readiness. He groaned again when he found her wet.

Her breath caught in her throat as he lowered his head and touched the sensitive nub at her center with his tongue, a slow, deliberate lick that made everything inside her tighten in glorious anticipation.

"Lachlan…please…"

He didn't respond to her plea, except to continue licking and nibbling her ultra-sensitive flesh, pushing her perilously close to the edge of climax.

She closed her eyes and fisted her hands in the sheet, biting down on her bottom lip as she tried to hold it together.

She didn't want to come apart like this. She wanted to wait until he was inside her.

But he was relentless, tasting and teasing, demanding nothing less than her complete surrender. As he continued his intimate exploration, she couldn't fight the desires and demands of her body any longer. The tension inside her built to a breaking point, and she shattered into a million pieces.

Lachlan held her close while her body continued to shudder

with the aftershocks of her pleasure, then he sheathed himself with a condom and rose up over her.

She gasped as he filled her, then lifted her hips to take him even deeper, the action drawing another low groan from him. Finally he began to move—slow, deliberate strokes that had anticipation building inside her again. Then the pace quickened. Harder. Faster. Deeper.

Her body moved in tandem with his, her fingernails biting into his shoulders as he drove them both toward the ultimate pleasure. As her muscles clenched around him, he tumbled with her into the abyss.

It was a long time later before either of them summoned the energy to move. When Lachlan finally rolled off her, he wrapped his arm around her middle and pulled her close, spooning her like they'd done at the Dusty Boots Motel the night of the storm. Except that they hadn't been naked then.

"Who were the bride and groom who canceled their appointment tonight?" Lachlan asked.

Finley twisted her head to look at him. "Is that really what you're thinking about right now?"

"Only because I want to send them a 'thank you' card."

She chuckled softly. "In that case, you can sign my name, too."

"Done."

She snuggled back against him. "I suppose you want your pizza now."

"I'm not in a hurry," he said—at the same time her stomach growled. "But apparently you are."

"I didn't have time for lunch today," she reminded him. "And that wasn't just an excuse to avoid sharing a meal with my mother."

"Then I guess we'd better feed you, because I want to ensure you have energy for round two."

"You don't have to worry about me," she told him. "I have energy for round two—and I can prove it."

Since her back was snug against his front, she knew that he could, too.

So they did.

And it was a long time later before they dragged themselves out of bed to refuel with pizza.

Chapter Fourteen

"**W**here's this mysterious Simon that I've heard so much about?" Lachlan asked, as he uncorked the wine.

"Most likely hiding under the bed in the guest room."

"Hiding from what?"

"You. Not you personally," she clarified, carrying plates and napkins into the living room. "But you being someone he doesn't know. He doesn't really like strangers."

"I hope I won't be a stranger for long."

"I do, too," she said, scrolling through the Netflix menu.

"There's a ball game on tonight." He settled on the sofa beside her. "The A's and the Orioles."

"I'm not in the mood to watch baseball tonight."

"Not in the mood for baseball," he echoed, with a shake of his head. "I might have to rethink this relationship."

"While you're rethinking, think about the red thong that you removed with your teeth," she suggested.

A slow smile curved his lips.

"Now what was it you were saying about baseball?"

"Is that the game where you kick the ball for a field goal?" She chuckled. "Eat your pizza."

"So what are we watching?"

"Four Weddings and a Funeral."

"Because you don't see enough weddings in real life?"

"Because it's one of my all-time favorite movies."

"You have a secret crush on Hugh Grant, don't you?"

"It's not really a secret."

Lachlan, having accepted that he wasn't going to win the battle for control of the TV, focused on his pizza.

Not fifteen minutes into the movie, Finley nudged Lachlan with her elbow.

"That's Simon," she said, as the cat ventured cautiously into the room.

"Does his presence mean that he's accepted me as a friend?"

"No, it means he's hoping I'll slip him a slice or two of pepperoni."

"Do you do that?"

"Sometimes," she admitted. "I know I shouldn't, but I feel guilty that I get to eat whatever I want, and he's stuck with the same chicken and rice every day."

Lachlan peeled a slice of pepperoni off his pizza and held it out to the cat.

Simon turned his head away and gave a dismissive flick of his tail.

"I thought you said he likes pepperoni."

"He likes when *I* give him pepperoni," she clarified. "He doesn't accept attempted bribes."

"Why would I be trying to bribe him?"

"Maybe because you think I'll be more likely to let you back into my bed if you make friends with my cat."

"I don't need to make friends with your cat, I've already made friends with your—"

She lifted her hand to his lips, her eyes narrowed. "Don't go there."

"I was going to say *pastry chef*," he told her. "I've already made friends with your pastry chef."

She had to laugh at his quick retort. "Are you referring to Domenic Torres at Bliss?"

He nodded.

"I don't think buying two cheesecakes from his shop constitutes a friendship."

"How did you know I bought two?"

"I was at the reception desk when the cake was delivered. What I don't know is why you bought a second cake rather than dropping off the one you'd bought the day before."

"Because Aislynn cut into that one."

"You only promised me a piece—not a whole cake. You could have just dropped off a slice."

"But a whole cake seemed like a grander gesture—and I felt like I owed you a grand gesture."

"Well, I did enjoy the cake. So did Julia, Rachel and Taylor."

"I'm glad." He topped off both their wine glasses.

Finley set her empty plate aside and settled back to watch the movie. And even if Lachlan wasn't paying much attention to what was happening on the screen, she appreciated that he was being a good sport about it.

At least until Gareth's funeral, when he decided to nuzzle her throat. The rasp of his unshaven jaw against her skin sent delicious tingles down her spine, but she managed to keep her voice even when she asked, "What are you doing?"

His lips skimmed over her jaw. "Moving on to the 'chill' portion of the evening."

"But…" she closed her eyes when he suckled on her earlobe "…the movie isn't over yet."

"How many times have you seen it?"

"So many that I lost count," she admitted.

"Then I'd guess you know how it ends."

"I know how it ends," she agreed, turning her head to meet his lips.

He captured her mouth then, kissing her long and slow and deep.

"And I think I can guess how this ends," she mused, when his hands slid beneath her top. (Because, much to his disappointment, she'd insisted on getting dressed in actual clothes for dinner rather than sitting around and eating pizza in a barely there babydoll.)

"A happy ending?"

"Very happy, as I recall." His thumbs brushed over her nipples, making her sigh. "Very satisfying."

"Well, tonight's feature might surprise you."

Her eyes popped open. "I'm not really big on surprises."

"You'll like this one," he told her. "Consider it a director's cut."

"An extra thirty seconds of previously unseen footage?" she teased.

"At least an extra thirty seconds," he promised. "And a brand new climax."

"I think I will like this one," she agreed.

He eased her back onto the sofa—or tried to, but there were too many cushions in the way. So he picked up one and tossed it aside.

The pillow hit Simon, who'd been snoozing on the back of the sofa. The startled feline screeched as he began to fall, paws scrambling for purchase—and finding it on Lachlan's back.

He swore ripely.

Finley gasped. "Ohmygod. Are you okay?"

"I'd be better if you could get your cat off my back."

"Right. Sorry." She carefully lifted the cat into her arms. Simon mewed pitifully.

"I know, baby. I'm sorry."

Lachlan swiveled his head. "Are you actually apologizing to *the cat*?"

"You scared him."

"He clawed me."

She gently deposited Simon on the seat of the chair to turn her attention to Lachlan's shoulder, where little drops of blood were seeping through his shirt.

"Come on," she said, taking his hand and leading him to the bathroom.

"Are we going to play doctor now?" he asked hopefully.

"I think you're already well on your way to recovery, but I'll clean it up and give you a Band-Aid."

She surprised him by turning on the shower.

"You want to wash my back in the shower?"

"Do you have any objections?"

He shook his head. "None at all."

He quickly stripped off his clothes as she did the same with hers, and they stepped under the spray together.

She squirted liquid soap onto a bath puff and instructed him to turn around.

He did as he was told.

"Shirla was right about you," Finley mused, as she lathered his back. "You are a bad boy and you've got the tattoo to prove it."

"It was supposed to be a skull and crossbones, but I didn't realize how much it would hurt to get a tattoo, so when I pleaded for mercy, that's what I ended up with."

"You wanted a skull and crossbones but ended up with an infinity symbol?"

"My regret is endless."

She chuckled softly as she continued to rub gentle circles on his back. "There's a date inside your tattoo."

He immediately stilled, holding his breath as he waited for her to ask about it.

A piece of advice—if you shared information beforehand, you wouldn't have to explain after the fact.

He opened his mouth, fully intending to heed her advice, but she spoke first.

"What's the significance of August second?"

The question gave him pause.

"It's Aislynn's birthday."

"I think it's really sweet that you have your daughter's birthday inked on your back."

"Well, it's no skull and crossbones," he said lightly.

"No, it's not," she agreed, moving in front of him to soap his chest…and stomach…and lower.

A piece of advice…

"The thing is—"

The rest of the words stuck in his throat when she dropped to her knees in front of him.

Finley had looked like a fantasy come to life when she'd opened the door in that sexy babydoll the night before. This morning she was no less of a fantasy, standing at the stove in the kitchen, wearing nothing but his shirt, her hips gyrating to the music spilling out of the speaker on the counter.

She did a twirl, halting abruptly when she saw him.

"Oh. Hi." Her cheeks flushed prettily. "Good morning."

He breached the distance between them and kissed her lightly. "Good morning."

"I probably should have asked you if you like pancakes before I mixed up the batter," she said. "But I can make eggs, if you'd prefer."

"I love pancakes." He reached for a strip of the bacon that she'd previously cooked and set aside. "And bacon."

And, as he nibbled on the bacon and watched her flip the cake in the pan, he realized that he could very easily fall in love with her, too.

In fact, it felt as if he was teetering on the precipice, as if all it would take was a tiny nudge and he'd be a goner.

In songs and poems, love was described as uplifting and exhilarating—the reason for being.

In real life, at least in Lachlan's experience, it was terrifying.

Because loving someone meant opening yourself up to the possibility of heartache.

But maybe what he was feeling for Finley wasn't love but lust. After the amazing night they'd spent together, it was understandable that his mind—and his heart—would be muddled by the surge of endorphins in his system.

"Then you're in luck," Finley said, oblivious to the tumultuous thoughts spinning in his mind. "Because those are both on the menu this morning."

"As much as I appreciate the home-cooked meal, I would have felt even luckier to wake up with you beside me," he said, nuzzling her throat.

"I thought about waking you," she confided. "But I figured that you deserved to sleep in after working so hard last night."

"That wasn't work. That was pleasure."

"A very definite pleasure," she agreed, smiling at him as she turned the pancake onto a plate already stacked high.

He took the plate and carried it to the table.

"Do you want juice? Or just coffee?"

"Just coffee, please."

She poured two cups.

"You have class at two today?"

"Nope," he told her. "I'm off this week. Summer term starts on Monday."

"Just when I was starting to learn your schedule, you had to go ahead and change it."

"I didn't change it, the college did."

"So what are your plans for the day?"

"I don't have anything specific on my agenda," he said. "Why?"

"Because it so happens that I was able to clear my schedule for the morning."

He looked at her in mock surprise. "Call CNN—I didn't think that was possible."

"Neither did I," she admitted. "But I'm finally realizing that I don't have to micromanage every detail of every event."

"Really?" Lachlan sounded a bit skeptical. "What's brought about this sudden change?"

Finley sipped her coffee. "I guess I've finally realized that I have an amazingly creative and hardworking team who are more than capable of doing the heavy lifting—when I let them. Which they proved when I was in Nevada, and which I'm letting them prove again this morning."

So they enjoyed a leisurely breakfast, then made love again and followed up with another shared shower—in the interest of water conservation, of course.

"Is it an early night for you tonight?" Lachlan asked, as they were toweling off.

He'd offered to help her dry, but Finley knew that if he did so, the chore would turn into something else, and she really did need to put in an appearance at the office today.

"It is," she confirmed.

"Would it be okay if I brought over some chicken to cook on your grill?"

"I'm never going to object to a man offering to cook for me," she told him.

"Six o'clock?"

"I'll be here."

When they were both dressed, he reached for the keys and phone he'd left on her nightstand, frowning as he looked at the display on his phone.

"What's the matter?"

"I missed three calls from Aislynn."

"Did she leave any messages?"

He shook his head.

"Then it probably wasn't anything important."

"You're probably right," he said, still staring at the log of missed calls. "But she never calls. She texts, sometimes too frequently, but she never calls." He tapped the screen to attempt a callback and sighed. "It's going straight to voicemail."

"Maybe because she's in class?" Finley suggested.

He glanced at his watch. "She should be."

"Then I'm sure she'll get back to you when she's on a break."

"Her next period is lunch," he noted. "If I head over to the school now, I should be able to catch her on her break."

Though Finley suspected that the phone calls were a deliberate effort by Aislynn to manipulate her dad, she wasn't going to say so. Because he wasn't likely to believe her and would probably question why she thought she had any insights into his daughter's mind when she'd only met the teen once.

But she probably understood the girl better than either of them could guess, because she'd been that girl—devastated by the breakup of her family and desperately wishing she could put the pieces back together again.

Instead, she only kissed Lachlan goodbye and said, "See you later."

When Finley got home at the end of the day and found Lachlan sitting on the steps, waiting for her, her heart did a happy little dance inside her chest. It might have been even nicer to come home and find him in the kitchen already, but she suspected it was far too soon—for both of them—to show him where she kept the spare key hidden.

After he'd assured her that everything was okay with Aislynn—a relief if not a surprise to Finley—they worked side-by-side in the kitchen to prepare dinner. Then they ate the chicken along with grilled baby potatoes and a green salad on the deck, enjoying a bottle of crisp sauvignon blanc along with the quiet spring evening.

"I could get used to this," Finley mused. "Unfortunately, the closer we get to June, the fewer opportunities I'm going to have for nights like this."

"Then we'd better make the most of them while we can."

"First—" she rose from her seat to stack their plates and cutlery "—I'm going to put these in the dishwasher."

"I can help."

"No. Sit." She gave him a quick kiss. "I'll be right back."

She wasn't gone more than five minutes, and when she returned Lachlan handed her the phone she'd left on the table.

"Mark called."

She frowned. "You answered my phone?"

"No. His name showed on the display when your phone rang."

"Oh." She set the phone down again and reached for the bottle of wine to refill their glasses.

"You're not going to listen to the message? Call him back?"

"Not right now."

"Are you going to tell me who he is?" he pressed.

"A friend."

"A childhood friend? A friend from work? A friend who's seen you naked?"

She lifted her glass to her lips, sipped.

"Mark and I did go out for a while, a few years back," she finally admitted.

"Wait a minute—are you talking about Mark Nickel? The ballplayer?"

"Yeah. But how did…you Googled me!" she said accusingly.

"Honey, I did a lot more than Google you last night—and this morning—and you didn't seem to have any complaints."

"That was different," she said. "I invited you to my bed last night. I didn't say you could snoop into my private life."

"It's not really private if it's on the internet, is it?"

"Which is one of the things I hated about dating Mark," she admitted now. "We were hardly A-Rod and J.Lo, but Mark was almost as popular with the photographers as he was with the fans, so even the most casual date ended up in somebody's column or blog."

"Wasn't he traded to a team on the East Coast?"

She nodded. "Baltimore."

"But you keep in touch?"

"Occasionally."

"And you see him when the Orioles are in town?"

"Sometimes. But not in the way you mean."

"That's why you didn't want to watch the game last night," he realized.

"Can you blame me for not wanting to snuggle up with my new boyfriend to watch my ex on TV?"

"So I'm your new boyfriend now, am I?"

She cringed. "Sorry. I didn't mean to slap a label on you. I know our relationship is very new and—"

He leaned across the table to silence her with a kiss.

"I don't have a problem with the label," he assured her. "Now what do you say about taking the rest of this wine into the bedroom, girlfriend?"

Of course, she said *yes*.

Finley said *yes* again when Lachlan called her the next day to ask a favor. He'd gone to Santa Cruz to have lunch with a friend and gotten stuck behind an overturned tractor trailer on the 85, which meant that he wasn't going to make it to the school to pick up Aislynn. (He'd tried calling Deirdre first, but his calls kept going to voicemail.)

It would be a stretch to say that Finley was happy to help—the truth was, she was more than a little wary, as Lachlan's daughter had given no indication that she might be warming up to her. But she did think it might be a good opportunity for her to chat with Aislynn without her father there as a buffer between them.

Of course, a conversation required the participation of two people, and the most she was able to elicit from Aislynn were monosyllabic responses to her questions—at least until she pulled into the driveway of Lachlan's house.

Then Aislynn dutifully intoned, "Thanks for the ride."

"You're not getting rid of me just yet," Finley said.

The teen's gaze narrowed. "I'm not a child—you don't have to wait with me for my dad to get home."

"He didn't ask me to babysit," Finley assured her. "Only to preheat the oven and then put the lasagna in."

"I can do that," Aislynn said.

"I'm sure you can, but your dad asked me to do it."

Aislynn pushed open the passenger side door and stepped out of the vehicle. "Did he ask you to stay for dinner, too?"

"No," Finley said. "And I didn't expect him to. I know Wednesday is your night with your dad."

"Every Wednesday *and* alternate weekends."

Finley just nodded as she followed the girl to the door.

"He spends a lot of time with me," Aislynn said, as she used her key to disengage the lock. "And some of his girl-friends didn't like that."

"Those girlfriends obviously didn't know him well enough to know how much his time with you means to him."

"You think you know him better?" Aislynn challenged.

"I'm hoping to know him better," Finley replied, aware that she was treading on boggy ground. "And I'd like to know you better, too."

"I don't really see that happening."

"I guess time will tell," she said lightly, refusing to let her-self be offended by the girl's dismissive tone.

Aislynn was scowling as Finley moved past her to the kitchen.

She found the lasagna in the refrigerator, where Lachlan had told her it would be, and checked the heating instructions on the packaging before programming the oven temperature.

While the oven was preheating, she opened the crisper drawer and found romaine lettuce, cucumbers and red peppers.

"What are you doing now?" Aislynn demanded from the doorway.

"I thought I'd make you guys a salad to go with the pasta."

Aislynn watched her tear up the lettuce and divide it into two bowls, offering no help or instruction as Finley rummaged around until she found a cutting board and chef's knife.

When the oven beeped to indicate it had reached the desired temperature, Finley placed the lasagna on a baking tray and slid it into the oven, then set the timer before returning her attention to the salads.

"I don't like red pepper."

"Then I won't put red pepper in your salad," Finley said.

"Why are you doing this?"

She shrugged as she began to slice the cucumber. "My mom always insisted on a vegetable at every meal."

"Dad says the tomato sauce on pasta *is* a vegetable."

"An interesting perspective."

She finished with the salads and returned the leftover vegetables to the refrigerator.

"I have homework to do," Aislynn said.

"Okay."

"I can't go upstairs to do it until I lock the door behind you."

Subtlety was definitely *not* the girl's strong suit.

Finley wiped her hands on a towel. "If your dad's not home when the timer goes off, remove the foil lid and put the lasagna back in the oven for another fifteen minutes."

Aislynn nodded. "Okay," she said, then added a begrudging "thanks."

"Anytime," Finley said easily.

Lachlan's daughter followed her to the door. "Goodbye, Finley."

"Good night, Aislynn."

She'd barely crossed the threshold when she heard the click of the lock at her back, an audible reminder that she was on the outside looking in.

Chapter Fifteen

It had been difficult to make plans with Finley in April, and May was proving to be an equal challenge. June, she cautioned Lachlan, was even more tightly scheduled. But now that their relationship had progressed to the next stage and the question of "will we or won't we" had been answered very much to his satisfaction—and apparently hers, too—Finley seemed comfortable asking him to meet her after an event or stopping by his place if she was on the other side of the Bay.

But she'd warned him that he wouldn't see her at all on the third weekend in May, as she had a rehearsal and rehearsal dinner on Friday, followed by a wedding with two hundred and fifty guests— "actually, two hundred and fifty-six now"—for which she'd contracted several additional helpers, and then a "morning after" brunch for the same number on Sunday. As it was Lachlan's scheduled weekend with Aislynn anyway, he decided to pick up the hint she'd dropped several weeks earlier.

"Planning a romantic weekend, I see," Ethan remarked, looking at the screen of Lachlan's phone over his shoulder when he met him at the campus coffee shop. "Don't you think a trip to Anaheim is a little... Mickey Mouse?"

"Ha-ha. Finley is going to be working all weekend, so I've decided to take Aislynn to Disneyland. I was thinking of splurging on an on-site hotel this time, but this late in the game, all that's available are suites and they're a little on the pricey side."

"A little?" Ethan echoed. "Jesus—is that the price *per night*?"

"No, that's the cost of a two-bedroom suite for Friday and Saturday."

"Still not much better," his friend said.

"You and Steph want to come? You could have the room with the king-size bed, Aislynn could take the one with the two queens, and I could sleep on the pulldown in the living area."

"Unfortunately—or maybe not—my wife and I have adult activities planned this weekend."

"You can spare me the details," Lachlan assured him.

"Not *those* kinds of adult plans," Ethan said. "Though after the wine tour, I'm sure things will move in that direction."

"I didn't think you were a fan of wine."

"I'm not really, but Steph is. And I'm a fan of the fact that wine lessens her inhibitions a little—" he waggled his eyebrows "—if you know what I mean."

"Nope. Don't know and don't want to know."

"Anyway, while you're snacking on churros and slurping Coke, we'll be sampling charcuterie and sipping chardonnay."

Lachlan was still staring at the number on his phone, as if he might will it to change. "I really shouldn't pay that much for a hotel room that we won't spend more than a few hours in, should I?"

"Knowing your daughter, I'd say that Aislynn would be happier with another pair of Minnie Mouse ears to add to her collection. And though it's really not any of my business, I'd also like to say that you shouldn't feel as if you owe her anything more than that just because you've been spending so much time with Finley recently."

"How do you know I'm feeling guilty?"

"Because you're a divorced single dad, and guilt comes with the title. Trust me—I'm Catholic, so I know about guilt.

Divorced Catholic single dads?" Ethan shook his head. "They have no hope of ever getting out from under that burden."

It turned out his friend was right—Aislynn was so excited to hear that they were going to Disneyland, she didn't even care that they were staying at a budget motel offsite.

"We're really going to Disneyland this weekend? Just you and me?"

"Unless you want to invite Harmony to come along?"

She considered for a minute, then shook her head. "I don't think so."

"Kendra?" he suggested as an alternative.

Another head shake. "No."

"I thought you said you wanted to bring a friend."

"I changed my mind," she told him.

"Any particular reason?" he asked.

"I guess I realized that I'm probably going to be going away to school in a couple of years, so we don't have a lot of father-daughter weekends left."

It was a fact of which he'd been painfully aware for some time now. And more specifically, every time she blew him off to hang out with her friends. He didn't ever complain, because he knew it was a reflection of her growing independence—and because he still saw her a couple of times every week. Wednesday nights, of course, but also on random occasions when she decided to stop by.

It was only recently, though, that Aislynn had given any indication that she valued those father-daughter weekends as much as he did. Since he'd started seeing Finley, in fact, and she'd realized that she wasn't always going to have his undivided attention.

Which made him wonder if she saw his new girlfriend as a threat to their father-daughter relationship—or as a threat to her fantasies of a reconciliation between her parents. But that, he decided, was a question for another day.

"Okay," he said now. "It's just going to be you and me. But you remember my rule, don't you?"

"I remember," she assured him. "No more than one ride a day on 'it's a small world.'"

"And you're okay with that?"

"I'm not a kid anymore, Dad. I'd be happy to skip 'it's a small world' altogether for another ride on Space Mountain."

"I don't know about skipping it altogether," he protested. "It is a tradition, after all."

She hugged him, laughing, and he found himself looking forward to the weekend, even if he wasn't going to see Finley at all.

By the time the "morning after" brunch was finally over, late in the afternoon on Sunday, and the last of the guests had departed, Finley's exhaustion went all the way to her bones.

It had been a fabulously successful weekend, and she was proud that Gilmore Galas had pulled off three days of back-to-back events without a hitch—or at least without a hitch that anyone else could see—and she had no doubt that more business would come their way as a result of the Parker-Chesney wedding.

But she would bask in that glory another day, because right now, she was too tired even for basking.

Julia and Rachel were similarly wiped out. And while the rest of their weekend staff had taken off at the earliest opportunity, the three partners decided to have a drink at the bar and do their usual debriefing of the event there rather than in the office the following morning.

Of course, they'd been so busy with the event, none of them had eaten throughout the day, so they ordered food to go with the drinks and ended up hanging around because that required a lot less effort than getting up to go home.

But eventually Rachel's husband came to pick her up and then Julia's fiancé did the same, leaving Finley alone, because her boyfriend (and it still gave her a little bit of a thrill to think of Lachlan as her boyfriend) was in Anaheim—or probably on his way home—with his daughter.

It was just starting to get dark when she finally summoned the energy to slide her feet back into the shoes that she'd kicked off under the table when she sat down and head out to her vehicle, unwilling to jeopardize the sterling reputation of Gilmore Galas by falling asleep in the hotel bar.

She'd just buckled her seatbelt when her phone chimed with a message, and her heart did a foolish little leap inside her chest when she saw Lachlan's name on the screen.

I'm back.

She immediately replied:

Did you have a good time?

It's hard not to have a good time at Disneyland. But I missed you.

I missed you, too.

I thought you might be too busy to miss me.

My days were busy. My nights were lonely.

Are you up for some company tonight? I could be at your place in twenty minutes.

Actually, I'm just leaving the hotel, so I could be at your place in ten.

Then I'll see you in ten.

She pulled out of the parking lot, suddenly not feeling so tired anymore.

R u home?

Harmony immediately responded to her text with a thumbs-up emoji.

Aislynn wanted to follow up by asking if Jarrod was home, but recently Harmony had accused her of only wanting to hang out at her place when her brother was there, and Aislynn suspected that it might be true.

She'd known Jarrod forever—and for most of that time as Harmony's annoying brother. But then, almost overnight, her feelings for him had changed. It was during the summer of her fourteenth birthday, after she returned from her annual camping trip with her dad and immediately raced over to see her BFF. Because she hadn't seen Harmony in a whole week and— thanks to her dad's stupid rules about unplugging to commune with nature—they hadn't even exchanged text messages.

When she arrived, Jarrod and a couple of his friends were in the pool. As she watched, he rose up out of the water, exposing surprisingly wide shoulders, a hard, flat stomach, neon orange swim trunks and muscled legs covered with dark hair. Her mouth went dry and her heart started to pound really fast. Then he gave a toss of his head, to flip his wet hair out of his face, and spotted her standing there.

His lips curved and her knees trembled.

Was it possible that he was feeling the same things she was feeling?

The hope had barely begun to blossom when he crushed it with a casual, "Hey, Squirt."

It was what he'd been calling her since she was eight years old. Not because she was little, even if she was in the eyes of a ten-year-old boy, but because she'd accidentally squeezed a juice pouch while trying to jam the straw in it and squirted fruit punch halfway across the room.

Shoving that embarrassing memory to the back of her mind, she slipped on her shoes and snuck out the back door. She didn't really need to sneak out. It wasn't as if her mom would have refused a request to go visit her friend, but she would have insisted on driving her, because her mom was as paranoid as her dad when it came to Aislynn being out on her own after dark. And anyway, it wasn't completely dark yet. Yeah, it would be, when it was time to go home, but she could call her mom for a ride if she needed one then. Or maybe Jarrod would walk her home.

He'd sometimes given her a ride in his Barracuda, if she'd stayed late to hang out with Harmony. But that wasn't an option now, as his beloved car was in the body shop while the insurance company decided whether or not to pay for the repairs. Jarrod assured Aislynn that he'd fix it himself if they wouldn't, but considering that his arm was still in a sling, she figured he should concentrate on fixing himself first.

"What's up?" Harmony asked, when she opened the door for Aislynn.

"I brought you this." She offered her friend a bag of Main Street popcorn—the Mickey Fruity Mix that she knew was Harmony's favorite.

"Thanks. You wanna come in?"

She nodded.

"How was Disney?"

"The Happiest Place On Earth."

"So why don't you sound happy?"

"Because when I got home, my mom and Philip were talking about their wedding plans."

"I want a destination wedding, so I can get married barefoot in the sand," Harmony told her, obviously having given the matter some thought.

"I'm not thinking about my wedding yet," Aislynn said. "And I don't want to think about my mom's, either." In fact, it hurt her stomach to think about it.

"I know you wanted your mom and dad to get back together," her friend said, not unsympathetically. "But maybe your dad will find someone, too. It certainly didn't take my dad long after he found out about my mom and Fernando."

"Actually... I think maybe my dad has found someone already," Aislynn confided.

"Really? When did that happen?"

"I walked in on them kissing a few weeks ago."

"And you're only telling me *now*?"

"I didn't want to talk about it. I *don't* want to talk about it."

Because while her dad had been great the whole time they were at Disneyland, she knew that when he dropped her off at home with a hug and a kiss and a lightning quick goodbye, he was rushing off to see Finley.

"You wanna play some *Mario Kart*?" Harmony asked, honoring her friend's request.

Aislynn nodded and followed her to the gaming room in the basement.

"Good morning."

Finley had hoped to sleep a little longer—especially as it was a rare opportunity for her—but she decided that waking up to Lachlan's sexy voice whispering in her ear was better than sleeping in any day.

She rolled over to face him. "Good morning."

He dipped his head to kiss her—a lingering kiss that led to leisurely lovemaking.

"I think I love waking up with you in the morning even more than I love falling asleep next to you at night."

"The two events kind of go hand in hand," she pointed out to him.

"They do," he agreed, linking their hands together. "Kind of like you and me."

"Somebody's in a poetic mood this morning."

"I really did miss you when I was away."

"I missed you, too, but even if you'd been here, I wouldn't have been able to see you."

"I know." He held her gaze for several seconds before he spoke again. "I think I was a goner the minute you walked through the doors of the Dusty Boots Motel."

"I'm not sure I believe that's true. You certainly didn't look too impressed that day."

"Because I knew you were there to take the last room."

"And then I shared it with you."

"Not just the room but your bed."

"And now we're in your bed," she noted.

"Which is much bigger than yours."

"More important, last night it was closer than mine."

"That is more important," he agreed.

"This morning, though, my priority is coffee."

"My coffee maker has an automatic timer, so it should be ready in the kitchen."

"You're not coming down?" she asked, surprised.

"I just need a couple minutes to shave first," he told her.

"I hope you're not doing so on my account."

"Only because I don't like putting marks on you," he said. "And you've got beard burn on your throat and probably... other places."

"Yes, I do," she confirmed, a smile tugging at her lips. "But I'm not complaining."

"Go pour the coffee," he urged. "And I'll be down in three minutes to scramble some eggs for you."

"An early orgasm and breakfast?" Finley's smile widened. "This is a very lucky day."

She was still smiling as she made her way down the stairs toward the kitchen, then halted in mid-stride when she spotted a woman standing by the counter, pouring what Finley coveted.

"Good morning." The woman—a stunningly beautiful woman with blond hair in a messy knot on top of her head, wearing spandex leggings and a matching sports bra, the strap of which was visible because her oversized T-shirt was worn off-the-shoulder, *Flashdance* style—greeted her.

"Um… Hello."

"I'm Deirdre—the ex-wife." She offered a smile along with the coffee she'd just poured. "And I'm guessing you're Finley."

Finley nodded as she accepted the mug.

Deirdre reached into the cupboard for another, obviously at home in her ex-husband's house. "You're the party planner, right?"

Finley nodded again.

"You did a wonderful job with the grandparents' anniversary party."

"Thank you."

Because the mug of coffee was in her hand, she lifted it to her lips and sipped, swallowing the question that she really wanted to ask—which was, what was Lachlan's ex-wife doing in his kitchen at seven thirty a.m. on a Monday morning?

Then the man himself was there, stopping short in the doorway, as she had done.

"Deirdre." His gaze jumped from his ex-wife to his current lover and back again. "What are you doing here?"

"I wanted to talk about Aislynn's birthday, as I said in the text I sent to you last night."

"Did I respond to your text message?"

"No," she admitted, handing him the second mug of coffee. "But I know you don't have an early class on Monday, so I figured you'd be home."

"Still, you could have called first," he pointed out.

"Why would I bother to call when I drive right by your house to and from band practice?" Deirdre filled a third mug from the carafe.

"And when you drove past the first time, did you not notice that there was another vehicle in the driveway?" Lachlan asked her.

"Of course, I did—and naturally I was dying to know who it belonged to," she said unapologetically.

"Now you know," Lachlan said. "And now you can go."

"Don't be rude," she chided.

"I don't think I'm the one being rude."

"Drink your coffee, Lach." Deirdre shifted her attention to Finley again. "He's always grumpy before his first cup. Though I'm sure you've figured that out by now."

"I wasn't grumpy until I walked into my kitchen and found my ex-wife here," he retorted.

"Aislynn's birthday is in ten-and-a-half weeks," Deirdre said. "And we need to figure out what we're doing for her party."

"I'll call you later to discuss it," he said.

"But I'm here now."

"And I should probably be going, anyway," Finley said, suddenly regaining her voice.

"You're not the one I want to leave," Lachlan told her.

"But I'm the one on a schedule," she reminded him. "And I need to stop at home before heading into the office."

"But you haven't had breakfast," he protested.

"I'll grab something on my way."

Lachlan followed her out to her car. "I'm sorry about Deirdre," he said. "I honestly had no idea she was planning to stop by this morning."

Finley turned to him then, and he could see that she was troubled. "How often does she do that—drop in unannounced and uninvited?"

"I don't know." He shrugged. "Once or twice a week."

"You see your ex-wife once or twice a week?"

"I realize it probably seems like a lot, but we've worked hard to maintain a cordial relationship for Aislynn."

"There's cordial and then there's codependent," Finley said.

He was taken aback by her blunt response. "What's that supposed to mean?"

"Just that it seems easier for you to apologize for your ex-wife's lack of boundaries than to actually set any boundaries."

"I've told her countless times to call before stopping by," he said.

"Have you tried taking away her key?" she asked him.

"I can't do that," he protested.

"Why not?"

"Because this is Aislynn's home, too."

"I'm not suggesting that you take away your daughter's key."

"You don't understand."

"You're right," she said. "How could I possibly understand when I don't have an ex-spouse with whom I share a child?"

Which was kind of his point, but something in Finley's tone warned Lachlan that what she was saying wasn't actually what she meant.

"Can we talk about this later?" he asked cautiously.

"I'd rather there wasn't anything to talk about, but sure," she agreed.

"Please don't go away mad."

"I'm not mad." Then she sighed. "I'm really not. I just didn't realize this relationship would be quite so...complicated."

"I know I've got baggage, but I've also got all the ingredients for my legendary enchiladas," he said, hoping to make her smile.

She gave him half of one. "Are you offering to cook for me tonight?"

"Well, you're running off without the breakfast I promised you, so it seems the least I can do."

"Enchiladas sound good to me," she agreed. "But we're sleeping at my place tonight."

He'd figured that was a given and kissed her gently before opening the door of her SUV for her.

He watched her drive away, then headed back into the house.

"You can't just use your key to barge in here whenever you want," he told Deirdre, who was sitting at the island now, drinking her coffee and thumbing through a Merivale College course calendar.

She closed the book to give him her full attention. "It's never bothered you before."

"You've never done it when I had company before."

"Maybe because you've never had overnight company before."

"I have so."

"Very rarely. And not in a long time."

He couldn't deny that was true.

"You really like her, don't you?"

"I'm not discussing my relationship with Finley with you," he told her.

"That's okay," she said. "You don't have to say anything. I can tell by the way you look at her—because it's the same way you used to look at me."

He sighed. "Dee—"

"No." She held up a hand. "It's okay. I know that was a lifetime ago. Aislynn's lifetime, to be precise. And, as I already mentioned, her birthday is the reason I stopped by."

"I don't know why you think we need to talk about her party, because you're going to do what you want to do, anyway."

"Because shared custody requires talking about the important decisions that affect our child."

"I'm not sure a birthday party falls into the 'important' category, but okay," he relented.

"The first thing we need to decide on is the venue. Kendra's sweet sixteen was at August Hall."

Lachlan was familiar with the Victorian Playhouse in Union Square. It was designed by celebrated architect August Headman and renowned for hosting the premier of Alfred Hitchcock's *Vertigo* in 1958, when it was known as the Stage Door Theater. He also knew that the hall came with a hefty price tag.

"No."

"I'm not suggesting August Hall," Deirdre assured him. "Having Aislynn's party at the same venue would be as tacky as suggesting she wear the same Bottega Veneta dress that Kendra wore."

"What are you suggesting?" Lachlan asked.

"Perhaps The Cliff House or Presidio Golf Club or—going in a completely different direction—a City Cruise."

"Let me further narrow down the options for you," he suggested. "Your backyard or mine."

Deirdre frowned. "It's her sweet sixteen."

"And I know everyone in her social group was talking about Kendra's party for weeks after the fact, but our daughter needs to understand that Silicon Valley executives are in a whole different tax bracket than college professors."

"Why does everything always have to be about the money?" Deirdre demanded.

"Because it doesn't grow on trees."

"I don't mind paying for the party."

Of course, she didn't. Because she came from family money, and even indulging her penchant for upgrading her vehicle every year, redecorating her house to follow the trends and filling her closet with exclusive designer labels, she didn't need to worry about burning through the trust fund set up by her grandfather.

"Just because you can afford to give her an elaborate party doesn't mean you should," Lachlan argued. "Or that I shouldn't be contributing. I'm her father, Dee."

She pouted. "She's only going to turn sixteen once."

"The same argument could be made for eighteen and twenty-one and—"

"And she's our only child."

"Who will hopefully be going off to college in a few years," Lachlan reminded her. "If you want to throw some of your money away, throw it into her college fund."

"This party is a big deal to her."

"Keeping up with Kendra Thornton is a big deal to her," he noted dryly. "And she needs to understand it's just not realistic."

"Okay. We can have the party at my place," Deirdre decided. "But I don't even know where to begin with the planning after that. Maybe Finley—"

"No," he said firmly.

She frowned. "You can't know what I was going to say."

"I can guess," he told her.

And Finley was right—their relationship was already complicated enough without letting her get tangled up in any birthday party drama with his ex-wife and his daughter.

Chapter Sixteen

Finley understood and accepted that Wednesday nights belonged to Lachlan and his daughter, and she never imposed on that precious time. The same was true of his weekends with Aislynn. Of course, she was usually busy with other things, but even when she had a free night or an early evening, she didn't intrude.

She didn't expect Lachlan to reserve the rest of his nights for her, but she would have appreciated Aislynn showing at least some consideration for the fact that her dad was involved in a relationship. Instead, it seemed to Finley that the opposite was true, because every time she was at Lachlan's house, his daughter just happened to find an excuse to drop by.

Tonight Aislynn had arrived as they were tidying up the kitchen after dinner. She claimed that she needed something for a school project and brushed right past them to head up the stairs to her bedroom.

She hadn't reappeared by the time dishes were put away, and Lachlan excused himself to participate in an online chat with the students in one of his summer classes.

Since he'd mentioned that there was ice cream for dessert, Finley opened the freezer to survey the options. She decided to go for the black cherry and began scooping it into a bowl.

She was nearly finished when Aislynn returned to the kitchen.

"Do you want some of this?" she asked, ready to give the girl her bowl and prepare another for herself.

Aislynn's only response was a scowl.

"I'll take that as a *no*," Finley said, putting the lid back on the container.

"I can get my own ice cream," the teenager said, removing a container of chocolate peanut butter cup from the freezer as Finley reached past her to replace the black cherry. "Where'd my dad go?"

"His office. He had an online chat scheduled with a group of students."

"A group of students? Or Zoe?"

Finley lifted a spoonful of ice cream to her mouth. "He said a group."

Aislynn dipped the scoop into the container of chocolate peanut butter cup. "Have you met Zoe?"

"I haven't met any of your dad's students." Though she'd been tempted to ask if she could hang out in his office during the chat—because she really liked how he looked in the glasses he only seemed to wear when he was reading or on the computer.

"Zoe's one of his grad students," Aislynn told Finley. "She's taken almost every course he teaches."

"I'd say that's a testament to his skill as a teacher."

"Or the fact that she's got a huge crush on him."

"Another possibility," Finley acknowledged.

"It doesn't bother you that another woman might be after my dad?"

"No. Because if your dad was interested in Zoe, he wouldn't be dating me."

"He might just be waiting for her to finish school," Aislynn said, adding another scoop of ice cream to her bowl. "So he can date her without getting fired."

"Would that make you happy?" Finley asked. "If he was dating Zoe instead of me?"

"As if you care what makes me happy."

"I don't want to be the cause of your unhappiness."

"Don't worry about it," Aislynn said. "You're not that important to me. Or my dad. You're just someone he's dating at this moment in time."

Finley dipped her spoon into her ice cream again. "Do they still teach Shakespeare in high school?"

"Yeah." Aislynn's gaze narrowed suspiciously. "Why?"

"I wondered if you might be familiar with the phrase, 'the lady doth protest too much.'"

The teen considered for a minute before responding, "That's from *Hamlet*, isn't it?"

Finley nodded.

Aislynn dropped the scoop in the sink and returned the container of ice cream to the freezer. "But what does that have to do with the price of Lego in Denmark?"

Finley appreciated the cleverness of her idiom. Lachlan's daughter was obviously smart—which made her a potentially dangerous rival. Finley had hoped they could be friends instead, but she wasn't going to keep setting herself up to be knocked down.

"It seems to me that if your dad had really had so many girlfriends, you wouldn't be so bothered by me being here."

"You don't know anything about my life or what bothers me."

"You're right," she agreed. "I just remember how I felt after my parents divorced, when my mom introduced us to her boyfriend. And how much I hated seeing her with anyone who wasn't my dad."

That revelation finally seemed to snag Aislynn's attention. "How old were you when your parents split?"

"Nine."

"I was three." She pulled a spoon out of the drawer and stuck it in her ice cream.

"Which might be even harder, because you likely can't even remember a time when they were together."

Aislynn lifted her chin. "They're always together. Every holiday and birthday and family event, they're together."

"Then you're lucky, because your mom and dad obviously put your needs first. Not all parents do."

Something else the girl obviously hadn't considered before now.

"Just some food for thought," Finley said, as Aislynn flounced out of the kitchen with her ice cream in hand.

"This is a nice surprise," Finley said, when she opened the door Tuesday night and found her stepmom standing there.

"You know you can send me away if it's a bad time."

"If that's a bottle of wine in your hand, it's definitely not a bad time."

Colleen chuckled as she stepped over the threshold. "Your dad's working late tonight, and I didn't see Lachlan's vehicle in your driveway, so I thought I'd take a chance that you were free."

While her mom uncorked the bottle, Finley set out some cheese and crackers and fruit to nibble on along with their wine.

They settled on the sofa in the living area and chatted casually for a few minutes, about some of Finley's recent events and her mom's volunteer work at the children's hospital.

"Something's on your mind," Colleen realized, when Finley had been silent for several minutes.

She shifted to face her stepmom. "I was just wondering if Haylee or me or Logan gave you a hard time when you were dating Dad?"

"Not at all," Colleen said. "And I'd braced myself for it—to be shunned and hated as a potential evil stepmom."

"That is how we depict second wives in fairy tales, isn't it?" Finley mused.

"Now, I'm not saying that Haylee and you and Logan didn't hate me behind my back, but you certainly never gave me any indication that I was unwelcome."

"I'm glad," Finley said sincerely. "Because you were the best thing that ever happened to Dad. And to us."

Colleen's eyes grew misty. "I feel exactly the same way about all of you. And I have no doubt that Lachlan's daughter will someday realize the same thing about you."

Finley sighed. "I wish I shared your confidence."

"She's giving you a hard time?" Colleen guessed.

"I can't blame her," Finley said. "She wants her mom and dad back together and sees me as an obstacle to that happening. I'd argue that the two-carat diamond on her mother's left hand is a bigger obstacle, but teenagers don't always think about things logically."

"And if she's always been daddy's little girl, then of course she sees you as a threat—especially if he hasn't dated much, and her mom is now remarrying."

"I don't know how much he dated, but I know he didn't usually introduce the women he dated to Aislynn."

"Which says something about the depth of his feelings for you."

She smiled and tipped her head back against Colleen's shoulder. "You really are the best mom."

"It's easy to be the best mom when you've got the best kids," Colleen replied.

Finley topped off their wine. "Can I ask you a personal question?"

"Of course."

"Did you and Dad ever consider having a baby of your own?"

Colleen nibbled on a grape. "As a matter of fact, we did."

"So why didn't it happen?"

"You mean, other than the fact that our hands were pretty full with the three kids we already had?"

It wasn't really an answer, and the way she didn't meet Finley's gaze told her that there was more to the story.

"Other than that," Finley said, pressing for more details.

Colleen tipped her head down to rest it on top of her daughter's. "The truth is, we did try. When Logan started school full-time, we decided it was the right time to add to our family. I got pregnant pretty quickly, and your dad and I were overjoyed.

"And then, at about seven weeks, I had severe pain in my abdomen. The doctor ordered an ultrasound and discovered it was an ectopic pregnancy.

"It wasn't a good time for me," Colleen admitted. "They managed to remove the fertilized egg and save my fallopian tube and promised I could try again. But I…struggled…afterward. So much so that, for several months, I couldn't care for the kids that I had. And when I finally got myself together, it seemed like too much of a risk to try again."

"I'm so sorry," Finley said sincerely.

"I was, too. But when my body healed… I realized your dad and you and your sister and brother were more of a family than I ever expected to have, and I know that I'm truly blessed."

"This seems to be the week for surprises," Finley noted, when Lachlan poked his head around the door of her office Wednesday afternoon.

"Taylor said it was okay to come back."

"To Taylor you will always be the sender of the cheesecake we gorged on, and she warned me that she'd snap you up in a second if she wasn't in a committed relationship."

"And if you hadn't snapped me up already," he said.

"I did do that, didn't I?"

"Yes, you did," he agreed, drawing her into his arms for a kiss.

"So what brings you out this way today?" she asked.

"I just wanted to see you. And to…" His words trailed off as he spotted the mail on her desk. "You got a postcard from Barcelona."

"Yeah." She glanced at the glossy image of the stunning La Sagrada Familia sitting on top of a pile of envelopes on the corner of her desk. "A lot of our clients send us postcards from their honeymoons or anniversary trips."

"Apparently they don't understand the purpose of a honeymoon," he noted dryly.

She rolled her eyes. "It only takes a few minutes to write a couple lines on the back of a postcard."

"But then you have to find a post office to buy a stamp and mail the card."

"Some people enjoy sharing information about their travels with friends and family back home."

"You mean some people like to show off that they're on vacation to those who aren't."

"And most people love getting postcards," she said, choosing to ignore his scathing remark.

"My grandparents were going to Spain as part of their European tour."

"I know," she said. "The postcard's from them."

"They sent *you* a postcard? They didn't send *me* a postcard."

"Probably because they figured you'd just toss it in a drawer."

"And you're planning to do something different with it?" he asked skeptically.

"We have a bulletin board in the conference room where we tack up all the cards our clients send to us. It's a tangible reminder to all of us at Gilmore Galas that what we do matters—maybe not to the world, but to the people who let us celebrate the important events in theirs."

"Speaking of events—I was wondering if you were free for dinner tonight."

"I'm not sure dinner qualifies as an event," she chided.

"It wasn't a good segue," he acknowledged. "But it is the reason I stopped by."

"To ask me if I was free for dinner tonight?"

He nodded. "I know it's short notice."

"It's also Wednesday," she pointed out.

"All day," he confirmed.

"You have dinner with Aislynn on Wednesdays."

"Also true."

"Did she bail on you for tonight?"

"No. In fact, it was her idea to invite you."

"And that wasn't a red flag for you?" she asked, her tone skeptical.

"Why would it be?"

"Because she doesn't like me."

"She doesn't *not* like you—she just doesn't know you. But if you have dinner with us tonight, it will give her a chance to get to know you. And for you to know her. Assuming you don't already have other plans, of course."

He was giving her an out.

If she didn't want to hang out with Lachlan and his daughter, she could simply say that she had a consult or an appointment or an event. And she was tempted to do so, because she was a little intimidated by Aislynn—embarrassing to admit but true nevertheless.

She was usually good with kids. She loved them and they loved her. The problem was, Aislynn wasn't a kid. She was a teenager, filled with angst and attitude like any other teenager, with an extra dose of attitude thrown in because she was the daughter of a single dad and understandably protective of that relationship.

But if Finley harbored any hopes of a potential future with

Lachlan—and she did—then she needed to not only get to know but get along with his daughter.

"What's on the menu?"

"Does it matter?"

"Not really," she decided. "But it might influence what I bring for dessert."

He grinned. "Aislynn is partial to cupcakes."

"Cupcakes it is."

Lachlan didn't blame Finley for being skeptical of his daughter's motives. He'd been a little taken aback himself when Aislynn suggested extending an invitation for her to have dinner with them. Prior to that she'd been…less than welcoming to the new woman in her father's life. Sometimes her attitude had been cool; other times it had bordered on hostile.

"Nobody likes change," Ethan had pointed out, when Lachlan expressed concern about his daughter's attitude toward Finley. "Add to that the fact that Aislynn's a teenager, with raging hormones and divorced parents, and it's understandable that she'd be resistant to welcoming someone new into your life."

But dinner had gone well. They'd had burgers and potato salad and then the cupcakes for dessert.

"Oh. My. God." Aislynn took another bite of the Black Forest cupcake she'd chosen from the assortment Finley offered. "I don't think I've ever tasted anything so good. Except maybe the cake at Great-Grandma and Great-Grandpa's anniversary party."

Finley smiled. "The cupcakes are from the same bakery."

"I'd love to get the cake for my birthday party from there," Aislynn said.

"That might not be in the budget," Lachlan warned.

Not wanting to get into the middle of a personal discussion, Finley got up to clear the table. Aislynn immediately jumped up to help her, but Lachlan insisted that he would take care of the cleanup so they could hang out and chat.

"I appreciate you letting me come for dinner tonight," Finley said, when Lachlan had disappeared into the kitchen. "I know your time with your dad is precious."

"It is," Aislynn agreed. "But I realized it's selfish of me to want to keep him all to myself when I'm going to be going away to college in a couple of years and he'll be on his own."

"That's very magnanimous of you," Finley said, not entirely sure she believed the girl's explanation but willing to give her the benefit of the doubt.

"Can I ask your opinion on something?" Aislynn asked, reaching into the bakery box for another cupcake.

"Of course," she immediately agreed, eager to grasp whatever olive branch Lachlan's daughter might be offering.

"I have to decide what kind of cake I want for my birthday, and I keep going back and forth between vanilla cake with raspberry mousse and chocolate cake with chocolate ganache."

"If you went with two tiers, you could have both," Finley said.

"I'd love that," Aislynn said. "But as you might have guessed from his earlier comment, Dad set a strict budget for the party and, based on prices I've seen posted on various websites, it's unlikely I can afford more than one tier."

"Cupcakes are always another option," Finley noted. "They're typically less costly, easier to serve, and they can be displayed to look like a cake."

Aislynn seemed to consider this. "These cupcakes are amazing, but cupcakes seem more middle school than high school."

"If you wouldn't think I was overstepping… I have some contacts through Gilmore Galas. I could maybe make some calls to inquire about a possible discount on your cake."

Blue eyes so much like Lachlan's went wide. "Really? You'd do that for me?"

"I'm not making any promises," Finley cautioned. "But I'm happy to see what I can do."

"That would be great. Thank you."

"Do you know how many guests you're going to have?"

They spent another hour discussing color schemes, decorations, flowers and food, after which Aislynn excused herself to finish her homework.

"What did you and Aislynn have your heads together about for so long?" Lachlan asked.

"She asked for some advice regarding her birthday party."

"She's not happy that I set a limit on the guest list—and the budget," he admitted.

"It's hard at that age," Finley noted. "Knowing her friends are going to be making comparisons and feeling as if there's no way her party is going to be as awesome as Kendra Thornton's."

"It's certainly not going to be as splashy," he agreed. "Her parents rented August Hall."

"There's one of those in every group," Finley noted.

"Did you have a friend like Kendra when you were a kid?"

"I knew girls like her," she confirmed. "But I was fortunate that my best friend was my sister."

"You hung out together at school?" he asked, surprised.

"It would have been strange if we didn't, considering we were in the same class."

"I thought she was older than you."

Finley nodded. "But only by eleven months. Her birthday is in January, mine is in December."

"December what?"

"Third," she said. "When's your birthday?"

"June fifteenth."

"That's in a couple of weeks," she noted.

"Yeah."

"Why didn't you tell me?"

"I just did," he pointed out.

"I meant, why didn't you tell me before now?" she clarified.

"Because I didn't want you to feel as if you had to make yourself available to celebrate with me."

"Maybe I want to celebrate with you."

"That's really not necessary," he told her.

"You already have plans," she realized.

"Not renting August Hall kind of plans," he said lightly. "Just the usual, low-key, family kind of plans."

"And you don't want me there."

"It's a Saturday. In June."

"I could make arrangements," she said, albeit not very convincingly.

"Which would only create more stress for you, and that's the last thing I want to do."

"Will you come over later that night—after your family celebration?" she asked hopefully.

"How many events do you have that day?"

"Just the Bracken-Ross wedding."

"That's your biggest one this summer, isn't it? With more than three hundred guests?"

"Close to four hundred," she admitted.

"You'll be exhausted."

"But I can sleep in on Sunday," she said. "It's one of those very rare summer Sundays when Gilmore Galas has nothing on the books."

"Then let's plan to do something Sunday," he suggested.

Lachlan was right. June fifteenth was a busy day. Still, Finley found herself occasionally peeking at her phone, because she was certain Aislynn would post photos on her Instagram account. And she was right.

When Lachlan said it was to be a family celebration, she'd

assumed that meant his daughter and maybe his parents. Possibly even his sisters and their families. And maybe they were there to celebrate with him, but in the dozen photos that Aislynn posted (#celebrating #bestdadintheworld #birthday #family), the only people she saw were Lachlan, his daughter and his ex-wife.

She was too busy to dwell on the pictures and speculate, but she couldn't seem to block the echo of Aislynn's words from the back of her mind.

They're always together. Every holiday and birthday and family event, they're together.

She texted Lachlan when she got home that night, to let him know it was okay if he wanted to come over. He didn't respond, which wasn't really a surprise considering that it was after midnight, but she was still disappointed.

So she got ready for bed, and she almost managed to convince herself that she didn't mind that he'd rather spend his birthday with his ex-wife than with her. Because she understood that Deirdre wasn't only Lachlan's ex-wife, she was the mother of his child. But when the knock sounded on the door, she knew it was a lie.

She wanted him to want to be with her. And she was so glad that he was here—because it meant that he'd chosen her.

She went to the door with a ready smile on her face.

Except it wasn't Lachlan she found at the threshold.

It was Mark.

Chapter Seventeen

"**I** like that kind of *hello*," Finley said against his lips, when Lachlan greeted her with a kiss the following morning.

"In that case, *hello* again," he said, and captured her mouth again.

He wrapped his arms around her and pulled her close, deepening the kiss. Her tongue danced and dallied with his as her scent, something fresh and distinctly Finley, stirred his blood and clouded his mind.

"You're out of bodywash, Fin."

The deep, undeniably masculine voice came from the hall, and Finley winced before she stepped out of Lachlan's arms—just as a towel-clad figure stepped into view.

"There's more in the cupboard under the sink," she responded to her apparent houseguest.

"I looked but couldn't find any."

"Then I guess I'll have to add it to my shopping list."

The mostly naked man deigned a glance in Lachlan's direction before commenting to Finley, "When I said I was up for a threesome, I was hoping you'd invite a girlfriend to come over."

"Don't be a dick, Mark," she admonished.

"Ah, the infamous Mark Nickel," Lachlan realized.

"Infamous?" Finley's ex echoed.

"Mark showed up here late last night and more than half-drunk, so I let him crash on the sofa," Finley explained.

"That's the story you're going with?" Mark said dubiously.

"It's the truth," she said, her gaze on Lachlan. "As you can see by the blanket and pillow on the sofa."

A neatly folded blanket and pillow, he noted. On top of which the cat was curled up, snoozing contentedly.

"It really doesn't look like anyone slept there," Mark remarked casually.

Finley glared at him. "I should never have opened the door when you showed up here last night."

Lachlan wanted to ask why she did, but he wasn't going to give her ex the satisfaction of questioning her in his presence.

She answered the unspoken question, anyway. "I only did because, when I heard the knock on the door, I thought—hoped—it might be you."

"You snooze, you lose, buddy." Mark's tone was smug.

Finley whirled to face him. "I will boot you out right now, wearing nothing but that towel, and call the *East Bay Times*."

He held up his hands in surrender. "I'm going to get dressed," he decided. "I have to head back to Los Angeles soon anyway."

"Good idea," Finley agreed.

"Would you really kick him out without letting him enjoy the breakfast you made for him?" Lachlan asked.

"I made breakfast for *you*," she said. "Pancakes."

He couldn't help but smile. "I have very fond memories of your…pancakes."

A faint flush colored her cheeks. "Why don't you help yourself to coffee while I get you a plate?"

He found a mug and filled it from the carafe on the warmer.

"Are those sprinkles in the pancakes?"

"Of course," she said. "That's how you know they're birthday pancakes and not just everyday pancakes."

"Do I get whipped cream, too?"

She lifted a brow. "For your pancakes?"

"Sure." He wrapped an arm around her waist and drew her close. "I could use it on the pancakes, too."

"Oh, honey, you didn't have to go to so much trouble," Mark said, striding back into the kitchen.

She smacked his hand when he reached for the pancake on top of the stack. "Those aren't for you, and you know it."

"I do prefer to avoid heavy carbs on game days," Mark confirmed, stealing a strip of crisp bacon from the tray on the table instead.

"That's not for you, either," she admonished.

"So how long have you two been together?" Mark directed the question to Lachlan.

"I don't see how that's any of your business," he replied evenly.

"Not long, I'm guessing," the other man continued. "Because you left her to sleep alone on a Saturday night, which suggests that you're not yet at the stage of regular weekend sleepovers."

"Ignore him," Finley said.

A honk sounded from the driveway.

"That's your Uber," she told Mark.

"I didn't order an Uber."

"That's why I did it for you."

"Okay, I can take a hint," he said, stealing another slice of bacon before heading to the door.

"I'm not so sure," she said.

But she walked him to the door and hugged him goodbye.

"So that's your ex," Lachlan mused when the man had finally gone and Finley returned to the kitchen.

She eyed him warily. "Not the only—or even the most recent—but probably the most recognizable one."

"Did you know he was in town?"

"He wasn't supposed to be in town. The Orioles are in Los

Angeles this weekend, but he hopped on a plane following their afternoon game yesterday."

"He just hopped on a plane and showed up at your door—confident that you'd let him in?"

"He's used to getting what he wants."

"And apparently that includes you."

"No." Finley shook her head. "It doesn't."

"Then why was he here?"

"I'd guess because he's been in a bit of a batting slump and trade rumors are swirling and he wanted his ego stroked."

"I don't think it's his ego he wanted stroked," Lachlan said dryly.

"He might be spoiled and self-absorbed, but I don't believe for a minute that he'd cheat on his wife."

"And yet he showed up here in the middle of the night."

"Because he knew that I'd deflect any passes he made."

Which seemed to confirm that the man had made passes.

Lachlan clenched his teeth.

"If he'd really wanted to step out on his wife, he would have stayed in LA and crooked a finger at a ball bunny or walked into a downtown sports bar."

"Do you really think it would be that easy?" he asked dubiously.

"I know it would," Finley assured him. "Because I saw the way women threw themselves at him when we were dating—even when I was right there."

"That must have sucked."

She shrugged it off.

He should have taken that as a hint to change the subject, but there was one more question that he needed to ask.

"Were you in love with him?"

She sighed. "You're not going to let this go, are you?"

"I'm only asking because I care about you and it occurred to me that I really don't know much about your past."

"Because it's not relevant to our present," she told him.

"Or maybe it is," he countered.

"Okay, if you really want to know—we were talking about a future together, and we wouldn't have been having that conversation if I hadn't believed I was in love with him."

"Then he got traded," Lachlan guessed.

"Then he *asked* to be traded," she clarified.

"And you didn't want to go to New York with him?"

"I wasn't invited."

He frowned at that. "But if you were talking about a future together—"

"He asked for the trade because he realized he was still in love with his ex-girlfriend—now his wife—who'd moved to Baltimore for a job."

"Oh."

"Yeah."

"I'm sorry."

She shrugged again. "Anyway, thank you for not fighting with me in front of Mark."

"Are we supposed to be fighting?" he asked curiously.

"I don't think it's necessary, but I thought it might be inevitable."

"I can't say I was happy to find him here, but you've never given me any reason not to trust you," he pointed out. "Besides, if you'd really tangled the sheets with him, I doubt very much you would have opened the door for me while he was in the shower."

"A very reasonable analysis of the situation."

"Don't get me wrong, when I saw him strutting around in that towel, I had some very unreasonable thoughts that might have involved my fist and his face."

That revelation seemed to surprise her. "You would have fought for me?"

"Absolutely," he said. "I mean, he's a professional athlete

and I'm a college professor, so I probably would have lost. Badly. But I'd have given it my best effort."

She kissed him lightly. "Thank you for that."

"Can I have my pancakes now?"

"I have a better idea," she said, picking up his plate. "What do you say to breakfast in bed?"

He grinned. "I say, don't forget the whipped cream."

Over the next few weeks, Lachlan spent more nights in Finley's bed than his own. In fact, he was at her place so much that he'd half-jokingly suggested moving his bed, so that they'd have more room for their nocturnal activities. Unfortunately, Finley nixed that idea, pointing out that a king-size bed wouldn't leave room in her room for anything else.

He didn't really mind her bed—and it certainly wasn't a hardship to snuggle up with her—he just wished she wasn't so opposed to sleeping at his place. He understood that she had concerns about Aislynn seeing her vehicle parked in his driveway overnight, but he suspected that she was even more uncomfortable with the possibility of facing his ex-wife over coffee again in the morning—despite his assurances that Deirdre hadn't used her key since the incredibly awkward morning after the first night Finley had stayed at his place.

So he was fast asleep in Finley's bed when his phone vibrated against the nightstand, jolting him awake. (He never activated "do not disturb" mode because he wanted to be sure that Aislynn could always reach him—anytime day or night.)

Beside him, Finley remained thankfully undisturbed.

And naked.

He loved that she slept in the nude, because he loved sleeping with her bare skin against his—and not because they were sharing body heat.

But he pushed those thoughts aside now, because middle-of-the-night text messages were rarely a good thing, and a chill of trepidation snaked down his spine as he reached for his phone.

Are you there?

Those three words identified the sender of the text even before he saw Deirdre's name above the message. His daughter never spelled out a word when a single letter would do.

But, of course, there was only one reason he could think of for his ex-wife to be reaching out in the early hours of the morning.

Aislynn?

She's fine. Sleeping.

His heart rate slowed to something approximating a normal rhythm.

What's up?

The three dots hovered on his screen, as if she was typing a really long reply. Then they disappeared, suggesting that she'd deleted her message. Finally she responded:

I just really need a friend right now.

He wanted to ask where Philip was.

Shouldn't her fiancé be the man that she turned to when something was bothering her in the middle of the night?

But he and Deirdre had been there for each other through all the highs and lows and milestone events over the past eighteen years, and he couldn't turn his back on her now.

On my way.

Of course, he had to find his clothes before he could dress—not an easy task in the dark when they were scattered all over the floor, a testament to the haste with which he'd shed them in his eagerness to get into bed with Finley.

He heard her shift now, and the sound of her hand sliding over the sheet as she reached for him.

"Lachlan?" she murmured sleepily.

"Sorry. I didn't mean to wake you."

Finley lifted herself on an elbow to peer at the glowing numbers on the clock on her bedside table.

2:18.

"What are you doing?"

"Looking for my sock."

"Why?"

"Because I have to go." He stood up to fasten his jeans.

"If you were the type to skip out in the middle of the night, I would have expected it to happen the first time we slept together, not three months later."

"I'm not skipping out," he denied. "I got a text message from Deirdre—"

She was immediately wide awake. "Is Aislynn okay?"

"She's fine," he said.

Finley exhaled a sigh of relief. Though she and Aislynn had gotten off to a rocky start, she thought they'd made progress in recent weeks and even bonded—kind of—during their extended discussions about her birthday party.

"So what's the problem?" she asked now.

"Can we talk about this in the morning? I mean, later in the morning—when I have the answers to your questions?"

"Let me get this straight…you have to go because your ex-wife sent you a text message and you're not even sure what the supposed crisis is?"

"I know she needs a friend," he said.

"You're serious," she realized.

He'd apparently located the errant sock, because he sat on the edge of the mattress to tug it on. "Why are you upset?"

"Are you honestly asking me why I'm upset that the man I'm sleeping with is running off, in the middle of the night, to be with another woman? And not just any woman, but his ex-wife with whom he clearly has a dysfunctional codependent relationship."

"You know it's not like that," he chided. "Dee and I have a history."

"As if I could forget."

He scooped his keys off the dresser, then hesitated. "If you really don't want me to go…"

She waved a hand. "Go. Be your ex-wife's knight in shining armor—you're good at that."

He leaned down to brush a quick kiss over her lips. "I'll call you later."

She wished she could tell him not to bother, but there was no point in fighting with him at two o'clock in the morning. She didn't want to fight with him at all, but she didn't know that she could tolerate always coming in second place to the ex-wife of the man she loved.

Because she could no longer deny that she'd fallen in love with Lachlan.

And even if she hadn't said the words to him, she couldn't ignore the yearning in her heart.

A yearning for more.

For a commitment. A future. A family.

Her desire for those things wasn't new—she'd wanted them for a long time. But now she wanted them *with Lachlan*.

But she was afraid to tell him. Afraid that he might not want the same things. Or maybe not with her.

Mark had told her he loved her, but he'd loved his ex-girlfriend more.

Lachlan hadn't made any declarations, and he still ran to Deirdre when she called.

Once again, Finley was in second place.

She honestly didn't mind taking a backseat to his daughter. In fact, his commitment to his relationship with Aislynn was one of the things she loved about him.

But she resented playing second fiddle to his former spouse.

For just once in her life, she wanted to be with someone who put her first.

Deirdre met Lachlan at the door, her face streaked with mascara and tears.

"What happened?" he asked, automatically enfolding her in his embrace.

She sobbed against this chest. "Philip and I...we had a big fight."

He'd never seen her so distraught and felt a surge of protectiveness rise up inside him. "What do you mean by a big fight? Tell me what happened."

Deirdre drew in a shuddery breath. "Ever since we got engaged, he's been pressuring me to set a wedding date and... I'm just not ready. So tonight I finally told him that, and he said that if I didn't actually want to marry him, why did I accept his proposal?

"I said maybe I shouldn't have and I gave him back his ring and...and he left." Her voice broke and she buried her face against his chest again. "He just tucked it into his pocket and walked out...without so much as a backward glance."

Lachlan drew back to look at her. "Are you telling me that you texted me—*in the middle of the night*—because you had a tiff with your fiancé?"

"Didn't you hear what I said? It was more than a tiff. I gave him back the ring. He left."

"Jesus, Dee. I thought something really bad had happened."

"He. Left," she said again.

"And he'll come back."

"How do you know?"

"Because he loves you."

Her eyes filled with fresh tears.

"Tell me," he said to her now. "Why did you accept Philip's proposal?"

She sniffled. "Because I love him."

"So maybe that's what you should have told him when he asked the question?" Lachlan suggested.

"Maybe." She rubbed the wet streaks on her cheeks with the heels of her hands and let out a long sigh. "He accused me of still being in love with you."

"And to prove him wrong, the first thing you did when he walked out was...call me?"

"Nobody else knows me the way you do."

"Probably because you don't overshare with anyone else the way you do with me."

"I don't overshare."

"Yeah, you do. But that's not the point. The point is that you've been with Philip for more than three years, and it's past time you opened up and let him know what you're afraid of."

"Who said I'm afraid?"

"I did. And I know that you are because I know you."

"Maybe Philip's right. Maybe I'm still clinging to hope that you and I might get back together."

"You're not," he told her.

"I loved you once," Deirdre said.

"I'm not sure you ever really did."

"I married you, didn't I?"

"We got married because we thought it was the right thing to do. But it wasn't. Not for you, not for me, and not for Aislynn. We made each other miserable."

She sighed again. "We did, didn't we?"

"The best thing we ever did—after having Aislynn—was get divorced."

"So why am I so reluctant to marry a man that I really do love?"

"Because you're afraid that you might get it wrong again. Because being with someone without that formal commitment—even being engaged and living together—isn't quite the same. It doesn't carry the same weight of expectation or the same risk of failure.

"And I suspect that's why he wants to marry you," Lachlan continued. "Because marriage is more. Making promises in front of your family and friends makes it more. It makes it real."

"Are you afraid, too?" she asked him.

"We're not talking about me," he said.

"Maybe we should."

"You were the one who called me in the midst of a crisis," he reminded her.

"And you're the one who came running," she countered.

"Because you said you needed me."

"I did say that. Because whenever I've encountered an obstacle in my life, I've turned to you. And for eighteen years, you've let me.

"And it has to stop," she decided, sounding uncharacteristically determined. "We've been in a codependent relationship for too long."

"That's eerily similar to what Finley said," he admitted. "Though she added the word dysfunctional."

"Well, she's right. And you're lucky to have her in your life."

"Yes, I am. Though she wasn't too happy when I told her I was coming over here tonight."

Deirdre's brows lifted. "You were with Finley when I texted?"

"Yeah."

She shook her head. "For a smart man, you really are an idiot sometimes."

"Are you saying that I should have ignored your message?"

"Yes." She sighed. "But also that I shouldn't have sent the message."

She picked up her phone.

"Who are you texting now?"

"Philip."

"It's after three o'clock in the morning," he felt compelled to point out to her.

"I need him to know that I want my ring back. And that I want to get married before the end of the year."

Only seconds after sending her message, she got a reply.

She smiled. "He's on his way."

"Then I should be on mine," he said. "I don't think your fiancé would be too happy to find me here when he gets back."

"Probably not," she agreed. "But I'm going to tell him that we talked. I don't want any secrets between us."

He kissed her forehead. "Congratulations on your upcoming nuptials."

"I'll make sure you get an invitation. Hey, do you think—"

"No," he told her.

Soft laughter followed behind him as he walked out the door.

Finley was distracted during her morning meeting with the linen rental company. Thankfully, the vendor didn't have an opportunity to notice, because Julia took the lead in the discussion to adjust the terms of their current contract. But the fact that Julia had taken the lead told Finley that her friend was aware of her preoccupation.

At the end of the meeting, smiles and handshakes were exchanged all around, then Julia escorted the vendor out. Finley didn't dare breathe a sigh of relief, because she knew that her friend would return with questions.

When she did, she also brought two mugs of coffee.

"I thought you could use this," Julia said, setting one of the mugs in front of Finley.

"Thanks."

Her friend sat across from her and sipped her own coffee.

"I dropped the ball today. I'm sorry."

"The ball didn't drop," Julia said.

"Because you didn't let it."

"Because we're a team."

Finley stared at the dark liquid in her cup. "I hate not being at the top of my game."

"I know," her friend commiserated.

"I should be able to keep my personal life separate and apart from business—and when I'm at work, I need to focus on work."

"That's a great theory," Julia said. "But it doesn't translate to the real world, because we're people, not machines, and people have feelings and feelings are messy."

"Maybe too messy."

"Do you want to tell me what he did?"

Finley gave her friend a brief summary of her middle-of-the-night argument with Lachlan. "It seemed like a huge deal last night," she confided. "But now, in the light of day, I wonder if maybe I overreacted."

"Really?" Julia said. "Because I think you *under*reacted. If that had been my boyfriend, I would have told him that if he walked out the door, he shouldn't ever expect to walk in it again."

Finley had wanted to say something very much along those lines—to force him to make a choice. But in the end, she'd been afraid to give him that kind of ultimatum. Afraid that he still would have chosen Deirdre over her.

"But maybe your professor is smart enough to have seen the error of his ways, no ultimatums required," Julia mused.

Finley followed her friend's gaze to where Lachlan was standing in the doorway.

Julia stood up with her coffee. "Should I finish this in my office?"

She directed the question to Finley, letting her know that she'd stay to provide backup if her friend needed it.

Finley gave a small nod of assent and Julia headed to the door.

Lachlan took a couple of steps further into the room. "I know you're probably tired of hearing me say that I'm sorry, so I'll tell you that I'm glad I went to see Deirdre last night, because we had a long overdue talk about some things—most notably our dysfunctional codependent relationship."

"Okay," she said cautiously.

"The bottom line is that she's always going to be part of my life because she's the mother of my child. And I can appreciate that it's inconvenient and maybe even frustrating to have to factor my daughter and my ex-wife into our plans, but if we're going to be together, that's something we're going to have to deal with on occasion.

"And I really want us to be together. When I'm with you, it's because I want to be with you. And when I'm not with you, I'm thinking about you and wishing I could be with you, and I'm sorry if at any point in time—and especially last night— I ever gave you reason to think otherwise."

"It's kind of hard to stay mad after an apology like that," Finley admitted.

"Does that mean I'm forgiven?" he asked hopefully.

"You're forgiven," she confirmed.

He took her hands and drew her to her feet, then lowered his head and brushed his mouth over hers. "Now we've officially kissed and made up."

"Not quite."

He drew back to look at her quizzically.

"The only good thing about fighting is the make-up sex that follows."

His gaze slid to the conference table.

She laughed. "No. Still no locks on the doors." She glanced at her watch. "Plus, I have another appointment in twenty minutes."

"And I'm definitely going to need more time than that," he promised.

Finley smiled. "I finish at eight tonight."

"I'll pick up the pizza."

Chapter Eighteen

Lachlan was on his way home, thinking about his plans with Finley for the night ahead, when his mom called.

"I need a favor," Marilyn Kellett said without preamble.

"Good thing it's my day off," he noted.

"That is why I'm calling you," she confirmed. "I need you to pick up your grandparents from the airport."

"I can do that."

"I told them that I'd be there, but I've been working with a couple who have viewed the same property in Hunter's Point three times and are finally ready to make an offer. The seller's agent is expecting another one to come in tomorrow, so I want to get in first."

"No worries," he assured her. "Just text me their flight information and I'll be there."

He'd had some reservations when his grandparents first mentioned their plan to tour Europe in celebration of their sixtieth anniversary. After all, his grandfather was eighty-one and his grandmother two years older than him. But they'd both remained active since their retirement—Douglas golfed at least twice a week, and Catherine participated in water aerobics—and were determined to celebrate in a big way.

"How was Europe?" Lachlan asked, after they'd exchanged hugs at the arrivals gate.

"Je suis tombé amoureux à Paris," she told him.

"You fell in love *in* Paris?"

She frowned. *"Avec Paris?"*

"De Paris," he said. *"Vous êtes tombé amoureux* de *Paris."*

"Show-off," she grumbled.

He grinned. "I'm happy to see you, too. And pleased to know that you had a good time."

"It was fabulous," his grandfather chimed in. "And something we both wish we'd done twenty years ago."

"Twenty years ago, you weren't retired," Lachlan pointed out.

"Fifteen years ago then," Douglas amended.

"In any event, we're already planning our next trip," his wife said.

"Well, hopefully you're going to stay put for at least a few weeks. I'm not sure Aislynn would forgive you if you missed her sixteenth birthday."

"Of course, we wouldn't miss her birthday. Are you planning a big party?"

"We're planning a party," he confirmed. "The size and other details are still being negotiated."

"You should get in touch with Finley Gilmore at Gilmore Galas," Catherine suggested, then she frowned. "But summer is prime wedding season, so she might not be able to fit another event into her schedule.

"Still, you should call her anyway," she decided. "She's really a lovely girl and I was so disappointed that I didn't get a chance to introduce you at our anniversary party."

"I appreciate the thought," Lachlan told her. "But I don't need my grandmother to introduce me to women."

"Apparently you do," she said. "Because as far as I know, you haven't dated anyone since Victoria and that was…how many years ago?"

"Four," he admitted.

"Four years." She shook her head. "Now I'm not naïve

enough to believe that there haven't been other women in that time, but clearly no one that you liked well enough to introduce to your family."

"Catherine." Her husband's tone was both admonishing and indulgent.

"I know you think I'm interfering—"

"You *are* interfering."

"—but I only want our grandson to find someone special to share his life with. To someday travel Europe with, strolling hand in hand across Tower Bridge, picnicking in Jardin des Tuileries, making love all night to the sound of the waves in Torre del Mar."

"Way too much information," Lachlan told her.

"I don't know why young people always think they're the only ones who get to have any fun."

"I never thought any such thing," he assured her. "But I wouldn't mind a change in the topic of conversation."

"You're the one who said you wanted to hear all the details of our trip," she reminded him.

"Have some pity on the boy and stick to the PG details," her husband suggested.

"Alright," she relented. "Why don't you tell us what's new with you, Lachlan?"

"Well, apparently you'll be surprised to hear this, but I've been dating someone."

"Why didn't you say something?" his grandmother demanded.

"Probably because he couldn't get a word in edgewise," Douglas said.

Catherine scowled at her husband before turning her attention back to her grandson. "So tell us now. What's her name? Where did you meet her? And when I am going to get to meet her?"

"If you promise to stop the interrogation right now, I might be persuaded to introduce you to her at Aislynn's birthday party."

She fell silent, but she grinned the rest of the drive home.

It felt strange, showing up at Deirdre's house, even if she was an invited guest. It might have been a little less awkward, Finley mused, if she'd been able to arrive with Lachlan. But he'd wanted to be there early, and she'd needed to do an airport pickup.

Transportation needs were usually handled by a car service, but this particular father of the bride required a personal touch. While the bride insisted that she wasn't particularly worried about his arrival, that was only because she'd been let down so many times by her father that she didn't actually expect him to show. In fact, she'd made alternate arrangements for a favorite uncle to walk her down the aisle in his absence.

It was a testament to the groom's affection for his bride that he'd made all the arrangements for his future father-in-law's travel and a personal plea to Finley to get him to the church on time for tonight's rehearsal. Once the father of the bride had been delivered to the church and the rehearsal had begun, Finley left Rachel in charge and slipped away to Aislynn's birthday party.

Of course, she was one of the last guests to arrive, forcing her to park halfway down the block, as Deirdre's circular driveway was already overflowing with vehicles. After she parked, she picked up the "bouquet" she'd brought for Aislynn. Wrapped in floral paper were sixteen cardstock "daisies," each with a gift card holder on the back. Finley hadn't gone overboard—she didn't want it to appear as if she was trying to buy Aislynn's affection—but she'd discovered, through conversations with Lachlan and his daughter, where the birthday girl liked to shop or hang out or grab a bite to eat, and so each daisy offered a unique surprise.

Deirdre answered the door herself when Finley rang the bell.

"You made it," Aislynn's mother said, sounding genuinely pleased to see her. "Come in, come in."

She led the way through the house to a wall of French doors that opened up onto a back deck as wide as the house and equally deep. The railing around the perimeter had built-in planters at six-foot intervals, and the royal palms that grew out of the planters had been wrapped for the occasion in twinkling lights, while more twinkling lights had been suspended above the deck to create a ceiling that looked as if it was made of starlight.

An arch of white and pink balloons stood over the gift and cake tables at one end of the deck, and a second marked the location of the food and drink stations at the other. Standing tables were draped with white cloths and wrapped with bows of pink tulle, and at the center of each table was a clear glass jar filled with white and pink peonies.

"The gift table is over there," Deirdre said, gesturing. "But I really wish you hadn't brought anything."

"I was hardly going to show up to a birthday party empty-handed."

"But you've already done so much, using your contacts and connections to help us put this party together—and keep us on budget."

"That was my pleasure," Finley said.

"I really do think you mean that," Deirdre said. "But honestly, it was a lot more work than I'd anticipated, and it gave me a whole new level of appreciation for what you do."

"Well, everything looks absolutely stunning."

"I was pleased," Deirdre agreed. "But more important, Aislynn was blown away."

"Where is the birthday girl?"

Deirdre pointed to a group of six girls near the cake table. "There's my baby," she said. "All grown up."

"You must be so proud."

"I am. I can't take all the credit, though. Lachlan has been there every step of the way. But, of course, you know that already."

"She's lucky to have both of you," Finley said sincerely.

"She's lucky, too, to have a solid group of friends, most of whom have been close since grade school." Deirdre then proceeded to identify Harmony, Kendra, Gabby, Sofia and Joy.

"And I swear Lachlan was around here just a minute ago," Deirdre said.

"Don't worry," Finley said. "I'll find him."

"Bryan and Marilyn are here somewhere, too," she said, naming Lachlan's parents. "And Catherine and Douglas are on their way. And this—" she said, as a man with sandy brown hair and warm brown eyes joined them "—is my fiancé, Philip Cohen."

Philip offered his hand. "You must be Finley."

"I am," she confirmed.

"You're also empty-handed," he noted. "What can I get you to drink?"

"Oh. Um…" She glanced around, not sure what her options were.

"There's nonalcoholic punch, which is what most of the kids are drinking," Deirdre said. "And an adult version with a little bit of a kick. We've also got champagne, soft drinks and sparkling water."

"I think I'll stick with the nonalcoholic punch," Finley said. "There's a slim chance that I might have to duck out to an event and a certainty that I'll have to drive home later."

"Champagne for me," Deirdre said.

"I'll be right back," Philip promised.

Deirdre watched him go, a look of pure adoration on her face that surprised Finley a little. Because Deirdre was a stunningly beautiful woman while her fiancé was handsome enough but not the type of man who, in a crowded room, would draw a woman's eye.

Not like Lachlan, who she'd been drawn to from the very first.

But where the heck was he?

When Philip returned with the promised drinks, Finley thanked him and excused herself, not wanting the couple to feel as if they needed to babysit her.

She added her gift to the pile on the table, then approached the group of teens that included the guest of honor. "I don't want to interrupt," Finley said, "but I did want to wish Aislynn a happy sweet sixteen."

"Thank you," Lachlan's daughter said, before deliberately turning to face one of her friends.

Ouch, Finley thought, and was about to walk away again when Kendra spoke to her.

"I don't think we've met," she said, in a much friendlier tone than the birthday girl had used. "Are you a friend of Aislynn's mom or her dad?"

Aislynn jumped in to answer the question before Finley could. "Finley's the party planner."

So much for thinking they'd bonded.

"Finley Gilmore," she introduced herself with a smile, determined to ignore the sense of betrayal evoked by Aislynn's words.

"As in Gilmore Galas?" Joy looked at Finley with renewed interest.

"You've heard of it?"

"Are you kidding? Since the Memorial Day party for Reese Scott at Venice Beach, *everyone's* heard of Gilmore Galas," Kendra said, dropping the name of a chart-topping pop star.

"I did a Memorial Day party at Venice Beach," Finley confirmed. "But it wasn't for Reese Scott."

"But she was there," Sofia insisted. "And she posted a ton of pics on Insta."

That part was true, and for a whole week after that event, Finley and her colleagues had barely been able to keep up with the requests and queries that had come into the office at Gilmore Galas.

"I saw those pictures," Harmony chimed in, sounding suitably impressed.

Aislynn stood by sullenly while her friends peppered Finley with questions about the event and the pop star. She was obviously annoyed that they were paying more attention to "the party planner" than the guest of honor, and while the situation was of her own making, Finley didn't want to be the cause of any distress for Lachlan's daughter—especially not on such a special occasion.

"It was nice meeting you all," she said, extricating herself from the group. "But I need to check on something in the kitchen."

She headed back toward the house, but she hadn't made it more than half a dozen steps before Lachlan caught up with her.

"There you are," he said, offering her a smile that warmed everything inside her.

"Here I am," she confirmed.

"Everything go okay with the airport run and the rehearsal?"

"Father of the bride did indeed arrive as scheduled and the rehearsal was just getting started when I snuck away."

"Does that mean you're free for the rest of the evening?"

She held up crossed fingers.

"Good," he said. "Because I have plans…"

"Don't look now, but your dad's flirting with the party planner," Harmony said.

"I'm definitely *not* looking," Aislynn assured her, though she couldn't resist sneaking a glance in their direction.

"Wait a minute," Harmony said now. "She's not just the

party planner, is she? She's your dad's new girlfriend. The one you said you walked in on him kissing."

"Yeah." She wouldn't have admitted it in front of Gabby, Sofia and Joy, but they'd wandered off to the food table, leaving her with only Harmony and Kendra, and they were her very best friends. The ones she didn't have any secrets from.

"So why didn't you say that she was his girlfriend?" Kendra asked.

She shrugged.

"Well, anyway, she seems really nice."

Aislynn shot her traitorous friend a look.

"I'm just saying—maybe you shouldn't be so quick to judge," Kendra said. "Especially considering that she knows people."

"I don't *not* like her," Aislynn said. "I just don't think she's right for my dad."

Kendra glanced over at the couple, whose heads were bent close together. They weren't actually holding hands, but Aislynn's dad was stroking the back of Finley's hand with his fingertips, a subtle caress that somehow seemed even more intimate.

"Obviously he disagrees," she said.

Aislynn turned away. "I'm going to get some more punch."

"Me, too," Harmony said, immediately falling into step beside her.

"Ignore Kendra," Harmony said, when they were far enough away that their friend wouldn't overhear them. "She only thinks she's an expert about this stuff because she's got a new stepmother."

A twenty-two-year-old gold digger, according to what Aislynn overheard her mom telling a friend.

"At least I know Finley isn't after my dad's money, because he's not rich."

"No, but he's hot," Harmony said.

"*Eww.*"

"I mean, for an old guy," her friend was quick to clarify.

"Still *eww*," Aislynn told her.

"Did I tell you how much I love all the fairy lights?" Harmony asked, obviously desperate to change the topic of conversation. "They make the deck look magical."

Finley's idea, Aislynn remembered.

But almost everything had been the party planner's idea. The lights, the balloons, the flowers, the cake. Finley had spent a lot of time talking to Aislynn—and later her mom, too—about what she wanted for her party, and then she'd helped make it all happen.

But that was her job, wasn't it?

So Aislynn hadn't been lying when she said Finley was the party planner.

But she hadn't been telling the whole truth, either.

She'd treated Finley badly and now she had knots in her stomach and it wasn't fair.

It was *her* birthday.

And not just any birthday—her sweet sixteen.

A special occasion, her mother insisted. A day that was supposed to be all about celebrating her.

But suddenly Aislynn wasn't in a party mood anymore.

Finley would be lying if she said that Aislynn's dismissive attitude didn't hurt. But she understood. She'd been that sixteen-year-old girl once, eager for parental attention and peer approval, desperate to feel as if she mattered.

And it didn't bother her to take a step back, to focus on helping with the party and support Aislynn's designation of her as the hired help. She appreciated that Lachlan tried to stick close, but the fact was, most of the people here were his friends—or at least parents of his daughter's friends that he'd known for years—and it was inevitable that he'd be drawn away to have a word with this person or confer with that one.

But he introduced her to Ethan and Steph—who were friends as well as colleagues of his at Merivale College—and, within five minutes, she felt as if she'd known them forever. She also spent some time chatting with his parents, who were both genuinely lovely people, and then with Catherine and Douglas, when they arrived.

Lachlan's grandparents were understandably surprised to find Finley in attendance at the party—and then overjoyed to discover that she was the mystery woman their grandson was dating.

"I knew you two would hit it off," Catherine said smugly.

"But you didn't know they'd hit it off before you had a chance to maneuver them together," Douglas remarked.

"Which proves that fate wields an even stronger hand than a grandmother."

"Unless that grandmother has a wooden spoon in hers," Lachlan said, wincing as he rubbed his derriere.

"Don't you dare," Catherine admonished, shaking her finger at him. "I *never* paddled your bottom with my wooden spoon."

"But you threatened often enough."

"And those threats kept you in line, didn't they?" she said.

Finley smiled, enjoying their banter, proof of the easy and sincere affection between Lachlan and his grandparents.

Before he could respond to Catherine's question, Deirdre came by to steal Lachlan away "for just a minute." It was the third such interruption in the forty minutes that had passed since his grandparents' arrival.

"You're being an awfully good sport about his ex-wife," Catherine remarked to Finley, after she'd sent her husband off to refill her glass of punch.

"I'm trying," she said. "The fact that I actually like Deirdre makes it a little easier."

"They've been partners in raising their daughter since she was born, so they don't always think about how other people fit into the equation—or even realize that they should."

"There have been a few bumps," Finley acknowledged. "But so far, nothing that's really thrown us off course."

"I'm glad to hear that," his grandmother said. "Because I've known Lachlan since he drew his first breath, and in all his years, I've never seen him as smitten with any other woman as he is with you. And it makes my heart happy to see that you're just as smitten with him."

"Is it that obvious?" Finley asked worriedly.

"Maybe not to everyone," Catherine said. "But a woman in love can recognize another."

"After three glasses of punch, I'm a woman in need of a bathroom."

His grandmother chuckled softly. "While you head off in search of one of those, I'm going to see where my husband is with my drink."

On her way back to the party, Finley took a wrong turn and found herself in what she imagined the architect of the home had referred to as a family room to distinguish it from the more formal living room she'd passed by earlier. This one was filled with comfortable-looking furnishings grouped around a massive flat screen TV, but what caught her eye was the array of framed photographs on the mantel of the fireplace.

She couldn't help smiling as she examined the photos of Aislynn through the years. Finley knew that every mom thought hers was the most beautiful baby in the world, but she suspected that Lachlan and Deirdre's daughter might actually have been worthy of that crown. Even as an infant, she'd been a gorgeous child, with dark wispy curls and big blue eyes.

There was a "First Day of Kindergarten" photo. A picture of Aislynn in a soccer uniform with a ball tucked under her arm and a wide grin that showed her front two teeth missing.

Then a "First Disney Trip" snapshot, with the little girl wearing Minnie Mouse ears and flanked by both of her parents. Fast forward a few more years, and there was Aislynn with her hair in a tight chignon, wearing a pink leotard and tutu. And then a more recent photo of her lounging against a doorjamb with a bass clarinet in hand.

"Did you get lost?" Deirdre teased from the doorway.

"I took a wrong turn," she admitted. "And then I got nosy."

The other woman smiled. "If I didn't want guests looking at the photos, I wouldn't have them lined up on the mantel."

"Did you take these?"

"Most of them."

"You've got an eye for photography."

"A hobby." Deirdre shrugged. "I have lots of hobbies, no real vocation. What's the saying—jack of all trades but master of none?"

Finley smiled—then her attention was snagged by a framed pencil sketch hanging on the wall.

"Do you dabble in art, too?"

"Goodness, no. Even paint-by-numbers are beyond me."

"So who did the sketch?"

"Oh. That was done by some street artist in Seattle when Lachlan and I were on our honeymoon."

"Dee?" Philip beckoned her from the doorway. "The birthday girl wants pictures with her parents before cake."

"On my way," she promised, following him out of the room.

Finley knew that she should go, too. Instead, she took a step closer to the drawing, her attention snagged by the date below the artist's scrawled signature.

Lachlan found her in that exact spot half an hour later.

"I've been looking all over for you," he said, offering her a plate with a wedge of vanilla cake with raspberry mousse filling. "What are you doing in here?"

"Developing an appreciation for art."

"You'd be better off at the Franklin Bowles Gallery," he told her. "Deirdre's taste is somewhat pedestrian."

"Interesting that you'd say that, because I got the impression her taste was similar to yours."

He followed her gaze to the sketch on the wall and winced.

"In fact, that looks like an exact replica of the infinity symbol inked on your shoulder."

"Actually, the tattoo is a replica of—never mind," he decided.

"I read the date as August second—assuming the standard format of month followed by day—which you said was Aislynn's birthday. And yes, I know it is. But the date is actually spelled out on the sketch as Feb 8."

"What do you want me to say?"

"I want you to tell me the truth—is February eighth your wedding date?"

"Yes."

The single word landed like a blow to her stomach. She closed her eyes, struggling to draw in a breath after all the air had been knocked out of her.

"God, I feel like such a fool."

"I didn't intend to mislead you," he said. "You asked me about the significance of August second, which *is* Aislynn's birthday."

"How convenient for you."

"And I realized, as soon as I said it, that I should clarify, but then…"

"Then *what*?" she demanded.

"Then you dropped to your knees in front of me in the shower and every other thought slipped out of my head."

Her cheeks burned. "So it's my fault?"

"No. Of course not. I'm just saying that there were…circumstances."

"You've had plenty of opportunities since then to tell me the truth, but you didn't."

"Because I didn't want to make it seem like a bigger deal than it is."

"The date you married your ex-wife is inked on your shoulder—I'd say that's a pretty big deal."

"Come on, Finley. It's not as if I'm your first boyfriend."

"No, you're not. But I didn't marry any of my previous boyfriends or have a child with any of them, and I certainly didn't tattoo my body with dates significant to our relationship."

"We were young and stupid," he told her. "Each of us barely twenty years old and expecting a baby. On top of that, Deirdre was freaking out about the fact that she was going to get fat and end up with stretch marks, so she wanted me to have a permanent memento, too."

"I understand why you got the tattoo," Finley said. "What I don't understand is why you still have it—and why you lied to me about it."

"Because it's a lot easier to remove a wedding band than body ink."

She shook her head, not sure whether she was feeling completely humiliated or just really angry. "All this time, I thought it was your ex-wife who couldn't let go. Now I know it's you."

Chapter Nineteen

"And then she walked out on me."

"That sucks," Ethan said sympathetically.

"It does suck," Steph agreed. "But it's not as if you really gave her a choice."

Lachlan looked at his friends, who'd followed him home after Aislynn's birthday party to find out why Finley had done a disappearing act.

"Can't you show some compassion, Steph?" her husband said. "The guy's obviously hurting."

"It's his own fault," she retorted. "He lied to her."

"She's right," Lachlan admitted. "Finley didn't ask for much from me, but she did ask for honesty."

"So why didn't you tell her the truth?" Steph asked now.

"Because I was afraid I'd lose her."

"And somehow, that's exactly what happened."

"Not helping," Ethan said.

"He needs to realize that he's getting in his own way."

"Huh?" Lachlan said.

"I know you haven't dated a lot of women," Steph noted. "And some of your missteps with Finley might be attributed to treading on unfamiliar ground, but from my perspective, your biggest problem is that you're afraid to let yourself be happy, and so you've been sabotaging your relationship with Finley every step of the way."

"That's ridiculous," he said.

"Is it?" she challenged. "Maybe you legitimately lost track of time the night you were at the hospital with Aislynn, but even so, you could have sent her a quick text message as soon as you realized you'd stood her up. And inviting her to your house without telling her that you had a teenage daughter who is in the habit of dropping by at random times? Then jumping out of her bed in response to a summons from your ex-wife? And lying about the significance of the date on a tattoo on your back?"

"Laid out like that, the evidence is pretty damning," Ethan agreed.

"I know I've screwed up, but none of it was on purpose."

"Self-sabotaging behavior is often unconscious. You grew up in a traditional family with loving parents, so you think you must be responsible for the failure of your marriage and don't deserve another chance at happiness."

"I'm sorry—isn't your doctorate in mathematics?"

"Psychology is a hobby."

"Well, perform your armchair analysis on someone else," he suggested.

"I don't know anyone else who is such an obvious textbook case," she retorted.

"So what's the textbook solution?" he asked.

"Forgive yourself," she said simply. "And open up your heart."

Finley didn't have time to wallow.

She had a job to do, so she put a smile on her face and did it, pretending all the while that her heart wasn't shattered into a thousand pieces.

After Saturday's wedding, both Julia and Rachel tried to talk to her, but she brushed them off. She wasn't ready to tell them what happened with Lachlan, to admit that she'd been fool enough to fall in love—again—with a man who couldn't let go of his past to move on with her. He'd claimed he wasn't still in love with Deirdre, but it seemed to her that permanent ink spoke louder than words.

On Sunday, after all the post-wedding hoopla had died down, she FaceTimed her sister. It was early evening, before the twins went to bed, and they were both eager to talk to "Auntie Fin."

"I can't believe how big they are now," she said.

"Growing like weeds," Haylee agreed.

"Wike fwowers, Gwamma says," Ellie announced, jumping up and down to see herself on the screen.

"That's right," her mom agreed. "Like beautiful flowers."

The little girl beamed.

Finley felt her heart pinch.

"I don' wanna be a fwower," Aidan protested. "I wanna be a dinosaur—Woar!"

"You are indeed a ferocious dinosaur," Finley told him.

The conversation lifted her spirits immensely.

And then, three days later, she opened the door and her sister was there.

"This impromptu trip was Trevor's idea," Haylee said, returning Finley's hug.

"And that's why he's my favorite brother-in-law."

"He's your only brother-in-law."

"Another reason he's my favorite." She looked past her sister. "But where is he? And Aidan and Ellie?"

"They'll be here on the weekend, because he knew that I wanted some one-on-one time with you first."

Finley's eyes filled with tears. "Can we have wine with that one-on-one time?"

"We can have whatever you want," Haylee promised.

So Finley opened a bottle and put out some snacks while her sister carried her bag into the guest room. When she came out again, Haylee had Simon snuggled against her chest.

"He's not happy with you," Finley warned.

"What are you talking about? Why wouldn't he be happy with me?"

"Because he knows you're getting a dog."

"It's Trevor who wants the dog, not me," Haylee said, speaking directly to the cat. "And we don't have one yet."

Simon didn't look impressed with her explanation.

Then again, he rarely looked impressed.

"Now tell me what happened with Lachlan," Haylee said, when they were seated on the sofa with their wine.

"Maybe I should tell you what didn't happen," Finley suggested. "Which is that he didn't have the tattoo with his wedding date removed."

Her sister winced. "When was he supposed to have that done?"

"Any time in the twelve years that have passed since his divorce."

Haylee sipped her wine. "Was this tattoo a recent revelation?"

"No," Finley admitted, and briefly explained to her sister her misreading of the date and, therefore, misinterpreting the significance.

"And you think the fact that he hasn't had the tattoo removed is a sign that he still has feelings for the ex-wife that he divorced a dozen years ago?" Haylee sounded dubious.

"It's at least a sign that he can't let her go," she said.

"Have you spoken with him since you left the party?"

"There's nothing to talk about."

"Fin." Haylee set down her wineglass to take her sister's hands. "I know you better than anyone else in the world, and I know—"

"Knew," she interjected to clarify. "You *knew* me better than anyone else in the world. Then you got pregnant and got

married and moved five hundred miles away. Now I hardly ever see you."

"Is that why you're freezing me out?"

"No. I mean, I'm not…" She blew out a breath. "Maybe I am freezing you out."

"I know things have changed since Trevor and I got married," Haylee acknowledged, "but you'll always be my sister and my best friend, and even when I'm five hundred miles away, you're always in my heart."

Finley teared up again.

"And because you're my sister and my best friend, I'm going to remind you of what you once said to me."

"What's that?"

"When you're dealing with a boatload of stuff, I'll be right there with you with the life jackets."

Finley was surprised—and just a little bit wary—when Taylor buzzed to tell her that Catherine Edwards was on the line for her.

"Catherine—how wonderful to hear from you." And it was true, because despite what had happened with Lachlan, Finley had nothing but sincere affection for his grandparents.

"It would be even more wonderful to see you," Lachlan's grandmother said. "When can we get together for lunch?"

"Lunch sounds lovely," Finley told her. "But before we make plans, there's something you need to know."

"If you're going to tell me that you're no longer seeing Lachlan, I'm aware."

"And you still want to have lunch with me?"

"I realize that I'm old enough to be your grandmother, but I liked you from the first moment we met. And since I'm at an age where a lot of my friends are dying, I could use some newer—and decidedly younger—ones."

Finley had to chuckle. "I'd be honored to be counted as a friend."

"Of course, as a friend, I'm going to expect some kind of discount when Douglas and I hire Gilmore Galas for our sixty-fifth wedding anniversary celebration."

"And you'll get one," Finley promised.

"Wonderful. Now when can you come for lunch?"

"You want me to come to your home?"

"Would you mind terribly?" Catherine asked. "On my way back from the spa last week, I had a minor fender bender. It really wasn't a big deal, but Douglas doesn't want me driving again until I have my eyes tested."

"I don't mind at all," Finley assured her. "In fact, why don't I pick up lunch and bring it to you?"

"I may be temporarily without transportation—by choice—but I'm perfectly capable of putting together a meal in my own kitchen."

"In that case, does Monday work for you?"

"It does," Catherine confirmed. "What time should I expect you?"

"One o'clock?"

"I'll look forward to seeing you then."

At the end of the summer term, Lachlan took Aislynn camping, as he'd done every August for the past twelve years. When she was a kid, she'd loved their summer retreats, but in recent years, she'd been a lot less enthusiastic about spending any time off the grid that fueled not only her electronic devices but apparently her very existence.

They spent the first few days in town with Ben's family, before heading up to his friend's cabin. Lachlan knew the first trip back after his friend's passing would be the hardest, and so he was grateful to have his daughter's company.

And he had to give her credit, she made it all the way to the evening of day four when they were playing cribbage by solar-powered lights before she said, "We don't have to stay the whole week, you know. If you want to go home, that's fine by me."

"This is our week," he reminded her, selecting two cards from his hand and setting them aside. "And I'm in no hurry for it to end."

She added two cards from her hand to his crib. "You're not missing Finley?"

It was the question he'd been simultaneously waiting for and dreading. And while he didn't always share the details of what was going on in his life, he tried to at least be honest about what he did share.

And yes, he didn't miss the irony of the fact that if he'd applied the same guideline in his relationship with Finley, they might still be together.

"Finley and I broke up."

"Oh." Her brow scrunched as she cut the deck. He flipped the top card, revealing the queen of spades. "When did that happen?"

"A couple weeks ago."

She led with a jack of diamonds. "Was it because of me?"

"No, honey." He tossed down a five and pegged two points. "It had nothing to do with you."

She added another five and pegged two for the pair. "Are you sure? I know I wasn't always very nice to her."

He added to the count with a king. "Except when you wanted her help with your party."

A guilty flush colored her cheeks as she dropped an ace on the table and pegged two more.

"So what happened?"

He started the count again with another king. "You mean between me and Finley?"

She nodded as she played a third king, securing two more points.

"Sometimes things just don't work out," he said, dropping his last card—an eight—on the table and pegging a single point for it.

"That's a totally lame answer," she told him. "If you don't think it's any of my business, just say it's none of my business."

"Okay, it's none of your business."

She scored her hand—nine points including the queen start card. He pegged eight from his hand and another four from his crib.

"Was it because you're still in love with Mom?" she asked, as she gathered the cards to shuffle.

He sighed. "Honey, I know this might be hard for you to accept, but I'm not still in love with your mom. She's in love with Philip and…"

"And?" she prompted, when his answer trailed off.

"And… I'm in love with Finley." It was the first time he'd said the words out loud. The first time he'd admitted the true depth of his feelings for her.

Unfortunately, it was too little, too late.

Not to mention that he'd made the admission to the wrong woman.

Aislynn frowned as she began to deal. "I don't understand. If you're in love with Finley, then why did you break up?"

"None of your business," he reminded her.

"Actually, I don't think that's true," she said now. "Because you're my dad, which means that what affects you, affects me."

"My breakup with Finley doesn't affect you."

"I don't like seeing you sad."

"I'll get over it."

She set the deck aside and picked up her hand. "Are you sure?"

"I'm sure."

"Because in the past five—maybe ten—years, I can count

on one hand the number of your girlfriends that you've introduced me to—with three fingers left."

"And I can count on one hand the number of my girlfriends that you've liked—with five fingers left."

She rearranged the cards in her hand, selecting two for her crib. "I might have been wrong about Finley."

"It doesn't matter now," he told her.

"It does matter," she insisted. Then, when he failed to respond, she asked, "Did you tell her you love her?"

He continued to examine the cards she'd dealt to him.

"You didn't, did you?" she pressed.

"I'm not talking to you about this, Aislynn."

"You need to talk to *someone* about it."

"Maybe I do." He tossed two cards down for her crib. "But it's not going to be my sixteen-year-old daughter."

"Then talk to Finley," she advised. "Because if you don't tell her how you feel, how will you ever know if your feelings are reciprocated?"

"You brought me flowers," Catherine said, smiling with pleasure when she opened the door in response to Finley's knock.

"Based on what you chose for your anniversary arrangements, I figured that dahlias were a favorite flower."

"They are indeed," Catherine confirmed. "And this color is absolutely stunning."

"It's called Frost Nip," Finley told her. "And I'll admit, I like the name as much as the white-edged pink flowers."

"They're going to look lovely in the center of the dining room table. Come," she said, taking her guest's arm and drawing her inside. "Let's eat and catch up."

And that's what they did. Over spinach salad with strawberries, toasted pecans and feta, Catherine regaled Finley with tales from her European travels with Douglas. The salad was followed by roasted lemon rosemary chicken with potatoes and anecdotes from recent Gilmore Galas. By the time they polished off their key lime tarts, more than two hours had passed.

"I can't tell you how much I enjoyed this," she told Catherine, as she carried the dessert plates to the kitchen.

"Hold onto that thought," the old woman said, as the back door opened and her husband came in, followed by his grandson.

Finley felt her heart squeeze inside her chest when she looked at Lachlan, who was looking back at her with an unreadable expression on his face.

Douglas, having quickly assessed the situation, sighed heavily. "You're meddling again, aren't you, Catherine?"

"I can see how it might look that way," she acknowledged. "But this wasn't my idea."

"And it wasn't mine," Finley said, so that Lachlan wouldn't think she'd set up this meeting in the hopes of crossing paths with him. Because why would she want to see him when doing so only made her heart ache again, longing for what she'd had and lost?

"I know it wasn't your idea," he said, taking two steps toward her. "Because it was mine."

"Yours?"

He nodded.

"I think I left…something…in the dining room," Catherine said, exiting in that direction.

The other three people in the kitchen didn't move.

"Douglas?" Catherine prompted. "I could use your help."

"With the…something?" he queried.

"Exactly," she said.

Sending an apologetic glance in Finley's direction, the old man followed his wife out of the room.

"So this was all your idea?" Finley said, when she and Lachlan were alone.

"Not the lunch part," he said. "My grandmother mentioned that she wanted to get together with you—because she really does enjoy your company—but she wanted to make sure that I was okay with it first. I suggested that she invite you to come here, so that we could talk after."

"If you wanted to talk to me, why didn't you just call?"

"Because I figured you'd blocked my number. Again."

"I didn't."

"Oh."

"I was upset when I walked out of Aislynn's party that day, but that didn't mean I wanted it to be over between us."

"There really should be a manual," he muttered.

"A manual?"

He gave a slight shake of his head. "I'm not good at this stuff," he confided. "Flirting is easy. And sex is pretty straightforward. But when it comes to relationships, I clearly don't have the first clue what I'm doing."

"I thought it was just our relationship."

He shook his head. "The truth is, Deirdre was my first serious girlfriend and, when she got pregnant, we got married."

"You told me that part already."

"What I didn't tell you is how much I hate to fail at anything, and failing at my marriage—something that was supposed to be forever—was major. So I put all my energy into being the best dad that I could be.

"I've dated since the divorce, obviously, but none of the women I've gone out with has tempted me to risk my heart again. Until you. And I hope I'm not too late in telling you how I feel, because the last few weeks have been hell, and I don't want to imagine the rest of my life without you in it. Because I love you."

Finley had always found it annoying when the heroine in a romantic book or movie would willingly forgive all kinds of transgressions simply because the hero uttered those three little words. Because she hadn't understood, until that very moment, how those words could change everything.

Because when Lachlan said, "I love you," her heart swelled inside her chest so that all the bumps and bruises it had suffered—recent and distant—were forgotten.

"You're not too late," she finally said, emotion filling her voice.

He breached the distance that separated them and lifted his hands to frame her face.

"I love you," he said again, looking into her eyes so that she could see the truth of his feelings reflected in the depth of his. Then he lowered his mouth to hers in a kiss that was filled with love and promise.

"I love you, too," she said, when his lips eased away.

He tipped his forehead against hers. "I'd almost given up hope that I'd ever hear you say those words," he admitted. "It was Aislynn who pointed out that if I wanted to know what was in your heart, I had to be willing to open up mine."

"Do you think your daughter's going to be okay with this?"

"She's already started to come around," he said confidently. "Oh, I almost forgot…there's something I want to show you."

"Have you forgotten that we're in your grandparents' house?" she asked, as he began unbuttoning his shirt. "And that they're probably just beyond that doorway listening to every word of our conversation?"

"Following the advice of my grandfather, I'll keep it PG," he promised, sliding one sleeve of his shirt down so that she could see the tattoo on his shoulder.

He hadn't had the ink removed—which she knew could be a time-consuming process—but had, instead, covered the date of his wedding with tiny flowers.

She tipped her head for a closer look. "Are those…?"

"They're violets," he told her.

Her heart skipped a beat.

"An unconventional choice," she noted.

"Do you really think so, Finley Violet Gilmore?"

She blinked. "How did you know my middle name?"

"It's on the diploma in your office."

"So…not a random choice?" she guessed.

"Not random at all," he assured her. "I didn't want to get rid of the infinity symbol, because it was always more about Aislynn than Deirdre, but I wanted to add something that represented you, to show how much I want a life and a future with you."

"Because you love me?" she prompted, wanting to hear him say it one more time.

"Because I love you," he confirmed.

Finley's heart swelled again in response to the words, so much that it almost hurt, and it was the very best feeling in the world.

Epilogue

In March, Finley made her annual trip to Haven to celebrate Aidan and Ellie's birthday. But this year, she had company on her journey. On previous visits, she'd always stayed at Haylee and Trevor's place, but this year, in addition to the twins, her sister and brother-in-law had a new dog and—surprise!—another set of twins on the way. Haylee had assured them that there was still room, but Finley and Lachlan decided that a hotel might be more peaceful for all of them.

Finley had voted in favor of a room at the Stagecoach Inn, because it was conveniently located in town, but Lachlan apparently had a sentimental streak, because he insisted on making a reservation at the Dusty Boots Motel.

"You know, this little trip down memory lane would be a lot more romantic if we'd met at five-star resort on a tropical island," she told him.

"I don't disagree," he said. "But we can only work with what we've got."

And what they had was the key to Room 6—handed over by Shirla herself—and a large pizza from Jo's.

"I'm experiencing the weirdest sense of déjà vu," she murmured, as she followed Lachlan into the room.

"Except that it's not snowing this year."

"I'm almost disappointed," she said, hanging her coat on

a peg by the door. "Because what possible excuse will I have to invite you to share my bed if the power doesn't go out?"

"Hmm...you could maybe try a more direct approach and say that you want to have your way with me."

"Do you think that would work?" she asked dubiously.

He set the pizza box on the desk and discarded his coat beside hers. "I guarantee it."

She turned to him and slid her hands slowly up his chest. "I want—"

That was as far as she got before he lifted her into his arms and tumbled with her onto the bed.

Afterward, they ate cold pizza and washed it down with (plastic) glasses of cabernet sauvignon, and Finley felt certain that she couldn't be any happier than she was in that moment— not even if they were at a five-star resort on a tropical island.

"This is a definite upgrade from last year," she said, gesturing with her glass of wine.

"Over the past year, I've learned a few things about what you like."

She had to smile. "And my favorite wine label, too."

"Speaking of upgrades," he said, taking the opening she'd given him. "I was wondering how you might feel about upgrading our relationship status?"

Her heart bumped against her ribs. "What kind of upgrade did you have in mind?"

"From girlfriend to fiancée seems like a logical progression to me."

"Very logical," she agreed. For the past several weeks, he'd been dropping hints that this moment was coming, and she was excited for it to finally happen.

"But most women seem to have specific ideas about how a man should propose," he continued, in a conversational tone.

"Certainly some women do."

"And what do *you* think would make the perfect proposal?"

She sipped her wine. "In my line of work, I've heard a lot of engagement stories, all of which have led me to the conclusion that the when and where and how aren't nearly as important as who's doing the asking."

"You're saying you wouldn't turn down a guy who got down on one knee in a roadside motel so long as he was the right guy?"

"Are we going to talk in hypotheticals all night or are you actually planning to get down on one knee?"

"I'm undecided," he admitted. "It doesn't look as if this carpet has been cleaned in the past decade."

"The one knee thing isn't a requirement," she said, silently urging him to move things along.

"What are the requirements—aside from him being the right guy, I mean?" Lachlan asked.

"Well, I'd want to know that he loves me."

"I do." He leaned forward to kiss her. "I definitely do."

"And I want a ring."

He reached a hand into his pocket. "How's this one?"

Her gaze never strayed from his. "That works."

"You didn't even look at it," he protested.

"Because I honestly don't care if it's stainless or silver or plastic or platinum," she told him. "I only care that you have a ring, because it proves that you're serious about wanting to marry me."

"I'm very serious," he said. "And FYI, it's a platinum halo engagement ring with a princess-cut center diamond."

She had to check it out then—and it was absolutely stunning.

"So what do you say, Finley Violet Gilmore? Are you ready to start planning *our* wedding?"

"I say, *yes*, Lachlan Patrick Kellett. Because the one thing I want even more than that ring is *you*. For now and forever."

After he slid the ring on her finger, they shared a lingering kiss, and it was a long time later before either of them noticed the fluffy white flakes that were falling outside the window.

* * * * *

Look for the next story in
Match Made in Haven,
award-wining author Brenda Harlen's
Harlequin Special Edition miniseries.
Coming soon, wherever Harlequin
books and ebooks are sold.